Spirit Of Independence

A Novel By
Keith Rommel

Published By
Barclay Books, LLC

St. Petersburg Florida
www.barclaybooks.com
A Spectral Visions Imprint

PUBLISHED BY BARCLAY BOOKS, LLC
6161 51ST STREET SOUTH
ST. PETERSBURG, FLORIDA 33715
www.barclaybooks.com
A Spectral Visions Imprint

Printed and bound in the United States of America
Cover design by Barclay Books, LLC

ISBN: 1-931402-04-3

Dedication Page

To my family, my friends, and to you, the reader: Thank you for taking the time and spending your hard earned money to share in my dream. A special thanks to Brantley and Becki at Barclay Books: Your continued encouragement and support with Spirit is appreciated.

Please visit: http://www.spiritofindependence.com

While there, take a moment to send me along your thoughts or any questions you may have.

Until Spirit of Independence: Repentance,

Keith Rommel

Part One

Introduction

My name is Travis Winter, but I go by the name Spirit of Independence. I'm dead, at least according to your beliefs. In simplest terms I'm a Spirit, though not just an ordinary spirit. For longer than your mind will allow you to remember, I've been around watching you. On many different occasions my interest in you has brought me dangerously close to your awareness, making me careless in my purposeful study of you. My recklessness has allowed you to see me, though just a glimpse. You would dismiss our brief encounters, thinking it was merely your mind playing tricks on you. Could you dare face the truth if I presented it to you?

Allow me the opportunity to explain things in some detail then. Maybe you can begin putting the pieces of this puzzle together.

At times when you were alone, occupied by one of the many things you enjoy doing, I would be near, watching you from somewhere within the room. Captivated by your creativity and ingenuity, I'd unknowingly drift into the physical realm and would be plainly visible to your eyes. You would take notice to something suddenly appearing in your hindsight that wasn't there before. You'd turn to see what it was that caught your eye and there would be nothing there.

Can you remember pondering the moment, trying to figure out what it was you saw? I can. After the brief moment of thought, you'd casually smile and lightly laugh aloud as your abnegation in what you did see was simply forgotten about. At the time I was thankful for this conclusion, but now I am even more grateful that I can use it as a tool to help you understand me. What you saw was a brief glimpse of myself. But I don't mean to cause you alarm by telling you this because there is nothing ominous about me; I'm here only for good.

Listen to everything I have to say to you; hang onto every word if you must to absorb its meaning. Your dedication will pay off when the end comes. I'm going to tell you of my last day as a human and about today's events and each day that passes hereafter. If you think the words you see before you are a compilation of fictitious events, I would like to emphasize how much you're mistaken; this is all very real and serious. So pay close attention to all you learn, and see here the reasons for which you will learn at a time when things are reasonably peaceful. Now, on to my story.

Chapter 1

The year of 1944 is the most relevant year to this portion of my story. I was part of a covert military team that was sent on a mission that, if successful, would change the course of World War II before the horrors of it ever really began. My company's orders were to sweep through a devastated town and gain control of a concealed military installation located in East Germany, in the countries former capital known as Berlin. That particular installation was, and would continue to be throughout the war, the main training grounds for troops and a supplier of ammunition throughout Europe. The United States first concentrated attacks that were undocumented on the installation using long-ranged bombing fighters known as P-51 Mustangs. At that time, Hitler had already begun to commit his troops to a bloody showdown for control over England, and this left his distribution operations vulnerable to our attack.

My company, the sweep-up ground unit, was jumped in approximately one mile outside the already battered city. By foot we advanced towards our target, walking through a devastated town that had no standing structures remaining, and no visible signs of life anywhere.

The citizens of the small town were scattered around the wasteland, appearing like lurid statues suspended in the image between fear and death forever. The visual impressions stained my mind and left me feeling paranoid. I knew that same fate sat silently, patiently awaiting me, the task to be carried out by someone that was born to kill me.

During our advancement, we witnessed the destruction of the P-51's powerful bombs step after step. Dead children held my gaze, reminding me of the senseless tragedy of war. What did they have to do with the politics of a madman? Some of the people were completely torn apart or had been crushed by the massive shower of falling debris spilt over by a building that toppled. But the most disturbing image of all was the one where a little boy clung to his teddy bear cradled within the cusp of his dead mother's stiffening grasp. His smiles were gone forever, his youth destroyed without the shedding of one tear. This was a harsh reminder of my wife and baby boy back home. What if this were my homeland and what if they lived in a town such as this one? I couldn't handle such a thought. I moved onwards with my squad, repressing my emotions no matter how loudly they screamed within, being a good soldier like I was trained to be.

Upon reaching our objective, my commanding officer, Arthur Steirheim, conveyed the impression that he was unaffected by the devastation around him by ordering everyone to clear away the debris and set up camp with decisive authority. Less than an hour after we began to settle in, my post was relieved when Captain Steirheim requested I accompany him due south to a small cluster of standing formations that hadn't yet been investigated for hostiles, an odd tactic by a team leader but one I wouldn't dare think to question—respect and obedience for the betterment of our country. What was best for our country.

Together, as quickly and as quietly as we could and always sticking close to cover, the Captain and I advanced to the serrated formations. The Captain was the first to disappear behind the structures. I nervously waited for his signal. My heart thundered, and my finger hugged the trigger of my rifle just in case the Captain was to find any hiding enemies. Moments later the Captain moved back into sight and waved me on, giving me the all clear it was safe to approach. I breathed a sigh of relief and slung

Keith Rommel

my rifle over my shoulder, searched my pocket for a much needed smoke, and casually approached the walls.

When I arrived on the opposite side of the wall, Captain Steirheim had his back to me and he was crouched low. I curiously approached him and when I neared, he quickly turned and pointed his 35mm pistol with a homemade silencer on it between my eyes. I stiffened at first, taking only a moment to note the devilish look in his eyes. "Run," my mind screamed, and understanding the urgency behind the order, I obeyed. The cement wall beside me exploded in a furious spray, sending pebble-sized stones splashing into my face. I frantically brushed at the dust that clouded my vision and tripped and fumbled as I tried to blindly run through the brick littered grounds of the demolished building. I fell forward. Stiffening before impact, I instinctively held my hands out to break the fall. My face thrust heavily into the bricks and dirt, and the dust rushed up my nose. My gun bounced away from me, clunking dully as it skipped away. I struggled to reach it and couldn't. I looked into the distance and could see the men from my unit that remained oblivious to my situation, continuing to build camp.

This couldn't have been happening to me; I wouldn't accept that and my mind wouldn't allow it.

My instinct to survive this unexplainable attack propelled me forward. I crawled, clawed the ground to pull myself within reaching distance of my gun. I reached to grab it but could only get a feel of the cold steel slipping off my fingertips. I reached further, stretching my shoulder, forearm and fingers to their limit to embrace the power of my weapon and even the score. But Captain Steirheim gave my feeble attempt a throaty cackle, knowingly telling me I wasn't going to reach my weapon. I dragged myself forward another inch and struggled again to reach.

The Captain stepped on my hand and pushed the barrel of his gun into my forehead. It was cold—deathly cold. He slowly pushed the impenitent barrel into my forehead, digging its' sharp curves into my skin, forcing my chin up. Eye to eye I looked at him and couldn't help but compare how his gaze and the cold gun barrel he held to my head was one in the same.

"I guess you can call this moment fate," he said like he'd

9

rehearsed the moment a thousand times. "You will be taught great things and will be prepared to become the savior of the world!"

He was mad, I was sure of that. The horrors of war could drive even the strongest willed man beyond himself; I'd seen it hundreds of times before. I looked deeply into his eyes and tried to find some compassion within, and hopefully make him understand that I was not his enemy.

"Arthur," I managed. "It's me, Travis Winter. Take it easy."

"It figures," he muttered angrily. I'd thrown my line in his play, but I had no time to rehearse my part. He didn't care; there were no second takes in his play. "I knew you'd think I'd gone insane from the horrors I'd seen. Believe me, the reasons for your death far exceeds anything you could comprehend. But I assure you, given time, things will be made perfectly clear."

His tone was brusque and impenitent and was accompanied by a stare that moved beyond me, beyond the moment. I knew I'd come to my last day, and strangely enough, the realization of this filled me with some peace. The world's problems were no longer my own to deal with. I would happily let everyone else deal with them. I wanted peace to fill me.

I knew what was to come next and I tried to hold strong—tried with all of my might to keep myself from looking away. I didn't want Arthur to relish in my fear—that satisfaction was not his to have. I had dignity and I was a happy man. I'd improved my life when the odds had been stacked against me. Defiantly, I looked deeper into his eyes, smiled sarcastically, and said, "What are you waiting for? Let's get this over with!"

Without hesitation he stepped away from me and pulled the trigger. I flinched just as the weapon was discharged. The bullet sped through the flesh and bone on the left side of my face, blowing a gaping hole underneath my left eye. I grabbed at the stinging pain and hopped to my feet. I danced around and skipped over my lifeless bleeding body. I froze in certain fear by this discovery.

Captain Steirheim dropped his weapon and approached me. How was it possible he could see me? I was a dead man, wasn't I? I watched him step over my dead body and walk directly to me. He stood before me in silence, then lashed out quickly. He plunged his fist into my chest and quickly withdrew it. My breath was pushed from my lungs and I reared back in fear. I grabbed my chest to cover the gaping hole I was sure was spewing blood. Suddenly, I was grabbed by the ankles and was pulled downwards through the many layers of the earth. Moments after my decent began, I was slammed to the ground, all air forced from my lungs. I gasped. Ugly little creatures grabbed me, stood me up, placed a spiked collars around my neck, ankles, and wrists, then chained me to iron rings set into the ground. The creatures were about three feet tall, hairless, and had hot pink skin. All had two fanged teeth that hung over their bottom lip and all carried pitchfork-like weapons.

Many souls that looked human were bound the same way I was. They were all reeling in agony and were being tormented by the demons and their pointed weapons. Things became clear: I was dead, and I was in Hell!

A tremendous blow to the back of my head took away my awareness and filled my eyes with cold blackness. Peace at last. I would embrace it, enjoy its' cold comfort. Within the blackness of my mind, a high-pitched scream echoed around and stirred my curiosity. Was it the peace calling out to me? Did it have a voice? It was within my mind somewhere and I happily searched for the source. If only I could find it . . .

I awoke to a demon hovering before my face continuing to scream while he slapped my cheek. I tried to lift my hands to thwart his blows but the chains that bound me restricted my movement. Once he had my full attention, he stopped his assault and flew off. Before me, a creature that was sitting in a throne made from stone cleared his throat and all around fell silent. The creature on the throne stood, slow and exact, and before me he paused and began to appraise me. Behind the throne, two giant bowls carved from stone roared with flame, spewing thick black soot that clouded the choking hot air. The creature appraising me was tall and skinny, having long stringy unkempt hair and pale cracked skin. His clothes were in tatters, hanging loosely over his bony body. I figured it was the Devil I was face to face with even though he was missing the razor sharp horns, fire red skin, spiked tail and hoof feet. If I had been given a moment to embrace my fear, I would've died.

At the moment I could only watch the foul creature and wonder what I'd done to be sent there—to Hell. There were many things I had done wrong in my life, but there was much more I felt I'd done right. I'd always believed that the good outweighed the bad. However, my perception may've been off, and it now seemed that I was going to spend an eternity suffering because of it.

The Devil moved himself closer, standing nearly nose-to-nose with me. I clamped my eyes shut and tried to turn away from him. The fear I felt was consuming. Paralyzing. After all, when I was a younger man, my parents had pushed me into religious study. Reluctantly, I'd gone to satisfy their wishes, but hardly ever paid attention to the lectures the priests had given; I'd found them boring, and a comfort only weak people sought and embraced. But the one thing that I had caught onto was that something that looked like the creature that was standing before me could be no one else other than the Devil himself. For what good that did me at the moment, I was glad I knew that much.

"Travis Winter," the Devil said. The whiff of his foul breath rushed up my nose and nauseated me. "You are the being that has been chosen to learn great things and to stand fast against my kingdom and dream." The creature turned his back to me and continued, "My name is Navarro, and I've requested you be brought here so I could try and persuade you otherwise."

His tone was surprisingly pleasurable, soft and merciful. I cracked open one eye barely enough to see out, and observed Navarro returning to his throne. Then he whispered, "Don't run from me, Travis. Just your hearing me out is all I want."

A demon approached me, quickly skipping across the uneven ground. Suddenly he stopped, his pointed ears pulled tightly against his head. He looked behind himself, then all around the room. I watched the other demons about the room begin to scurry. And then I heard what they had been hearing—grumbling sounds, like rolling thunder. It was a distant sound, but approaching quickly. Navarro began to yell to his demons but the broadening noise drowned out his voice. Then suddenly silence came. And then a sudden crash followed by a swarm of all male Angelic creatures that had descended into Hell. Violent battles began to break out all around me. The Angels had majestic wings that were covered with bright white feathers that flapped with authority and grace. A glowing aura seemed to surround the Angelic creatures, making it easy for me to follow their every move throughout the dimly lit pit of Hell.

As the room became consumed with the bloody battle of good versus evil, an Angel came to me. He wrapped his soft wings around me, providing impenetrable protection, and asked, "Are you Travis Winter?"

I became consumed with a certain calm that he, the Angel, was going to make everything all right. I reached forward, needing to touch him. But the chains that bound me continued to restrict me.

"Answer me!" the Angel said, and he shook me. "Are you Travis Winter?"

"Yes," I answered, remaining distant in the comfort that surrounded me, protected me. The Angel retracted his wings and broke the chains that bound me.

"Go!" he told me. The sudden exposure to the chaos dizzied me. "Go up to the surface as fast as you can. Don't look back and never return here!"

I was hesitant in my confusion. I had so many questions I needed to ask him, but couldn't decide which to ask first.

"Go now!" the Angel demanded, but that time he followed with a shove.

A group of demons attacked the Angel and in my fear I ran from there. As I fled, I could hear the Angel's cries of pain as the demons began to tear him apart. I did as the Angel had ordered and found my way to the surface and never looked back. And, at that moment, when things around me finally became quiet and still, though lost and confused, I began my reluctant existence as the Spirit of Independence. I never knew what had happened to the group of Angels that had been sent to rescue me or what the fate of the souls remaining behind had been, trapped in the steamy bowels of Hell. With any luck, I hoped they'd escaped during the diversion the Angels had created when they'd first attacked. If not,

I hoped they had all perished. I know that sounds like a cruel wish, but I knew death would be a better fate than spending even one moment trapped inside that hell.

Chapter 2

DemAngel

Now that the Spirit has gotten his introduction out of the way, allow me to introduce myself. My name is DemAngel. I received my name because I was once an Angel from Heaven who, according to legend, had been turned into a demon. Be wary of the word "demon" and don't let it sway you to Spirit's side so quickly. You may come to understand that things aren't exactly as they seem.

I haven't prepared a speech like Spirit has, and I needn't tell you that there is nothing ominous about me. I will simply allow you to decide what I am for yourself; I offer you to exercise freewill. Freewill is the structure behind fate. Fate can kill you or offer you great things. Isn't freewill the whole reason why the Angels fell to begin with? It is responsible for a lot of things in this world and it could be responsible for your success or failure today. I, like Spirit, will be coming to you and showing you things I feel are important to properly educate you about the functions of our society. I don't want you spending unnecessary time wondering why we've come to you, because even if you were to find out, you couldn't possibly change what is to be. Your fate lies within these very pages, so stay smart and when it comes time for you to choose sides, make sure you decide wisely because the consequences of your decision could be catastrophic. Now, let us begin, shall we?

I had been sent to Westinger Maximum Security Prison. The facility was made strictly of concrete, bars, and bad attitude. Only the criminals that were extreme offenders of the law, committing crimes such as murder and rape were sent there. It's a cold desolate place, a place where people's souls scream out in agony.

When I first walked its' corridors, I immediately noticed the mood inside the facility had been mournful and drab. It was a different feeling from the normal raucous that usually went on—inmates complaining and carrying on about their unfair punishment, and pleading their innocence to the brick walls that couldn't hear them. Well, what else did they have to do?

During the time of my arrival, I observed the inmates holding a silent vigil for a friend that used to offer a sermon to those who needed to hear one. His service would be watched through angled mirrors held beyond the bars that confined the prisoners. Though his teachings were a bit eccentric, they were entertaining nevertheless. For this "friend" was about to take his final walk after being locked away in his cage for ten years on death row. His last meal of steak and potatoes had been served and consumed and his final few moments of "life" were ticking away rapidly with each slam of the second hand pushing forward on the clock.

Two tall muscular security officers unlocked a cell door and stepped inside with the prisoner as two other guards remained outside the cell, keeping watch. The small cubicle the three men crowded was no larger than 4x6, and it housed a single bed with a pillow and no sheets. A metal toilet bowl and sink was located in the rear of the cell. The barest of the minimal was offered in the high security prison that presented little opportunity for the prisoners in either escape or suicide.

A tall skinny man with a shaven head wore an orange uniform with the words "inmate" printed on the back in big bold black letters. He sat motionless on the edge of the bed, awaiting the guards' orders.

"Time to go, Ice," one of the officers said.

Ice stood from the bed and waited in silence. One guard

immediately began placing the required shackles on the inmate's ankles and wrists. He said, "It seems you've been losing some weight. How much do you weigh now, 150 pounds maybe? That's too damn skinny for a man of your size. But I guess that really doesn't matter now, does it?"

The guard had gotten no response from Ice other than a slight smirk. This reaction seemed to unnerve all the guard's standing both inside and outside the cell. One of the guard's outside the cell said, "You've come to the final walk, Francis, I don't see what you have to smile about!"

Ice merely turned to the guard and winked at him. The guard responded in turn by saying, "Wise ass."

The guard placing the shackles on Ice gave the chains a tug to reaffirm their security. He then gave the inmate a shove from behind, sending his feet into motion, then said, "Come on asshole, it's time for you to meet the Reaper!"

Neither fast nor slow did the prisoner walk the long hallway lined with dozens of death row cells. The hallway was brightly lit and bland. Bright white floors and walls added to the lustrous shine of the final walk. Ice walked casually and smiled openly, but thought quietly, wondering if the lights were purposely that bright to prepare the lucky few that would get to see the brilliant bright light in the afterlife. A mirrored glass door was in the far distance, reflecting the approaching four guards and the accompanied inmate.

"I can't feel pity for you, Francis," a guard said. "You've taken a lot of lives and affected even more for some ludicrous purpose. I'm glad the jury saw through your insanity plea; you deserve this. You act as though you don't care for those you victimized. But, that's okay—this is your victims payback."

The guards and prisoner continued to walk down the hallway, their feet moving in perfect unison. The clacking sound of their shoes rattled loudly, symbolic of something significant to come. Ice spoke, his tone soft, unaffected by the impending finality the walk would bring. He said, "What is it you want me to feel? Remorseful?"

The guards gave Ice a grazing glance. Ice returned a neutral stare to them all. He studied them. "That would be it, wouldn't it? How many times must I go through this with you all? I am a servant to a higher being. A being so powerful, so godlike you couldn't possibly comprehend the significance of his call. He has soldiers, people like myself that do his bidding for him on the realm of the flesh. Once I die and leave this world, I will be rewarded for my dedication to him. I'll be called to his side where I'll be able to continue to serve him until his dream becomes a reality. When that day comes, I'll be able to sit back and relax."

The lead guard unlocked the mirrored door, pushed it open, and entered the hollow room. Hearing the clacking sounds of his shoes echoing throughout the tight room reminded me of a drum being pounded for an ancient ritual sacrifice, my heart thundered in anticipation. The guard inside the chamber held the door ajar for the other guards to enter the execution chamber with the prisoner. One guard remained in front of Ice while the remaining two stayed close behind him.

The guards led the prisoner over to the chair in the center of the musty smelling all tan room. The chair had several straps dangling open in the area of the ankles, upper calves, mid thigh, waist, mid torso, upper torso, head, wrists, and biceps.

A guard removed the restraints that had been placed on the prisoner for the walk, and then they sat him in the chair. Without sound, the guards began fastening the straps around each limb they were specifically designed to hold, and once all the straps were securely in place, the guards moved beside the prisoner.

A priest entered the chamber and began reading the prisoner his last rights. "Lord, I ask you to have mercy on this poor man's soul . . ."

Ice's eyes narrowed, instantly filling with rage. His cheeks burned red and veins bulged from his scrunched forehead. "Your Lord, not mine!" he screamed at the priest. The priest backed away, the guards stepped forward. Ice paid them no mind. He continued to scream, "I don't want your damn lord's mercy! Just keep the hell away from me! And to the rest of you . . ." he turned his attention to the mirrored window before the chair. "I'm not looking for absolution. The rules made in this world no longer concern me. I am not done with his purpose and I will not rest until I fulfill my calling. I know where I belong, and that's in my Lord's perfect world. I need to ask you people who so bravely hide your face from me behind that glass, and to each and every guard, shrink, and judge that mistreated and condemned me a question. Do you think you are worth the perfection my Lord is striving for?" He chuckled and shook his head back and forth. "I shall rest now."

The prisoner closed his eyes, seeming content with his retaliation against the immoral. He relaxed his body, causing himself to sink ever so slightly into the chair.

The guards escorted the priest outside the chamber and shut the big steel door behind them. Metal banging against metal bounced around the chamber, and the sound of metal grinding verified the guards slid the locks into place. It was time for Ice to die and I couldn't help but rub my hands together.

After the guards departed, there was a dead moment of silence. Reverberating inside the walls, the sound of levers being slammed tensed Ice. Seconds following, he restrictively bounced in the chair, the skin on his face rippled, and the room filled with the rank smell of his burning flesh.

When the current of electricity stopped flowing through the prisoner, Ice pulled the straps off his body and stood from the chair. He walked to the window and raised his hands high in the air. Victory!

"You cannot kill me," Ice shouted. "He won't allow it!" He turned around and faced the chair while saying, "That piece of shit doesn't even . . ."

His frantic rave ended instantly. To Ice's disbelief, he saw his human body still strapped in the chair. The guards unlocked the chamber door and escorted a doctor inside the room, passing by Ice without notice. The doctor took the pulse from Ice's human body while he watched on in confusion. The doctor looked at his watch, jotted down some notes on paper attached to a clipboard, then looked to the mirrored window, verifying to the onlookers that the execution of the prisoner had been successful. Curtains slowly dropped, covering the window.

From a darkened corner that I chose to observe Ice's final moments in, I spoke assertively to him. "You're dead," I said. "And now it's time for you to come with me."

I grabbed him and pulled him through the floor. Though resistance was expected, Ice submitted to my touch. Onwards I dragged him to the vast chambers deep within the earth. During the way I couldn't help but think that maybe the Lord was right about this man and his dedication to serve the cause.

Chapter 3

Spirit

I was inside a jewelry store silently observing people that were browsing well lit glass display cases that fit the spacious room in a perfect u. Security cameras moved side to side, canvassing the entire sales floor.

The sound of a buzzer resonating inside the store alerted the lone woman behind the counter that potential customers were outside wishing to come inside. She pressed a button hidden on the underside of the counter and unlocked the door, allowing two young men to enter the store. Once the door clicked shut behind the men, one of them started to draw the shades, and the other pulled out a gun and waved it over his head. "If everyone cooperates, no one will get hurt," the one yielding the gun shouted. Tauntingly he pointed his weapon at the people. They screeched from fear, pleaded for their lives and scrambled for cover. I could tell the robber was rehearsed. He didn't pause as he headed to the rear of the store, deliberately searching for the woman that worked behind the counter. On the floor, trembling violently he found her. He pushed the barrel of his gun into the back of her head, and said, "Get yourself together and open the safe. If the cops show while we're still here, people are going to die. Do as we say, and we leave without anyone getting hurt."

The woman gathered herself as best she could and calmly walked to the back room with the robber sticking close to her side. She walked to the rear of the room and pushed on the corner of a framed painting that portrayed a beautiful sunset. It clicked and popped open to reveal louver doors. Pulling them open revealed the face and knobs of a bulky safe. The woman fumbled clumsily as she turned the dial from left to right, her hand unsteady and awkward, the fear unhidden; her face contorted into a mask of frustration and she began to weep. Knowing full well her attempt was futile, she hit the lever to open the safe and nothing happened. She backed away from the safe rattled, and said, "I can't do it. I can't remember the combination!"

The man that stood beside the woman at the safe turned to his partner that was watching over the people and said, "Choose someone special and bring them here. We're going to show Miss Forgetful here what she gets for not cooperating."

Robber Two rubbed his chin and searched the people scattered around the sales floor with consideration. He grabbed a young woman by her wrists and tugged her off the floor. She went limp in his arms, it being her only stance against the fear that gripped her. Robber Two fought diligently to stand her up. While they struggled, the woman at the safe pleaded, "Please, give me one more chance. I can open it." With a hesitant nod of approval from the man, she began flipping through the numbers on the dial again. She hit the lever to open the safe again and nothing happened. Backing away from the safe, the woman looked to the robber and entreated, "Please, if you put the gun away I would be able to do it. I'm so scared."

The robber's face contorted and he gave his friend a hard stare. "Damnit," he shouted, and raised his weapon. He turned the butt of the gun and swung it towards the woman's head.

Propelled into action, I moved. In a blur to the people around, I charged the robber that swung his weapon and hit him with a stiff shoulder. The force of the impact sent him crashing to the floor with bone crushing force. I ran to the store's center and appeared partially translucent, looking to be made strictly of soft light. As I began to repress the light, my body began to take on a more solid form, becoming tangible to the people around. My loose fitting cloak that wrapped my body flowed gently behind me although there was no breeze inside the store.

Robber Two gasped in surprise, mindlessly raised his pistol, aimed and fired it. The weapon discharged a single shot that headed straight for my chest. I fizzled out—a term we Spirits use meaning to make the transition between the physical realm and the spirit realm. Disappearing completely from sight, I was within the spirit realm. Terrified and tense, the two men frantically searched the room for my whereabouts.

I fizzled in behind one of the men and slowly began to tie his shoelaces together and, once finished, I tapped him on his shoulder. The robber turned and found himself face to face with me. I lightly whispered, "Boo!" and startled him. He turned to run and fell heavily to the floor. I turned my attention to the other robber and found he'd taken the opportunity to flee. He was a quick thinker. My attention shifted to the woman before the safe who looked to me as if she were in a trance.

"Amanda!" I called out, trying to gain her attention. She trembled where she stood, remaining unresponsive to my call. "Which way did he go?" I asked her, and slowly, she raised her arm and pointed.

I fizzled and exited the store. Using Amanda's lead and pursuing the scent of the man, I followed his trail to stairs that descended into the subway system. Downwards I went, knowing my prey was hiding somewhere within; my heightened senses told me so.

As I headed down the crowded steps, I examined each person and searched their faces. As each unknowing person walked through me, a deep chill went through them, causing their bodies to shiver wildly from the sudden intense cold. He wasn't where I was, but he was near; his scent was getting stronger.

From the stairs, I saw the robber standing on the platform trying to blend with the ocean of people. I quickly moved to where he stood and fizzled quickly in and then out, just fast enough for him to notice me before him. He began to scream madly and he pushed his way through the crowded platform and jumped onto the tracks. He ran down the poorly lit tunnel and I followed close behind, waiting for the opportune time to strike. Once he was beyond the stare of the inquisitive commuters, I acted. With a simple command from my mind I hurled a board that had been discarded on the trackside. It hit the thug in the upper thighs, tangling his legs, knocking him to the ground. His momentum sent him sliding across the gravel that made up the tunnels bed. Without warning, the robber vanished, seemingly into thin air.

Halting my chase, I fizzled in and retrieved the board I'd used against him. I examined it and determined the board was ordinary. I walked over to the area where the man disappeared and hurled the board and it also vanished.

"Damn!" I said, feeling exasperated and began to release the energy I used to construct my form on the physical realm. The particles began to swirl in a counterclockwise motion and formed a funnel. When I shed enough of the energy from my decaying physical form, I threw the energy outwards and stepped into the spirit realm.

I quickly left the tunnel by ascending through the earth. Once on the surface, I headed to my lair inside an abandoned church on the lower east side. I respectfully kept the dark, stale smelling interior of the church as it had been some twenty-five years past. Mounds of dust had accumulated on the pews, altar, and the open confession booths. Sunlight that broke through the stained glass windows smeared a portrait on the floor as it had every day before.

The abandoned disheveled church had been the center of controversy within the neighborhood it was located in for years. Some called it a landmark, and others called it a hazard. Two sides with very different point of views fought over the church's future with no resolution in sight. I wouldn't leave its sanctity unless I absolutely had to.

I descended through the floor of the church and entered its basement. There, waiting for me was an ordinary human soul I'd befriended years before named Eidolon. The day I found him he was so lost and confused, but was aware enough to know that getting to the light would take him to the other side. Before the light, he pleaded with me for some more time to sort through his confusion. It was real, his confusion, but viably fixable through self-exploration. Finding his request to be reasonable, I reluctantly agreed to his wishes and didn't send him through the light. Since that day, we've built on an awkward relationship that now categorizes us as friends.

"I was inside Amanda's store, watching her as I always do," I explained to Eidolon, and paused a moment to reflect. I continued. "She's grown up so quickly . . . Anyhow, two men attempted to rob her store and I intervened. One of the men ran from the store and I chased him into the subway system where he disappeared. I have to find out why. I'll need you to look over Amanda for me while I'm gone. Please, make sure she's alright."

Eidolon nodded, and said, "Sure, Spirit, I can do that."

I knew he could. I had all the confidence in him that no matter what I was to ask of him, he would do it. "I will meet you back here once I'm done."

I left the church and returned to the void where the robber disappeared. I stepped before the invisible hole and felt around for something to grab onto. I acquired the firm outer edge and pulled on it with all of my might. I struggled against its inflexible hold before a thin clear fabric that seemed to be as flimsy as tissue paper, yet as firm as iron, began to lift. I gave the fabric one last solemn tug before it broke away and revealed a blackened pit.

I pushed my head inside the hole to see if I could get a glance at its' interior. Unexpectedly, a forceful air grasped me and began to pull me in. Catching the outer rim, I struggled to pull myself out, but its force was overpowering and my muscles tired quickly. I let go and was pulled into the blackened abyss where I was violently tossed about and jiggled around before I was spit out of the void and onto the hard ground that crunched beneath the weight of my body. I was face down in a bed of leaves. Feeling no pain from my rough journey through the void, I pushed myself to my feet. Surveying the strange place I was in, I found I'd landed inside a dense forest.

Aimlessly, I set off, wandering trails overgrown with tree branches, shrubbery and weeds. Luckily, I found a break in the trees, and through the opening I spied my first glimpse of a large building that towered high above the tree line. I pushed aside some remaining tree branches that obscured my vision and the entire building in all its immensity came into sight. The building resembled a castle from the days of Medieval Times; a time I'd been intrigued by through the years of my human life and death. The building was constructed entirely of cobblestone brick and two huge towers with crowned tops were located on either side of the structure. Several windows were in the center of the building just above a balcony that ran horizontally across the entire length of the building. Each window was made from stained glass, and each contained a picture that had no meaning to me. A man with no head, but above the body where the head was supposed to be was the sun. Another window showed a picture of Navarro, the creature that had approached me in Hell. Unable to decipher any meaning from all this, I shrugged my shoulders and moved onwards in my inspection of the building. Beside the buildings' entranceway were two big stone demons, squatting, keeping guard of the castle's secrets.

The intense curiosity to see what was inside the building propelled me to look left and right. When I saw I was alone, I cautiously exited the cover of the forest and walked into the entranceway of the beautiful yet eerie looking castle.

As soon as I entered the building, I grabbed some energy and concentrated it into my fist. I juggled the energy around which caused a spark that ignited the energy I controlled. A dull flame surrounded my fist and provided me with enough light to see my way around the darkened hallway. The flickering light cast shadows on the walls that danced mysteriously. Even in the comfort of the light I felt uneasy, like I was being watched.

The entranceway was long and sinuous, seeming endless in my exploration. But soon I emerged into an immense chamber that housed a large table and four overly large chairs. Strange. Candleholders mounted on the walls held lit candle's that flickered, providing me with enough light to see the entire room and its' contents. This meant someone had been here moments before my arrival. The hand I lit the darkness with, crackled and popped as I extinguished the flame. I stepped into the room, immediately taking notice of the platform in the corner of the room. I walked there and found a coffin that had been hallowed from a trees' trunk and placed on a stand. I approached the coffin with careless curiosity and cleared away the cobwebs that blanketed the interior. I froze in horror at my discovery. Inside the coffin were my human remains, carefully laid and still dressed in my WWII uniform. I brushed more of the cobwebs aside from the right breast pocket and muttered the words, "My God," when I eyed the patch that read "Winter" still sewn onto the uniform.

Abruptly, I peered towards the same hallway I used to enter the room and noted someone was approaching. I ran off the platform and hid behind a stanchion that was in the least lighted part of the room. I tried to fizzle and found I couldn't. Pulling myself against the brick-supporting beam, I remained as still and quiet as I could.

Hearing the being, that probably lived within the building, enter the room, I casually peered out from behind the stanchion to see a tall-cloaked creature moving about, seemingly oblivious to my presence. I pulled myself behind the cover of the supporting beam and tried to calm my pounding heart. The follies I'd made that had cost me my life during World War II came into mind; it was those mistakes I vowed never to make again. Keeping my head was what was going to get me out of there unscathed. I had a plan, and that was to stick to cover and work my way over to the hallway and sprint for the outside once the opportunity presented itself.

When I looked again from behind the stanchion to see where the cloaked being was, he turned and faced me. Quickly, I pulled myself behind the cover of the pillar and angrily mouthed the word, "Shit." I'd been spotted and knew nothing good could come from it.

"I knew you had come the moment you landed in the forest," the cloaked beast said, his voice like an ordinary man's. "I was using the trees as cover while I watched you. After you entered the castle I willingly gave you some time to look around. Come out now so I can see you."

Reluctantly, I stepped out from behind the pillar and raised my hands in a kind gesture. "If you'll show me the way out of here, I'll move onwards without trouble."

The shrouded being took a step towards me. He looked to the casket on the platform, and then to me. "Travis Winter, the Spirit of Independence . . ."

I felt uneasy and took a step to the side and started creeping towards the hallway. The shrouded creature anticipated my action and stepped in front of me, blocking my path. I stopped and felt the uneasiness of the situation beginning to unnerve me. The situation felt life- threatening. The creature spoke, his voice deep. "You're ready and there are things we need to take care of."

His actions continued to appear aggressive as was the tone and obscurity of his words. I allowed anger to consume me, to guide me. I shouted, "If you want to take care of something, how about we start with your explanation of what you're doing with my bones!" Then I lunged forward, attempting to catch the creature off guard. He groaned like an untamed beast and swatted me to the side. I fell to the ground, the force of his blow skidding me across the floor. Using this opportunity to try and fizzle, but finding I still couldn't, I jumped to my feet and started running for the hallway. I ran into something unseen, bounced backwards, and flopped heavily to the floor. The creature walked to where I was sprawled, his probable anger-filled expression hidden by the darkness of his hood, and he pulled me to my feet. I swung at him, missing him grossly. I was grabbed around the neck with a grip so powerful it paralyzed me. Struggling for breath, the creature lifted me off my feet and thrust me backwards. I was slammed into a brick wall that cracked around the contour of my body. I was doomed.

"You, Spirit," the creature said winded, "are going to relax and listen to what I have to say."

I was choking, and struggled desperately to free my airway. I barely managed to say, "Okay, anything you want."

"Good," the cloaked being said, loosening his grip. "Because I am not an enemy of yours. I am here to protect your body."

I relaxed myself in response to his repose. I gasped hungrily at the air I was allowed to breathe. The beast lowered me to the ground, released me, and said, "If someone is to destroy your bones, your existence will cease forevermore. If I wanted harm to come to you then I would've done just that."

I could still feel his crushing grasp wrapped around my throat though he no longer held me. I started choking, knowing full well if I were still an ordinary man, I would've been broken by his attack.

"Your life essence is within those bones on the platform," the creature continued without pausing to show concern for my condition. "And anyone that can gain control of a Spirit's bones can control the Spirit's fate."

I silently considered his words while pondering the probability I'd stumbled upon this creature. A human disappeared into thin air, revealing an invisible entranceway to a fantasyland. The odds were unlikely. Maybe I was walking on the heels of predestination . . . Answers I'd been seeking for so long were being divulged, and I didn't want to defer his willingness to volunteer such precious information by questioning such odds. I would allow the path I'd begun walking on to take me anywhere it would lead me so as long as the answers I sought were revealed along the way.

"Once your bones have been buried, then your existence will cease, but this doesn't mean indefinitely. Your bones will have to be recovered in order for your awareness to return. Navarro knows the circumstances surrounding your weaknesses. He knows full well how to destroy a Spirit and has been searching for your remains day and night."

He paused in thought, muttered the word, "Weaknesses," and contemplated in silence for a while longer before saying, "You are no longer of the flesh, but we are still vessels inside a shell. And the shell you're in now has many weaknesses and as many strengths. There will be more death for you as there will be life. I wish not to overwhelm you with too much information. You will learn the necessary things as time goes on."

The creature fell to silence again, and when I was sure he wasn't going to speak anymore, I prompted him, by saying, "I am willing to learn what you have to teach me."

"And I wish to teach you much. I am eager," he said. "Understand,

I've waited for your coming for a long time. The circumstances that brought you here were Heaven sent."

I nodded, half in understanding and half doubtful. He continued. "This Land, this castle, everything you see here was built with my own hands. I built it to be special. This place is unlike the spirit and physical realms you roam, in a few different ways. It is impossible to fizzle while you're here. It helps me in the fight to keep your bones safe from Navarro."

"I want to help you in the fight against Navarro."

"As you must. Understand if Navarro or one of his hordes follows you here, your very existence will be in danger. Probably over for good. Navarro found the Spirits before you under tougher circumstances. Don't under estimate his abilities or over estimate your own—your life depends on it."

I barely heard a word of what he said after he mentioned there were other Spirits before me. What were their roles in the scheme of things, what was their downfall? I questioned this, and he said, "You are eager to find answers, to finally understand your purpose and I like that. But first you need to learn to have patience. Too much information too soon can confuse you. Overwhelm you. It'll make you make unwise decisions. I believe you are the most promising Spirit to come along since they began coming. Perhaps you will be able to accomplish the things that need to be done."

"Tell me," I said without hesitance, "what needs to be done?"

He chuckled and shook his head. "You're also persistent in your quest to understand. Very well, to whet your appetite: the destruction or dethroning of Navarro is what needs to be done. As time goes on, the violence in the world worsens. This is mainly due to Navarro's influence and his ability to control people on the subconscious level. I know he goes to men and women in their sleep, invades their dreams, establishes a relationship with them. His choices in people are always right one's, and the people do his bidding; some knowingly, others completely oblivious. They'll kill and be killed in his name. Each person that dies in sin is another soul for his army."

Silence befell, and he allowed me to absorb the information I'd learned. It was all so mind-boggling. Unbelievable. Bet yet, it was all so knowingly true.

"Take everything I say into consideration," he said. "Heed my warnings and you may survive the onslaught of Hells' minions. If you've been fortunate enough to remember any part of your human life, push it out of your mind. Things aren't safe within the confines of your skull—it can be invaded by beings much more powerful than yourself. You're no longer a human being and the people you left behind need to live their life without the interferences and misfortunes your function in the afterlife can bring."

"Why, why have I been chosen to be one of your Spirits?"

"My Spirits?" He chuckled, seeming genuinely amused by my confusion. "No, Travis, this is much larger than you know, maybe much larger than you could ever believe."

The creature wrapped in cloth began to walk away, drifting into the hallway. His parting words were softly spoken, expectant that I would return again. He said, "My name is Divination and I believe you are the one that can stop Navarro before the final war between the two opposing forces commences. The power you wield radiates off you; I can feel it. You've learned a great deal today, but you still have a lot to learn. I will make a promise to you: in time, everything will become perfectly clear to you. Be patient in your quest and never careless. For all of our sake."

I ran to catch the cloaked being, and when I did, he escorted me in silence to a cave covered by moss and greenery from the forest. Without uttering another word, he departed and I stepped into the cave he brought me to, and in an instant, I was returned to the train tunnel I originally started from. Without delay, I returned to the church to meet with Eidolon.

Chapter 4

Amanda

I've been given the honor of being able to contact you so I could share events in my past relevant to you and your future quest. My name is Amanda, and to clear up any confusion you may have as to who I am, I am the woman from the jewelry store.

Not too long after Spirit intervened in the robbery attempt and chased the man that ran from the store, the police arrived. They discovered the one robber lying face down on the floor, unconscious from his fall. They immediately cuffed him and called in paramedics to tend to his injuries.

I was still standing beside the safe when a police officer approached me. He asked if I was hurt and I responded kindly, saying, "No, no I'm not."

He pulled a chair to me and asked if I wished to sit. I did, and he told me to try and relax as if that were a possibility after having a gun pushed into my head. Being sure I was comfortable, the officer disappeared into the ocean of bodies. About five minutes later, a big rugged looking man with a predominant square jaw came over to me.

"I am detective Bowman," he said. He was holding a large cup of coffee in one hand, and he extended his bulky free hand, offering it for me to shake. I was obliged to react to his offering and he pumped my hand up and down twice, released it, then said, "I know now is a bad time for you and all, but I need to ask you a few questions. While things are fresh we like to roll with it. This gives us a better chance of catching all the people involved."

He patted his pockets and came out with a cigar. He popped it in his mouth, chewed it, and then asked, "Do you mind?" I shook my head in response and he quickly retrieved his lighter. He lit his cigar and puffed away in silence for a moment. Blue smoke clouded the air around us and the fine smell of cherry tobacco scented the air.

"First round of business is those camera's. Are they hooked up to a taping system, we can't seem to locate one?"

"No, it's only used as a deterrent," I said.

He took a few more puffs on his cigar, inhaled the smoke, and said, "I see." Smoke oozed from his mouth and nose and while it continued to ooze, he said, "Have you seen these men before?"

"No, I haven't."

He nodded his head towards the man that was being tended to by the paramedics, and said, "He had a friend with him?"

"He did. He ran away."

The detective studied me expressionless; what was he thinking? He chewed his cigar and the ash end dropped onto his shirt and rolled onto the floor. "Crap," he muttered, looked to me and said, "Sorry."

Was his apology for the language or the ash he dropped on the floor? I figured for both.

He swatted the ash off his shirt then ground it into the rug with his shoe. "An officer will be over in a few minutes to take a statement from you, and he'll need a description of the other suspect. I thank you." I gave him a fake smile, and he walked away.

Alex, my boyfriend, sprinted into the store calling my name with a desperate tone. I stood from the chair and called out to him. He stopped in the center of the sales floor and spotted me. He shot me an analyzing stare and I smiled to reassure him I hadn't been hurt.

Seeming relieved, he ran to me, squeezed me in his arms, and whispered, "I came as soon as I heard. Are you alright?"

"Just shaken," I said, feeling comfort in his strength. He kissed the side of my head, and said, "I'm here for you now. Things will be just fine."

I believed him.

After the police took all statements and cleared the store, Alex and I were left alone. I was too tired to work the rest of the day out, and looked to close up shop, at least for the rest of the day. I wrote up a sign explaining how the store would be closed until tomorrow and hung it in the window frame of the door. Alex came behind me, rubbed my shoulders gently, and said, "I'll close up the store for you and meet you at your place when I'm finished."

I reluctantly agreed with him and allowed him to walk me to my car. He opened the door for me and closed it once I was situated. "Please, put your safety belt on and drive carefully. I'll see you in a bit."

We kissed goodbye and I watched Alex walk to the store. Fifteen minutes later, I arrived at my apartment and thought to call Alex to see how he was fairing. The telephone within the jewelry store was answered after the second ring and was dropped. The receiver clunked loudly which provided temporary cover for a commotion coming from within the store.

"Alex?" I questioned, growing increasingly concerned with what I was hearing. I pushed a finger into my free ear and pressed my other ear tightly against the receiver. Unidentifiable sounds were coming through the phone, a tiff of some sort? I listened intently.

A terror filled scream boomed through the phone and rattled my head. I reared and began screaming into the mouthpiece, "Alex, what is it, what's wrong?"

I pressed the telephone back to my ear and heard someone handling the phone then hang it up. I listened until the hum of the dial tone compelled me to slam the receiver down and run to my car. I raced to the store.

When I arrived at the store, I noticed the front door was slightly ajar. The closed signs had been placed in the door and the shades had been drawn, covering the interior of the store in darkness. I stood before the door and contemplated opening it. Should I go for the cops first, or should I peer inside? The thought that the robber that escaped earlier in the day might've returned unnerved me. The door swung open without my touch.

Frozen in place and emotionless by the unexplainable, I waited to gaze at the unknown. When the door opened fully I wanted to run away, scream at the top of my lungs and cry out for all the tragedies in the world. But I remained choked in movement and in voice and could only examine what was before me in anguished silence. Alex was hanging from a ceiling beam by a cord that was wrapped around his neck. His head was slumped forward and his eyes were wide and aware though glassy and red. His skin was a pale white and purple patches stained him. Blood still trickled from his nose, mouth and ears; his death still fresh.

As if something had begun to control my emotions, without fear, I stepped inside the store and pushed the door closed behind me.

"Amanda," a low sibilant voice familiar to me called out. I looked around and saw something move quickly in the rear of the store.

"Amanda," the voice called again. It sounded as if the lips that spoke were pressed against my ears. I spun curiously, still unafraid.

"Amanda," the voice called again, but this time yelling. "Look at me when I'm talking to you!"

A chill coursed through my body and I suddenly knew where it reluctantly. "Alex?" was coming from. I slowly moved my eyes upwards and questioned

"Look what has happened to me because of you!" he said.

I deniably shook my head. I could feel the fear entering my body, building, compelling me to flee. I watched Alex reach his hands upwards and try and loosen the cord that had begun to slice through the skin on his neck. I began backing away, my self-control hanging by a frayed thread. I bumped into something hard. I turned to see what it was that blocked my path. A beautiful man stood before me, a soft glowing light surrounding his body. Inner peace surrounding his presence held me still. I looked to his bare chest, the muscles so perfect and strong. His long flowing hair dangled around his shoulders, and his young vibrant face so innocent and gentle looking. Lust was not an option but love was.

"Don't worry about him, my dear," said Angel Face and I was completely enamored. His voice was like a chorus of a thousand people singing the gospel and my heart their metronome. "Alex has died, but you are alive. You've made some powerful enemies, enemies that are looking to drive you mad. They're doing this by showing you things that are beyond human understanding."

I began to weep. Angel Face wiped the tears from my cheeks, and said, "I beg you not to cry. The evil that surrounds you is playing games with your mind and to defeat this evil you need to stand fast. I want you to know I tried to help Alex but his fate was beyond my control. He loved you very much and he doesn't want you to remember him like this."

Angel Face pointed to Alex and I looked. His appearance was dreadful . . .

I turned to see Angel Face, and as mysteriously as he'd come, he disappeared. Beyond my reasoning I exited the store, locked its' door, and went home.

Chapter 5

DemAngel

After I delivered the soul I gained from the execution chamber to our Lord, I was immediately sent on another assignment. Its objective was to make the woman named Amanda aware of us and to inform her of others that may try and manipulate her.

I traveled hastily to the place I'd spent much time observing her unseen to her eyes: her jewelry store. My timing couldn't have been any worse. A most unfortunate robbery attempt sent Amanda home early and her boyfriend, Alex, was in the store closing out the register, preparing the bank deposits, pulling the shades and placing the closed sign in the door. When he shut the lights off, I entered the physical realm and observed him from the cover of shadows. Unfortunately, his insight was profound and he was aware of my presence and he requested, no, demanded I show myself as he peered into the covering darkness.

I didn't answer his call and remained perfectly still. I was hoping his curiosity cured when he'd gotten no response from me and he would simply take his leave. But he didn't. He marched towards me, insisting he knew I was there, continuing to demand I reveal myself. I was diffident at first; it had been some time since I had any direct contact with a human. I knew it was forbidden for a divine knight to show himself to mortal eyes. Dismissing my concerns, going against my better judgment, I stepped forward and illuminated the outermost portion of my body so his wondering eyes could see me.

He stepped back and groaned in astonishment. I continued forward and reached out to him with my mind. I put him in a dreamlike state, tricking his senses so he couldn't separate reality from fantasy. I then went to take Alex from the store, to bring him to his own nest where he would wake and believe his visions to be nothing more than a dream. But, before I could move myself close to him, Travis Winter, the Spirit of Independence, manifested from the spirit realm to the physical realm. His very presence shook me to the core. His powers far exceed my own and his personality is most unpredictable.

He stood before me, silent and cognitively scrutinizing my union with the human. I didn't dare say anything to him because I knew the slightest irritation could set him off. I stood still, looking away from his accusing gaze. He circled me like a vulture would dying prey. He demanded an explanation of my actions.

I answered him, being careful to keep my voice soft and respectful. I told him how Alex had laid eyes upon me and that I temporarily confused his mind so I could take him to his home. The Spirit was outraged by my intentions. He approached me, his wide chest filled with air, his arms bulging from his sides. He circled me and roughly brushed against me. After some tense moments of preparing myself for his fury, Spirit stopped behind me and angrily whispered how it is forbidden to allow any human to see a celestial knight, and how if any human does, they must perish by any means necessary without delay.

I pleaded for the human's life, begging the Spirit to lay his eyes on the helpless man before us and to find the love he once had for them and to show mercy. Spirit laughed at the man whose eyes were transfixed on the nullity before him. His mouth was dripping drool like he was a helpless child without yet gaining awareness of his life.

My pleading enraged the Spirit even further. He turned to me and raised his voice to a deafening level. He accused me of being weak, a coward for not slaughtering the man. He reached to grab Alex by his throat, but I leapt forward and knocked Spirit off balance, temporarily keeping the man safe. I wouldn't allow anything to happen to that man. The Spirit's vengeance turned towards me. The look his eyes held was intense, surprised, angry and ready to exact punishment. He closed his eyes and tilted his head back. He began to chuckle, and while he did so, I felt the strangest things happening to my innards. They felt as if they were moving around, churning like they'd been turned to living snakes. I had no doubt the Spirit was slowly pushing my insides into my stomach and up my throat. He was turning me inside out and the agony I was in was unbearable. I began to choke and vomit blood. I found myself completely defenseless against Spirit's onslaught.

The telephone rang with a roar, distracting Spirit. He went to the phone, picked it up and dropped it on the counter. He walked over to Alex and beat his body for a hellacious minute, the assault pulling him from the trance I'd placed him in; my sacrifice was in vein. Once Spirit was satisfied with the results of his attack, he hung up the telephone and strung Alex up with a cord. He was strangled to death.

While Alex was still flailing on the end of the line he'd been hung with, Spirit demanded I dare not attempt to interfere in his business again or he would finish what he started. Spirit pulled me from the physical realm and discarded me on the floor like a piece of trash. To my relief, he departed without punishing me further.

By the time I healed myself enough to move, Amanda had arrived in her store and discovered Alex's body. I shielded her emotions best I could and took some time to explain to her the dangers lurking around her. I told her to go home and she did without hesitance. Beside Alex's body I remained silent at first, then my emotions gripped me and told me to speak. I told Alex how sorry I was about his fate and how I wished I could've changed it.

Chapter 6

Spirit

When I left the mysterious Land of Chova, I made a swift journey to the abandoned church I'd called my home for nearly fifty years. Upon my arrival I was greeted with the most unfortunate turn of events. The building that had sheltered my companion, Eidolon and me had been engulfed with raging fire. It had grown out of control, destroying the entire buildings insides without prejudice. By the time I'd arrived, the fire was working hungrily on the church's frame. I stood transparent, invisible to any human's eyes, staring helplessly at the inferno. My body shivered at the notion of being powerless to put a stop to such a thing and brought my mind back to the day my commanding officer held his pistols' cold barrel to my forehead. Damn that day.

I watched on as firemen fought their small war against the flames and felt a changing feeling consume me. The love I felt for each person hugged my heart and brought a compassionate tear to my eye. They all were so beautiful, but in their own right. If I could somehow get them to understand what their life was all about, what awaited them in the next life. But ignorance and pride within the human heart would only bring despair, intolerable suffering and confusion for the people of the world. I hated knowing that and wished there was something I could do to change it.

A loud thunderous explosion erupting from the blaze pulled me from my thoughts. A fireman began to yell at the onlookers to back themselves up. I pulled my garment tangled around my legs and pushed it behind me. I examined the surrounding area with passionate determination to see if I could find something from the ordinary. I figured Navarro finally found where I retreated to and he attempted to capture me by sending his demons for me. Unable to find me within the church, I thought the demons might've taken Eidolon and burnt the church as a message to me. But if they'd gone for Eidolon, then they would've gone for Amanda too! So quickly I pushed onwards, journeying to Amanda's den.

I discovered Amanda lying on her bed face down. Her breathing was gravely shallow and her skin had turned a sickening purplish color. Knowing death was near, I quickly acted. Fizzling into the physical realm I placed both my hands on top of her head and opened her mind to my own. I saw how she discovered Alex's body inside her store and didn't realize it until she returned home. No recollection remained within her mind as to why she went to her store, or why she returned home after seeing his body. I pried into her mind deeper, trying to loosen her wrapped experiences that remained stubbornly strong against my intrusion. Inside her psyche I plummeted, and this is what I saw:

Amanda was gazing at her night table that sits alongside her bed. The table held a digital alarm clock, a lamp, and a bottle of sleeping pills. She took the bottle and shook it to determine its' contents. It gave off a loud rattle. Satisfied knowing her plan could be carried through, she opened the bottle and dumped a generous amount of pills into her palm. She shuffled to the kitchen and retrieved a glass of water. In the time it took her to get from her bed to the kitchen, she maundered the choice she decided to settle on to ease the pain associated with losing her loved one. It was a bad choice, against her beliefs even, but it is what would ease the pain she felt inside her heart. She returned to bed and began to take one pill at a time and washed it down with a swig of water until her hand was completely empty of pills. Fearful for her soul's judgment but satisfied to be done with the world, she lay back down, reached out to the lamp and grabbed the dangling chain and gave it a tug. The darkness consumed her tired mind and quickly brought sleep.

I took my hands from her head and paused momentarily to regain my equanimity; entering someone's mind is an experience that leaves me feeling spent and nauseated. After my belly settled and the cobwebs cleared some, I shook Amanda and called out her name loudly. She stirred slightly and mumbled something indecipherable. I shook her again and moved her feet off the bed. I pulled her up to a sitting position. With a thought I churned her insides and she vomited violently several times. Acidic liquid and half digested food splashed on the floor in front of her and she stroked her chin. The bile smeared on her face and clung grossly to the back of her hand.

I called to her again and slapped my hands in front of her face. Her eyes opened for a moment and closed again. I repeated the action and her eyes fluttered open and closed. I pulled her to her feet.

"Come," I told her with a soft tone.

"Alex?" she questioned, hopeful in her inquiry. "I don't feel so good."

I took her souls hand into my own and asked her to come along with me. Unbeknownst to her, she stepped from her body. I led her into a small room and positioned her before a closed door then left her sight.

"Open the door, Amanda," I told, and without hesitation she turned the knob and pushed the door open. At first she stood and looked into the room in awe. Clouds rolled around on the floor and drifted overhead. A cool-warm breeze swooped gracefully past her body.

"Go inside," I coached, and she did.

"So peaceful," she whispered, closed her eyes and breathed deeply. Satisfied, she cracked a smile.

"Amanda," a male calling voice echoed from the distance. With brief hesitation she opened her eyes and searched the distance with curiosity.

A bright light containing the silhouette of a man approached Amanda from the distance. Amanda dug at her eyes with the palms of her hands, disbelieving what she was seeing. When the illuminated sphere settled before Amanda, it dimmed, revealing an ordinary man.

"Remove your hands from your eyes, Amanda," said the man. "This may be the last chance we get to see each other for a while."

She slowly removed her hands but kept her eyes tightly shut.

"Please," the man begged, "look at me."

Frightened, she hesitated, but had to look. "No," she said at first glance, struggling to make sense of things. "This cannot be, I saw your dead body today!"

"Reach out and touch me," said Alex. "Then tell yourself I'm not really standing here before you."

"Just a dream," she muttered and reached to touch him.

When Amanda made physical contact with Alex, she weakly fell to her knees and began to weep. "It can't be!" she muttered and repeated.

"But it can, Amanda. You felt me with your own hands. How do you explain that?"

"A dream, a very realistic dream, that's all. You're dead, I saw you."

"My human body died, Amanda, not my soul. Not what makes Alex, Alex."

She looked up to him and pouted understandingly. A million thoughts raced through her mind all at once, but one was clearer than any other. The thought moved to her lips. "I love you, Alex. I never thought I'd get the chance to tell you that again."

Alex was moved, choked up with emotion. This was hard for him as I told him it would be. But he wanted to see her, to add importance to her life. "Alex," I called while remaining deaf to Amanda's ears and blind to her eyes. "It's time. I must take her back."

Alex nodded in understanding. He knew the importance in my words and all hesitation left him because of it. "It is time you leave, Amanda, return to your life."

"No!" she shouted and began to bawl hysterically. "I want to stay here with you; I miss you. It's so peaceful here, we can build on that, recapture what we had before the madness entered our life!"

"Amanda," Alex said, the hurt evident in his soft tone. "I want you to know I love you. I also want you to know how important your life is. To do what you've attempted to do is unthinkable, unforgivable from the side I'm on. Embrace the life you've been given and the memories of those who loved you during it."

Alex hugged Amanda, kissed her forehead and simply turned and walked away. My heart sank, feeling the pain of both people. But this is what I needed to do; it's what would help save Amanda's life and ultimately her soul. Knowing this kept me going.

I filled the room with a blinding light. Amanda recoiled and tried hiding her eyes within the cusp of her arm. This presented me with the perfect opportunity to act. I quickly scooped her up and returned her soul into her body that had been moved to the ICU in a local hospital.

There I sat, waiting for Amanda to come back to me, to the world. Her thoughts were jumbled most of the time, and the rest of the time there were no thoughts at all. Death was so close to Amanda; I was angry at her for attempting something so foolish. I hoped what I'd done would change her.

Abruptly, Amanda sat up in bed and let out a powerful cry for Alex. Two nurses hurried into the room and pushed Amanda back down onto the bed.

"It was only a dream," one nurse told her. "I need you to lay down, Amanda, your body is weak and needs rest. The doctors will be pleased to hear you've regained consciousness."

When both nurses left the room, Amanda sat back up and cradled her face with both hands. "Everything seemed so real . . ."

I slowly plucked the emotions away that allowed her to fear and grieve; everything in the world was just perfect to her. When it was gone, fully under my control, I fizzled into the physical realm and stood at the foot of her bed. She looked to me with an astonished stare. Curiously, she removed the covers that wrapped her body and got out of bed without removing her gaze from my eyes. She reached her hand out and touched the back of my hand.

"You," she said. "You're the man I've been seeing all my life . . ."

My heart thundered and my palms became clammy. "I'm . . . I watch over you."

"Why? Why do you cover your face?"

I shamefully turned my head away and she quickly looked to comfort me. She reached her hand to touch the side of my face.

"Amanda!" a nurse said, her displeasure evident. She escorted Amanda back to bed, and said, "We told you you've got to lie down. Your body needs the rest and your heart monitor must be on at all times. Now give me your finger."

Amanda stuck out her pointer finger while scanning the room. She said, "He was here, I touched him."

"Who was here?" the nurse asked and finished placing the heart monitor on her finger. She fastened it with medical tape.

"The man that wears the mask, the one that was at the store. The one that I've seen in my room."

The nurse gave the room a once over and retorted to Amanda's claim by saying, "Well I can assure you there is no one in here now."

Amanda snickered. "If he doesn't want you to see him, you won't. I'll bet he's here watching us right now."

A tall thin male doctor with a shaven head entered the room and took Amanda's chart off the footboard and studied it. Returning the chart from where he got it from, he turned his attention to Amanda.

"And how are you feeling today?" asked the doctor.

"Okay," said Amanda.

The nurse interjected, saying, "Apparently she feels well enough to stand and move about."

The doctor nodded and walked to the side of the bed. "Well that's good to hear," he said, and looked down on Amanda. He tightened his face playfully, and said, "Though you're not to do that. I need you to sit up for me."

Amanda shot a distasteful glance towards the nurse and sat up. "When can I go?" she asked.

The doctor's attention shifted to the nurse. "Didn't you tell the patient?"

Perplexed, the nurse replied. "Doctor?"

The doctor quickly lashed out and grabbed the nurse by her throat. She flailed in his grasp, the meaning behind the doctor's motive not yet registering. He cocked his fist back and punched her in the face. A sickening thud and furious spatter of blood made my grip on Amanda's emotions slip. The nurse fell assumingly dead, and Amanda screamed for her life. The doctor turned towards Amanda, and I fizzled into the physical realm. Catching the doctor off guard, I sent a furious barrage of fists at his face. The doctor simply shook the blows off and smiled defiantly.

"I've been warned about you," he said. "But be aware that Ice has come prepared."

I was completely baffled to see that this was no ordinary man standing before me; I never suspected one from the other side not being the elite would be sent over to the physical world. It seemed Hell was getting desperate. My perplexity kept me from continuing with my assault, giving the doctor time to respond. I was punched on the chin and knocked to the ground. My head buzzed from the blow and the room around me blurred. Knowing Amanda was in immediate danger, I forced myself to stand. Catching movement forming all around us from inside the spirit realm, I cried out to Amanda, telling her to run from the hospital.

Hundreds of demons began to swarm, hungering to please their master. But I knew if I kept Ice busy, Amanda would be able to escape freely. The swarming demons weren't able to enter the physical realm; therefore they didn't present any danger to Amanda, just Ice did.

Desperate to buy Amanda some time, I sent a punch towards Ice that landed on his chin. A loud thud accompanied the impact of the blow and a heavy thump followed as Ice's body dropped to the floor.

"Run, get out of here now!" I shouted before I pulled Ice into the spirit realm. Amanda remained within the room, alone and frozen with fear as the swarming demons piled on top of me. They clawed me, kicked, punched, bit, and filled every orifice with their fingers, spiked tails and forklike spears. I couldn't resist the oppressive amount of demons that were relentless in their pursuit to pull me downwards, into the caverns that belonged to those of the underworld. Defiantly I sank . . .

Chapter 7

Navarro

My name is Navarro and I am sure you've heard a lot about me by now. No doubt, all bad, but as you come to know me and find the true reasons behind my actions, you'll see I'm not as bad as some would lead you to believe. The only thing I ask you to do is hear me out and don't be so quick to prejudge me; that's all I've ever asked from Travis. If only he would've listened to me that day, things would've been so much easier. If you can accomplish what I ask of you then you've already surpassed those who came before you. Yes, there were some before you, just like there were other Spirits before Travis. Like Travis, you are the most promising to allow me to present my side of things. It's what you've been bred for since birth, and I think on the subconscious level, you recognize this and embrace it. Think back on your life, all the answers to your reading this are there. All the questions stirring inside your mind led you to this. But enough blathering for now, allow me to move on to the events on hand.

After the Spirit had been removed from the hospital, I watched Amanda standing within the room, alone, frozen with fear. I didn't count the time that elapsed before the poor girl tilted her head backwards and looked pleadingly to the sky. She raised her hands high above her head and opened her arms wide. "Why? Why me? You won't answer my calling either, will you?"

I reached my pale-clawed hand out and lightly rested it on her shoulder. "No, He won't," I said, "but I will." My penetrating voice startled her, sending her scurrying away from me. From across the room, she turned and looked to me. Repulsed by what she saw, her face distorted and she began to scream. Admittedly, my appearance has a little to be desired. I stand well over six feet tall and I'm sickly thin. I have long scraggly unkempt hair and my skin is pale and split like the deserts dry surface. My clothes are charcoal black from years of dirt and soot being ground in; trying to save the soul of man leaves me no time to keep clean.

"Jesus!" she screeched and ran from the room. I walked out the door and continued to speak to the foolish girl as if she'd never left my side. "It is sad that your prayers will never be answered. Your god doesn't give a crap about you or your cries for help. He never has, and unfortunately, never will."

I stood and watched Amanda run down the empty hospital corridor that I, moments before, posed as a police officer to the staff, had ordered them to clear out all patients and doctors using a story that a dangerous madman had escaped from the mental ward and was thought to be active in that particular wing. I know that may sound ridiculous, but my influence is strong. So strong, in fact, I could move mountains with a mere thought. Thanks to the ensuing chaos and a touch of my influence, the room Amanda occupied so happened to be passed over.

But now that I was finally able to meet with Amanda, she frantically ran away from me, searching for an unlocked door throughout the hospital wing. She found one at the far end of the hallway. When she entered the room, I quickly fizzled into the spirit realm and journeyed to the room she was scrambling around in, frantically searching for a hiding spot.

In the rear of the room, a bronze coat rack held a sports jacket and white smock. A finely polished lacquer finished oak desk with a maroon leather chair with wheels on the legs was pushed neatly under the desk. Three matching fluffy leather chairs were positioned before the desk, and several framed diplomas hung on the wall, proudly displaying the level of education the doctor of this office had reached.

Invisible to her eyes, I watched Amanda pull the chair out and crawl beneath the desk. She reached out and grabbed hold of the chair's leg and pulled it in, making it appear as if it was left undisturbed.

Being bilateral (becoming two separate entities at one time), I was able to keep one form within the spirit realm to watch Amanda from within the room she hid in, and was able to move my other form before the door to the doctors office concurrently. Though I am weaker when I become two, there are many advantages to the trick that has taken me many human lifetimes to master.

I observed Amanda pushing the chair away and peek her head out from underneath the desk and look to the door; her hopes for losing me were so high. But it wasn't I who was the enemy. The door she looked to had a wavy glass window making anything on the other side have a kaleidoscope appearance. And there, unclear through the glass, my other form waited. By my command, I knocked lightly.

"Amanda," I said diligently. "I know you're in here and you're scared. I understand, but I'm not going to hurt you. Please, come out or I'm coming in."

She cupped her mouth to conceal sound and as quietly and quickly as she could, she retreated beneath the desk. I bowed my head in indecision, and moved my other half away from the door.

"Oh, thank god," she said in relief, hearing my person departing. She relaxed, her stampeding heart suddenly discernable through the drumming in her ears. She looked out from beneath the desk, verifying my departure. She breathed a sigh of relief and seconds afterwards she became placid. I swung the door to the office open and pushed the head of a CPR dummy into the room. "Amanda," I made it say. "May I come inside to talk with you instead of that creepy looking guy that was around you earlier?"

Amanda screamed and quickly retreated again. I laughed at the simplicity of fear and what it brings; what sort of protection would the underside of a desk provide for her if I was truly evil? None. I rejoined my two halves on the physical realm knowing full well my playfulness was wrong. I sat the dummy on one of the chairs and sat myself on the desktop. I knocked on it lightly, saying, "I know you're under here, Amanda. I mean you no harm, I want to help you but cannot if you refuse me."

"God, please," she whimpered, "Help me!"

I leaned over the side of the desk and looked directly into Amanda's reddened eyes. "If you mean the God above you can forget it. He doesn't want me, you, or anyone on this world."

Amanda struggled to move her big 200-pound frame from beneath the desk. She ran around the room without direction, pulling open the first door available to her and revealed a closet filled with white robes and gauze pads. I stood from the desk, and calmly said, "Amanda, please, calm down."

"Leave me alone," she screamed and found her way out of the room. Again, I used my gift of becoming bilateral and split myself into two. One half stayed in the physical realm while the other half retreated to the spirit realm. I would use the one on the spirit realm to spy on Amanda.

I caught up to her just as she reached a dead end in the hallway where a set of swinging doors stood before her. She turned to run back in the direction she came from, but saw my other half approaching from the hallways end. She reluctantly pressed on, pushing her way through the swinging doors.

The room was filled with metal gurneys and almost all the tables were occupied with dead bodies covered with baby blue sheets. At the rear of the room, a slanted metal table had a stream of water flowing on it. Just above the table, clean stainless steel handsaws, knives, and an assortment of power tools hung from a rack.

"An autopsy table," Amanda muttered, troubled by the tasteless coincidence. She located an empty gurney and laid on it. She pulled a sheet over herself and lay perfectly still. I admired her creativity.

My other entered the room through the swinging doors and once again rejoined with its other half on the physical realm. "I just want to talk," I told her while standing at the foot of the gurney she laid on. "All I ask in return is that you listen. I understand that my looks may be frightening to you, but I can assure you that is only skin deep. I intend to do you no harm. I know you've noticed a man following you. He intends on doing you harm like he has Alex and I am here to prevent that from happening. In time, Amanda, I am confident you will see that I am telling you the truth. I understand your fear and can't blame you for it; it's what He promised would happen after all."

I turned and walked away and stopped at the double swinging doors. "He sent someone to do you harm, but I knew all about it and intervened. He's been taken into custody now so you're safe for the time being."

I turned to walk away when Amanda shrieked in terror. Spirit had somehow escaped those who held him, and he'd returned to barbarously attack Amanda and attempt to do so in my presence. His arrogance would be the death of him. He held her down, one hand was wrapped around her throat and the other was cocked back, ready to slash down with a knife.

Without thought my body split. One part remained on the physical realm while the other quickly entered the spirit realm. My physical form charged Spirit and knocked him down before he could harm Amanda any further. We wrestled around, each struggling to gain control of the sharpened blade. His strength was even to my own if not greater. I needed to act and do so swiftly. I wrapped Spirit and fizzled, dragging him into the spirit realm where my other self waited readied, knowing its other half intended on bringing Spirit there. My spiritual form pulled the Spirit from me, fighting to restrain him. I quickly returned to the physical realm to check on Amanda and found she was badly shaken, but not physically hurt in any way.

"Leave here now!" I commanded. "He's dangerous and has come here for you!" I pulled her to her feet and pushed her. Her feet continued moving, quickening to a run. I knew for the moment she would be safe so I returned to aide my other half in the spirit realm. No sooner after I engaged the battle at full strength did the Spirit flee with the promise of revenge.

Chapter 8

Spirit

When the demons dragged me into the vile smelling depths way beneath the earth's surface, I was forcefully slammed to the ground. The air was forced from my lungs and I struggled to breathe as the demons that attacked me in overwhelming numbers pinned me down and placed a leather collar with long thick chains dangling from it around my neck. I was forced to my feet and held still by the chains that'd been pulled tight. A large muscular demon approached me through the crowd and I appraised him. He was filthy and wore no shirt or shoes. Through the grit and grime that caked his body I could see the creature was a creature of beauty.

Moving all around the beautiful creature stole my gaze. I saw a countless amount of human souls chained to the walls and floor, and all were crying out in anguish. Demons were scurrying about, torturing the restrained souls with their weapons. In the center of the cavern I saw a cement throne. Its' memorable details resolved any questions I may've had as to where I was. It was that throne I saw the Devil, Navarro, sitting upon when I was dragged through the earth some fifty years ago. The designs on the armrests and backrest were something I failed to acknowledge my first trip to

Hell. But this time I couldn't miss it. Demon heads engraved on the arms and Navarro's devilish stare peering into the calamitous cavern atop the backrest seemed to follow my every move.

"Look at me, boy!" said a commandeering voice. I looked to its' source and saw the large demon had moved before me. Or was he a demon? His face was flawless and his deep blue eyes seemed compassionate, unfitting of the filth that desecrated his body.

The demon thrust his face into my own and he spoke with a passive tone. "Travis Winter, the Spirit of Independence . . ." He turned and took a few steps away. "It has been long since I uttered that name. But maybe it hasn't been long enough, though. Since the day you were born I watched over you, watched you grow into a man, and watched you fight and die in that war. I know all about your fear and desires, your likes and dislikes. I know the power you control and the amount you're capable of utilizing. I know who selected you and killed your human body so you could be brought into our war. This interests you, doesn't it?"

It did, but I didn't dare admit to it. It showed I had a weakness. "What interests me is to know why you attacked Amanda. What does an innocent human have to do with any of this?"

The demons expression turned into stone and the tone of his voice fell into a raspy growl. "Attacked Amanda? You have no idea what is going on here, do you, Travis?"

"Apparently not," I said, struggling to break free from those who held me, but was rendered immobile. Fearlessly, the large demon stepped to me and took hold of the leather collar around my neck and pulled me close. "You are an unappreciative bastard, Travis, and I should take it upon myself to destroy you before Lord Navarro returns from paying Amanda a visit."

I frenzied at the mention of her name. I thrashed and tried to strike anything within arms distance but was held at bay by the demons and their tested restraints. "Let him go, my pets," the large demon commanded and stepped away. The demons released me and scurried behind the large demon. I reached into the air and gathered as much energy as I could. I shaped the energy into a ball and threw it at the large demon. Hitting him in the center of his chest, the ball of energy burst in a fury of sparks, knocking the large demon off his feet. The small demons charged without hesitance. I thrust my hand forward, sending a gusting wind towards the disorderly group. It swept away each one, tossing them about. The big demon rose to his feet and began to titter.

"Silly me," he said. "It seems your creativity exceeds the credit I give you."

"Next time I'll send a force towards you so powerful, it'll tear you in two," I rebutted, partially believing I could do as I said.

"Don't fool yourself, Travis. I sacrificed myself for you, therefore I understand everything you're capable of doing. Destroying me is not something you're capable of. You should try to never forget the faces of those who helped you out of this place. You should be grateful for the things others have done for you, not dealing threats. You're a misguided fool like I once was. You look around you and see things as being chaotic and cruel here, don't you?"

"You torture . . ."

"You don't know what we're doing and the reasons why they're being done! You make accusations off of uneducated assumptions!"

The demon turned his back to me and displayed two stumps in the center of his back that were stained with blood and smut.

"There were once wings there--pure white one's that opened wide and carried me to your side."

"It was you?" I said flabbergasted.

"Me. I'm the one who surrounded you with my wings, provided you with comfort when you needed it. What we'd been sent for was accomplished, but for what? What have you done since then that deemed you so important? Nothing! And look what has happened to me as a result of it. I was shamed in the Heaven's. The mission was a simple one, and because of the casualties and your whereabouts unknown, my wings were taken, done so before the entire populace of Heaven. I was shamed, Travis, never to return there again. If you wanted to prove your worth to me, you should've come back and tried to help those that helped you. But, you didn't and I hate you for that. You deserve nothing less than the humility I suffered."

"I didn't ask for this and didn't leave anyone! I did exactly as I was instructed to do! I was scared, confused, and didn't know what was happening. My human life was stolen from me, and for that, your fate changed too. Everything surrounding my fate seems tragic..."

"Fate!" the demon shouted. He huffed and didn't speak until he calmed. Composed, he said, "How ironic you speak of fate. My abhorrent feelings towards you keep me from helping you change your fate, from coaxing it into another more positive direction. Besides, Travis, you act like you're my enemy. You are my enemy, aren't you?"

I shamefully hung my head, and sadly said, "I didn't ask for any of this . . . "

"I don't feel pity for you, Travis. The sacrifices that were made for you are unspeakable. And now that you know this, what difference has it made to you? None. I can feel it. Wallow in your pity while I show you humility. Get him!"

Hundreds of Hells' demons attacked me with great fierceness. I struggled to fight my way through the overpowering wave of pink bodies but the odds were too overwhelming. I was quickly overtaken and brought to the ground. The pain of the assault I was suffering was numbing but I fought back, killing the closest demons with my bare hands. I knew Amanda's survival ultimately depended on my own, and that thought alone gave me the strength and will to fight against insurmountable odds.

A muffled roar resonated throughout the cavern, and immediately following the distorted command, the demons that smothered me halted their attack and quickly disbursed.

"Don't say anything to me," the large demon said as he looked down on me. "I want you to leave here while I'm giving you the chance to do so. Go to your precious one, I'm sure she's in need of you. Don't question my kindness and don't mistake it for weakness. If I'm given a moment to think this through, I'll probably change my decision to let you go."

The demon turned from me and I seized the opportunity to flee. I ascended to the surface and tried to find Amanda by hearing her thoughts. I soon found she was still inside the hospital, but had fled to the morgue. Navarro was after her. I hurried there and fizzled into the room, bringing a thunderous resonance with me to gain Navarro's attention. He was looking to me by the time my transition into the physical realm completed, and he was holding Amanda in the air by her throat. He dropped her, and said, "The pawn plays into my plans perfectly. Finally, Travis, you're becoming interesting."

I grabbed some energy, bunched it into a ball, and threw it at Navarro. He leapt out of the way and I ran to Amanda's side. I helped her to her feet and said, "If you hesitate, you're going to die. Leave here now, I'll find you wherever you go!"

Amanda cringed, and shouted, "He's behind you, look out!"

Before I could react, I was grabbed from behind with one arm that tightly wrapped my neck and the other that pulled back on my hair. "You see!" Navarro shouted at Amanda. "He has the true face of evil! Look long and hard and remember what you see here!"

Navarro released my hair and pulled the mask that covered my face and threw it to the floor. I hung my head, trying to shield my deformities from Amanda's gaze, but Navarro tightened his hold around my neck and tugged on my hair again. I couldn't breathe. My hands went to his forearm to try and clear my airway.

Amanda gasped at the sight of the torn purplish flesh beneath my eye that oozed puss.

"Do you see the evil that consumes his face?" the Devil raved. "It's eating at him from the inside out!"

"No! I don't believe you!" Amanda shouted and ran from the morgue. Navarro tightened his hold around my neck, allowing Amanda to flee. What game was he playing? He pressed his lips against my ear and began to speak with a sudden calmness, saying, "I don't know how you escaped my demons. I told them to hold you until I returned. It's of no matter, I suppose; here is as good as anywhere. If you remain calm, I can grant you detailed explanations as to why we war."

He loosened his grip enough to allow me to respond. I said, "We war because you are evil and you try to tempt those that are virtuous. And within your demented mind you actually believe I'll buy into your lies. I won't, and I know how this annoys you because my presence interferes with the growth of your hell. My immortality grants me the right to interfere in your perverse cause forever!"

My words infuriated Navarro and his choke on my neck became like a vice. He lowered his lips to my ear again; his words to come were of ridicule and scorn. "One thing you'll eventually learn, Spirit, is that even an immortal can die in this war! Be careful who you trust, they may not be who they seem to be. How can you call yourself the Spirit of Independence when you can never be independent of the things you were designed for? If you fail to obey your calling, then surely someone will be sent for you, and when they locate you, you will be ousted or destroyed!"

I allowed him to prattle on while I bunched together a handful of energy. I reached my hand back and ignited the energy beneath his chin. The blast that would've taken an ordinary man's head off sent Navarro to the floor; my ears buzzed from the explosion. Unfazed, Navarro began to stand and I knew I had to act quickly. I began to release the particles that gave me solidarity on the physical realm, and released them to step through to the other side. Once my transition to the spirit realm was complete, hoping Amanda found safety, I fled and listened intently for Amanda's thoughts.

Chapter 9

DemAngel

The wounds inside my body from Spirit's attack I'd sustained inside the jewelry store took several hours to heal. And almost an entire day later, my innards still burned, feeling as though they were on fire. When I finally got myself to leave Alex's body behind, I journeyed to Spirit's lair located inside an old abandoned church. There, in its musty basement, a lost soul sat fearful and alone. I cautiously approached this soul, trying desperately not to frighten him. Knowing the Spirit was his controlling tormentor I wanted to assure him I was there for reasons undefiled. I remember the conversation well . . .

"Is Travis here?" I asked.

"No," he said in a whisper, looking left then right. "He left hours ago, but he'll be returning soon, I'm sure. If you like your existence then you'll take heed and leave here before he returns. And whisper when you speak, you never know where he may be."

"So what if he is near! Why should I fear the Spirit?" I whispered, remaining heedful to his request, remembering the Spirit's attack well.

"Because he is evil and he has regard for no one. Who are you, and why have you come here?"

"My name is DemAngel and I am a servant to Navarro. I have come to take you from here."

I extended my hand out to him, and he forcefully slapped it away. "Don't you touch me!" he shouted, forgetting his need to whisper. "Spirit may be evil but his wrath is nothing compared to that Devil and his children. I'll go nowhere with you!"

"The Spirit has taught you lies," I said, myself also forgetting to whisper. "You would rather believe lies and stay here so you could continue to live this life of torment?"

"Yes."

"Don't be a foolish soul, Eidolon. Navarro is not the Devil! Can't you see the Spirit has you brainwashed? Navarro has sent me here to free you while the Spirit is occupied. He has heard you crying, heard your prayers to be saved from the Spirit's oppression. If you choose not to come with me then allow me to show you a way to get away from the Spirit and not have to return to Navarro's lair until you've had plenty of time to think things through."

"Surely, if such a thing were possible and I were to leave here, the Spirit would find me and punish me severely for my disloyalty."

"You will never have to return if you don't want to, and I can grantee he'll never be able to find you again."

"That's impossible!"

"Only for someone who doesn't know the secrets I do. Come with me and I'll show you."

He shook his head, denying my request, but not truly wanting to. He said, "I don't trust you!"

He needed coaxing. I said, "And you trust the Spirit after all he's put you through? I should go then . . . that's if you're sure you don't want your freedom."

Eidolon's eyes brightened at the mention of the word freedom. He considered my words and understood my offer was the best he would get. He asked me to show him how to escape. His courage made me smile; finally, he would make a stand against the Spirit.

I proudly brought him to a house where five teenage kids had gathered around a table. All the lights in the house were off and two lit candles were in the table's center, on the outside of a board game. The candles flickering light caused shadows all around the room to dance dauntingly, twisting and distorting the expression on all the faces around. The game board in the table's center read Ouji. It had a plastic pointer sitting unmanned, and letters of the alphabet were spread about the surface of the board. The numbers one through ten were scrolled across the bottom of the board, and the words yes and no were in the upper left and right portion of the board.

One young boy playfully teased a friend sitting across the table from him by saying, "You look like you're shitting in your pants man. Are you scared the boogie man is going to come and get you?"

"No, I'm not scared! You can be such an asshole sometimes," Pete said, shaking his head in disgust. Though he fooled his friends into not thinking he was scared, I knew better. I could feel his fear like it was heat from an oven.

"Would you two knock it off," another boy interjected. "We need everyone to keep quiet and we have to be serious if we want this to work."

All the boys placed their fingertips lightly on the plastic pointer, and one began to speak, saying, "Are there any Spirits on the other side willing to speak to us?"

I turned my attention to Eidolon. I said, "This is your way through to the other side. If you want it, you've got to answer them."

"What?" he asked oblivious to what he must do. "I don't understand what you mean."

"Watch," I told him and began pushing the plastic pointer around the board in a clockwise motion. Fear and doubt struck each boy, all wondered if one of their friends were coaching the object; the naïveté of children can be a blessing to the tormented sometimes. As their eyes jumped nervously around the room, I stopped the object over something on the board. All the boys looked to the board and read the response aloud.

"Yes."

Some of the boys smiled, two others felt like running from the room. Pete was one of them. One boy said, "Are you a good ghost?"

I pushed the pointer in circles and stopped it over the word "yes".

The same reaction from each boy followed this action. The gateway was opening.

"And what is your name?" I was asked.

I turned to Eidolon, and said, "I can give you that chance to escape right now but you have to tell me you want it."

"I want it," he said anxiously, suddenly believing in me.

"Then follow my instructions exactly," I said, "and it'll be done. Once I strike fear into the boys, a temporary bridge will open between our world and theirs. When this happens, you will be able to cross the bridge and jump inside one of their bodies. Ready yourself."

Moving the object strategically around the board, I responded to their last question by spelling out the word: death. Then I made both candle flames crackle and pop, and all the light bulbs began to burst inside the lamps.

Every boy released the pointer and jumped from their seat. "Now," I shouted to Eidolon, and he jumped through the temporary bridge and ran across it. The bridge collapsed, and all the boys ran from the house, but before the boy named Peter made it out, he gasped and fell to the ground. I've seen the affects of a spirit using the fear method to hide inside a human's body. Peter's sudden weakness was the result of Eidolon entering his body. Satisfied knowing I may have saved Eidolon's life, I left the house and returned to the place I call my home. When I arrived there, I discovered Navarro kneeling beside Ice's badly beaten body. He cradled him in his arms and rocked him back and forth. As I approached Navarro, the demons watching on cleared a path for me. When I stood over my Lord, he looked up to me with reddened eyes and spoke with a trembling voice.

"He was murdered protecting the girl Amanda," he said. "The Spirit knew to remove his eyes to kill him. He is a sinister being, DemAngel, and now I have the fire of vengeance burning within me. I want to avenge Ice's death."

I knelt beside Navarro and placed a comforting hand on his back.

"No, Lord," I told him. "Your ways are better than that. The Spirit is expecting revenge for sure, so let us not seek it. Instead, we should continue on the path we're on so your dream can reach fruition. That, my Lord, would be the ultimate revenge."

He wiped the tears from his eyes and casually smiled at me. "Perhaps you are right, DemAngel. Sometimes I don't know what I would do without you." Navarro gently placed Ice's body flat on the ground and stood to his feet. "My little demons, please, handle him with care and give him the proper burial he so duly deserves."

The demons flocked around the body and picked it up in their tiny hands and began to rapidly flap their tiny wings. They took to flight, lifting the limp body up and carrying it away. Navarro shuffled to his throne with his head down and sat. He shook his head from left to right and cradled his face in his hands. I approached him, and troubled by the despair he wore on his sleeve, I asked, "Lord, will you be alright?"

He looked to me with saddened eyes, and said, "I fear this Spirit. He is powerful and shrewd. I am afraid I am now forced to do something most drastic. I have no other choice but to do this because my actuality is in danger. And by doing this, I am ensuring my dream continues on. As usual, DemAngel, I will need your help to pull this off."

"Anything, Lord. I will follow you to the final day and fight by your side. I am honored to have that glory."

"I thank you, DemAngel. I require getting the girl Amanda alone. What I need you to do is occupy the Spirit for me. I know such a request is dangerous, but it is important. Do you think you can do that?"

"I can and will, my Lord."

Chapter 10

Spirit

Upon departing from the morgue and avoiding a full-blown physical confrontation with Navarro, I located Amanda with the power of my mind. She'd safely retreated to her apartment, but while there, she stumbled on something that caused her great duress—something her mind wouldn't reveal to me from such a great distance. I journeyed swiftly to her side and found her laying facedown and unconscious. Her breathing was steady but her mind was inactive, locking itself away from the world and its evils.

Blue flashes of light filled the room and I turned see where it was coming from. A mysterious soul that had acquired unexplainable powers and had gained access to the physical realm shot small charges of electricity about the room, causing random objects to burst into flames and explode.

Before the soul could focus on me, I charged him and tackled him. His looks were strangely familiar to me, and as I struggled with him, I searched my memory to place his face. The protruding cheekbones, his shaven head . . . where had I seen him before?

Suddenly I knew. He was at the hospital. He was the doctor that punched the nurse and tried to drag Amanda into the spirit realm. The recollection of his actions both recent and past enraged me.

"What have you done to her?" I shouted and latched onto his neck. I choked him as hard as I could. His eyes bulged out of his head and his face was reddened. He flailed, fought against my hold, but was unable to move. My fury could've taken the lives of 1,000 men that day. Unmercifully I watched his eyes glaze over and his jaw dangle open as it tried to produce sound, tried to utter a plea for life. The fear he felt, the suffering he was experiencing was payment for what he tried to do to Amanda. I would show him no mercy as he had Amanda.

I released his neck and he paused to gasp the air. I moved my thumbs over his eyes and pushed down on them. I felt his eyes squishing around my fingers as they sank inwards. The tendons and ligaments that held them popped as they broke under the pressure I applied. Frantically he thrashed and tried to resist my assault. I switched tactics and began draining his body of its precious life energy. When I depleted enough of the energy, he involuntarily moved into the spirit realm. I followed, persistent in my assault, relentless to see him pay. I continued to drain his energy until he could no longer defend himself. I plucked the eyes from his head and pushed him downwards, returning him to the hell that created him. There, in Hell, was where he was going to die. For without the eyes the soul cannot live. It was what he deserved for obeying the requests of a demon. I'd let his death be a message to those who would take me lightly.

I quickly ran to Amanda's side and placed my palms on top of her head. I opened her mind to my own, and witnessed everything that transpired after she fled the morgue.

She'd flagged down a cab and told the driver the destination. The driver acknowledged her request with a nod and pulled away from the curb. Amanda slid back in the seat. Feeling uneasy she chewed at her nails and kept looking out the back window for anyone that may've been following. She couldn't find anything from the ordinary.

Some minutes later Amanda leaned forward and tapped the glass that separated the front portion of the car from the rear. The diver slid the glass panel to the side and listened.

"Please hurry," she said.

The driver looked her over using the rearview mirror. "I'm going as fast as I can, lady. Traffic is hell. Relax we'll be there in a few minutes."

Amanda threw herself back in the seat and placed her elbow on the armrest. She cradled her chin and stared impatiently out the window. Her mind drifted to my face; questions came and screamed for answers. The wounds on my face, were they symbolic of my corruption as the Devil suggested? No, she fought internally and ultimately decided it was the creature that held onto me who was the evil one.

The cabby slowed and directed the yellow station wagon to the curb, and told Amanda they'd arrived at their destination. Amanda flung the back door open and jumped out of the car. Amanda rifled through her pocket and found a ten-dollar bill. She threw it to the driver and ran up the walkway that brought her up to a small white house with black shutters. Colorful flower beds were on either side of the stoop, and within my vision, I could smell the aroma they emitted. Unmindful of such details, Amanda ran up the steps, opened the front door, and stepped into a foyer. She ascended a second flight of steps, unlocked the door at the top and entered the apartment.

She walked down a short hallway and entered a living room/kitchen that had been modernized with black glossy counters, mirror top tables, and wavy chairs that seemed too weak to hold someone's body weight if they were to sit on them. Amanda plopped down there and thought to cry. Flickering light coming from behind her caught her attention. In the living room portion of the apartment, an entertainment center held a television set that'd been left on without sound.

"I could've sworn I shut that off before I left the house," Amanda thought, and walked to the television and jabbed her pointer finger at the power button. The picture blinked off.

"Why are you shutting that off, I was watching that!" someone said from behind her. Fear wrapped her spine and traveled down her legs. Her stomach rubbed with pain and her heart paused in its rhythm.

Amanda looked to the couch and saw a man lying there; it was the doctor. He had propped his head up with several pillows, and filled the gap between his skinny legs with several pillows to keep his bony knees from clunking together. He pushed the pillows aside and sat up. He rested his elbows on his knees and rubbed his eyes. Amanda watched him in disbelief.

"Never mind," he said, stretching his arms over his head and yawning. "There are other, more important issues that need my attention. I beg you to forgive me for my appearance, I haven't had any time to change." He looked himself over, admiring the orange jumpsuit he wore. "Or maybe it's the fact that I might've grown fond of this getup."

Amanda began to back away, her breathing heavy. Tripping clumsily, she fell to her laurels. She paused long enough to break into tears before she shifted her weight to her hands and knees and crawled into a corner where she wrapped herself into a tight ball.

"Guess what?" Ice questioned as he approached her. "I was told Alex was sitting just like that when he began pleading for his meaningless life."

Amanda's heart sank, her tears turned into a wailing fit of anguish.

Ice grabbed a chair from the kitchen table and positioned it in front of Amanda and sat. "The doctors told me I was sick, but I'm not, you know. They said the voices I was hearing were from within, that if I took their medication and participated in their sessions, I would get better. But they didn't understand, wouldn't listen to a word I said. I explained how it all started through dreams about five years ago. I would dream about things of biblical proportions: the end of the world, Angels fighting Angels, human souls suffering eternally for their sins. You get the picture, I'm sure. But the only problem with these dreams was I wasn't exactly seeing things as I'd learnt when I went to church and studied the Bible. There was this man in my dream, a man I'd interpreted as being the Devil. He was the one showing me everything I was seeing. I was fearful of this man and of the horrifying visions he was sending me. I couldn't see his reasons. Really, who was I to him? I questioned this but no answers came, just more visions. For some time I remained fearful of the devil from my dreams and of his horrific message of end times until the day came that I was finally able to see, to understand what he'd been trying to show me. The answers were there all along, and they were all around me, always in front of my face. My own ignorance was keeping me from the truth. The corruption in the world and of its people was like an incurable disease, destroying the lives of everyone. How bad can society get before someone starts to question where we're headed if things don't compose themselves? I saw this and started to question it, and like a benumbing miracle, I was shown something miraculous. Navarro's dream, his vision of a perfect world, of peace and harmony was the answer to the madness around me, around us. I wanted his dream and the rest of the miserable world needed it. I gave myself to him and begged for his acceptance.

"My acceptance was granted in a vision. I was asked to take my family's life away so he could have their souls to preserve, to use in his army, to place in his Heaven. I did his bidding without contention and took my wife and two children's lives. Their deaths were so peaceful, so beautiful. Over their bodies I cried. Not because I was unhappy, because I wasn't, I was elated knowing they were at peace, away from the noise of the world and all its problems. They were with my Lord, being watched over and kept safe. I wanted to join them. I gathered several guns with plenty of ammunition and went to a local mall where I killed as many people as I had bullets. By the time the law arrived, my guns had been emptied, and every piece of ammunition spent. Without that I was overtaken and was arrested, tried and convicted. I was sent to prison to face death by electrocution. I was elated that I would soon join my family. Years of appeals by lawyers I never wanted delayed the process; if I could've killed my lawyers to speed things up, I would have.

"Shrinks would come and pick at my brain, treat me like I was a science project they had to dissect and interpret for their final exam. I told them many times why I killed but they only laughed at me, told me I was constructing fable's to delay their sessions and efforts to finding what was truly wrong with me. They didn't believe anything I told them. I eventually learned to listen to them prattle on and tell them the things they wanted to hear. They told me I'd committed one of the most heinous crimes they'd ever seen, and for that, they dubbed me: Ice. Whether the name is for my emotions or my heart, I'll never know. The nickname has stuck with me through the tabloids and through the terrified populace of the prison. I don't mind the nickname, in fact, I think it's fitting. Both my emotions and heart have no feelings for the world and the people of it who judge.

"So now that I've gotten the introduction out of the way and I feel we're acquainted, I must take you with me to Lord Navarro. He's expecting you. Unfortunately, this leaves me the task of killing your human body. Understand this is nothing personal. I know you think death is something terrible. But it's not. In fact, life doesn't truly begin until your soul leaves the body it's trapped inside. What Navarro has planned for you is pure, you'll see. Take my hand," he said, extending his hand to her.

Amanda slapped his hand away and shouted, "Get away from me, don't you touch me!"

"Please, Amanda, I want to make this as pleasurable as I can for you. The time I spent in jail was a lonely time. It has been ages since I had the pleasure of a woman."

Amanda was repulsed by the advance and cowered into the corner deeper. "Don't do this," she said, the anger leaving her voice, replaced with desperate appeal.

Ice was growing impatient. He growled, "Take my hand and come willingly or I'll take you forcefully and not worry about the pain you'll have to endure."

He reached to touch her. She fended him off with a few wild swats and attention grabbing shouts. Ice's patience quickly dwindled to nothing and he stood from the chair, grabbed Amanda by her hair and dragged her from the corner. He pushed her to the ground and pinned her down. With closed fists he struck her. Instantly, Amanda's mind sought out the comfort of the dark and went there. I pulled my hands from her head and sat uneasy next to her.

When I was well enough to move, I scooped Amanda into my

arms and called her name. I said, "Amanda, granddaughter? Awake for me. I'm here with you now, I'll protect you."

Her eyes fluttered. I fizzled with her into the spirit realm. I said, "I would've allowed you to stay with Alex longer, but it's dangerous for a human to enter the spirit realm for long periods of time. It could cost the person their life. Don't watch the passing landscape, it'll make you sick."

"Who?" she whispered, her eyes unable to find focus.

"I'm your grandfather, Amanda."

" . . . But grandfather was killed . . . "

"Yes, some fifty years ago. When I first past, I could remember nothing of my human life besides the few moments before my death. Flashes of my life would come and go but would never make any sense. As the years past by the visions came to me more frequently, allowing me something to piece together. I understood I'd left a wife and baby boy behind when I went off to war. I searched for them and discovered my boy was already a full-grown man with a wife and child of his own. Though I was happy my former life was remembered, I was melancholy I'd acted on the visions knowing I'd placed all those I'd loved in harms way. And now here I am, six month's after the recollection of my past has fully returned, I am running from those who wish to see me destroyed and desperate to protect those I love."

"Why, Grandpa, why are they after you?"

"Because I stand against the evil manipulators and deceivers that spread their hate and fear."

Amanda smiled proudly and for the moment all the turmoil seemed worth that one smile. I placed her on her feet and slowly returned us to the physical realm.

"It's dark," Amanda said. "I can't see a thing."

I gathered available energy and concentrated it into my fist. The energy crackled and popped to life and gave off a soft glow, providing us with limited light. "Once you arrive inside the forest," I said. "Call the name Divination. He will come for you, but fear not, his appearance will be strange to you."

Her eyes pierced me, her voice suddenly rose, and she asked, "A forest?"

There was no time for explanations. I lightly shoved her and she stumbled backwards. Reaching to grab me I pulled away and she fell into the void that would take her to the Land of Chova. Once she disappeared into the blackness of the void, I knew she was safe and quickly moved onwards, journeying to my son's home.

Chapter 11

Divination

I am Divination, the keeper of the Spirit's bones, a servant of the Heaven's. I, like Navarro, have been around since before time was. I understand you are not fully aware of the depth of the things that are going on here and why you are involved in this. Given time, all things will make sense.

When Spirit sent Amanda through the void, she was dumped inside the forest, landing softly but oddly on her belly. The void in which is used to gain access to the Land of Chova is somewhat of a nauseating experience. It tosses you about and spits you uncaringly inside a dense forest in the middle of nowhere. Amanda's stunned condition was a symptom of such a journey.

"Divination," she bellowed and listened to her voice echoing into the distance. I heard her call from the House of Chova and sent my servants, the Dezrects, to retrieve her. Moments after her call went out to me, the shrubbery surrounding the small clearing in which she laid in began to shake. Unidentifiable squeaking sounds began to roll randomly from bush to bush. She followed the sounds with her eyes, and asked, "Who's there?"

Sixteen bald, little pale men that stood no higher than three feet tall, all wearing blue silk robes with red lapels gathered in front of Amanda. They all turned and looked at her, then back to each other. With a squeak of their voices and a nod from their heads, the Dezrects surrounded Amanda, put their hands underneath her body and picked her up over their heads. They rolled her like a log until she was face up and began to run her through tunnels burrowed in the forests thick brush.

The branches whizzed by her head and the sounds of sticks snapping underfoot went on for several moments before she was brought out into the blinding suns' light. She reached her arms out as a sudden degree shift in her positioned changed; the Dezrects were running up the front steps of the House.

"Don't move, Amanda," one of the pale men told her and she quickly pulled her hands against her side. The Dezrects continued up the steps and ran into the darkness of the House. Amanda gagged from the stale musty smell that looms within the House, and bile dripped from the corner of her mouth; though it would take some time, I knew she would get used to the smell.

The Dezrects entered the dimly lit main room within the House with Amanda still hoisted over their heads. They lowered her to the ground and set her down carefully. The group of Dezrects gathered into a tight circle and exchanged a few words. They disbursed and headed back into the darkened entranceway they'd brought Amanda in from. I paused and listened palatably to the pattering of their little feet fading away as they ran deeper into the curving hallway. I always enjoyed that sound, it reminded me of organized soldiers marching with honor.

"Welcome to the Land of Chova," I greeted Amanda happily. "Please, take my hand so I can help you stand. The floor is awfully hard and I'm sure most uncomfortable."

I extended my hand down to her and she hesitantly placed her hand into mine. I helped her to her feet and brought the back of her hand up to the hood of my cloak and gently kissed it. "I am Divination and you're inside the House of Chova."

She smiled and remained quiet. She was shy, respectful. I liked that. She panned the dismal undecorated room, chewed her lip, and then said, "I'm not sure why I'm even here."

I stepped away for a moment and returned with a lantern. I

held it before her, and said, "Take this. You're going to need it to find your way around. You'll find there are matches in the drawer on the base." She took the lantern from me and began to inspect it. "You are here for security reasons," I explained. "Your life has been in danger, and while you remain here, it will no longer be. Follow me outside, I have some things I wish to show you."

I turned from her and entered the hallway that led to the outside. She lit her lantern and caught up to me, keeping her pace with mine. After walking the full length of the hallway, the stale smell of the House's innards was replaced with a fresh meadow breeze. The bright days sun replaced the pitch-blackness of the hallway. I turned to Amanda and took her hand, helping her down the steep steps of the stoop. I took the lantern from her hand and extinguished the flame with a blow. "The Land of Chova is much different than your realm, but it's still flammable. Now," I said while peering into her squinted eyes. They hadn't yet adjusted to the bright sunlight. "The building in which we just exited I built many human years ago. If you look to the stained glass windows you'll see they contain pictures. The pictures you see are historical moments from the place that I come from. I'm sure you'll notice the Devil, Navarro, is within those pictures. He comes from the same place I do, but his story is one I will tell you some other time. For now I will stick to what you need to know.

"I'm here to protect the Spirit's human remains and have since the beginning of the war. I'm sure you know by now your grandfather is a Spirit; a new breed of Angel. I watch over his bones because I've been assigned the honorable duty of defending his one true weakness. If anyone were to gain control of his bones and they were to be buried or destroyed, then his existence would end. But being Navarro can't find Spirit's bones he's decided to go after his second weakness: you, Amanda."

She looked to her feet and deniably shook her head.

"I know," I said, understanding how difficult all of this was for her. "It is hard to accept but vital for you to know and learn. Your survival may depend on what knowledge you have.

"Now, if you're standing at the entranceway to the House of Chova and you're looking towards the forest, you'll come to find it is there where all arrivals must exit from. Don't ever go in there, you may never find your way out. Behind the House there is a path that leads to a waterfall and lake. You can go there whenever you wish, but again, never wander off the path because you may never find your way out of the forest. The lake is a lovely place. You'll find it is peaceful and relaxing. If you wish to look around, please do, I have business to attend to. But always remember never to enter the forest."

I turned from her and entered the House. I walked beyond the light that shined inside and waited for her to depart. She walked to the rear of the House and I followed her, keeping clear from her sight by using the cover of the forest. Her journey on the dirt path was uneventful with the occasion of picking a flower or kicking a rock until it left the path.

Towards the paths end the trees began to drip with moisture and a fine mist floated gracefully through the air. Heavy pounding sounds thundered in the distance and the paths surface became muddy and slick. She pushed onwards, walking carefully to ensure she didn't fall.

When she emerged into the clearing beyond the forest she paused and stared in awe at the sparkling lake and the giant mountain that spilled a curtain of white water from its' peak. The mountain was rocky and bare of any plant life, and an obvious path had been worked in starting alongside the lake and running up the mountainside. From there it stretched horizontally across the full bulk of the mountainside and disappeared behind the waterfall and emerged on the other side, continuing around to the opposite side of the mountain.

Amanda walked to the lake and stood before the waters edge. She looked into the rocky, moss free water and searched for marine life. She would have no luck, I never stocked the lake. She picked up a small rock by her feet and noted it was flat, moist and dirty. But mostly she noticed it was perfect for skimming. She cocked her right arm back and hurled the stone side-armed, skipping it across the waters surface some six times before it lost its momentum and sank.

She placed the lantern she was carrying on the ground and

chose another rock, this one being much larger than the first one. She needed both hands to steady it, and when she did so, she lunged forward, hurling it high in the air and outwards towards the water. Watching it sail through the air, her attention was stolen by the sight of the waterfall that splashed heavily into the giant pool before her. Closing her eyes and taking a deep breath in, Amanda embraced the tiny droplets of water that soaked her skin. Licking the air and rubbing her face with her hands, she ran her fingers through her long blonde hair, opened her eyes and followed the path up the mountainside and across its' great bulk.

She shook her head, trying to snap out of the trance the beautiful meadow had placed her in and she picked up the lantern by her feet. She left the shoreline and journeyed the path before her. I followed her with my eyes until she disappeared behind the falling veil of water.

Chapter 12

DemAngel

In the quiet suburbs of Long Island, New York, in the town of North Bellmore, a two family house sat inactive and dark in the mid hours of the night. I entered the house with a companion of mine named Joy, one who'd been serving Navarro for many years. We crept around the house staying within the spirit realm.

Going to the second floor and into the master bedroom where two individuals slept beneath the covers, we stood over them, quiet and intrusive. An air conditioner was inside the window, blowing cool air into the room, keeping the humid night air outside. Heavy breathing and indecipherable chatter stirred from the bed top, bringing a playful chuckle into Joy's throat.

"You stay here and try and keep quiet while you watch over them," I told Joy. "I'm going to check the rest of the house to make sure nobody else is around. Remember, Joy, no harm is to come to them. We are here only because the Spirit will undoubtedly turn up and when he does, we are to stall him. I'll be right back."

When I left to inspect the rest of the house, Joy had entered the physical realm and paced the bedside of the sleeping couple. He soon grew tired of his simple task and decided to grab and shake the leg of the frail woman that slept soundly. He said, "You wouldn't last but a minute in the heat of our home. Nope!"

"What, sweetheart?" the woman asked as she stirred from her sleep. Her eyes never opened and she rolled from her side to her back. Joy settled on the foot of the bed and giggled childishly, amused by the woman's confusion.

The woman heard Joy's laughter and it took precious moments for it to register. Strange. Unfamiliar. Spooky. She abruptly sat up and tried to focus her eyes in the consuming darkness. "George?" she questioned, hoping.

"No, not George, I'm Joy. I said you could never stand the heat in my home. Nope!"

The woman pulled her legs to her chest and scooted towards the top of the bed. She slammed her back against the giant wooden headboard and the bed shook violently; the sleeping man next to her stirred. "Tammy? What's wrong dear, another nightmare?"

"No!" she shrilled and grabbed her husband's shoulder and shook it. "Get up, George, wake up!"

George jumped up and flicked on the lamp next to the bed that only required a touch. "What dear, what is it?" His heart raced and his hands became clammy. He scanned the room and saw nothing. Joy had left the physical realm and watched from the spirit realm.

George turned to his wife and saw her shaking wildly. Her eyes were transfixed on something he couldn't see. But what was it? He was desperate to know, and asked, "What is it? What do you see, darling?"

Her eyes remained at the foot of the bed and she rambled without taking a breath, saying, "This was no dream, George, everything was way too real. I felt something grab me, shake me, trying to wake me on purpose!"

George gently crawled onto the bed and sat next to his wife with his back against the headboard. He placed his arm around her shoulders and pulled her head to rest on his shoulder. "Sweetie, it was just a dream. I know what the police discovered in Amanda's store and her unexplainable disappearance has been hard to deal with. It is for me. The stress is causing your mind to play tricks on you, nothing more." He leaned into her and kissed the top of her head.

She lightly returned the kiss on the back of his hand, and said, "I saw a clown. A very evil looking clown."

"Let us try and get some rest," he said dismissively. He lifted the covers away enough for his wife to slide in and patted the bed invitingly. Sluggishly, she scooted beneath the covers and sank into the soft mattress, considering the logic behind her husband's words. Maybe the stress was influencing bad dreams. George rolled to his side and shut the light off, rolled back to his wife and pulled his body tightly against hers. "Goodnight, sweetheart, sweet dreams."

A flirty giggle erupted from the comforted woman as she burrowed her body into the bed. A heavy sigh came whimpering out of his wife, and she said, "I'm not tired. Nope!"

George groaned and pulled away from his wife. He fell out of the bed and hit the floor heavily.

"Are you afraid of me?" Joy asked from the bed top. "You shouldn't be. Nope!"

George grabbed at the stabbing pain that consumed the left side of his chest. He reached out with his right hand and tried to find the lamp on the night table above his head. Everything sitting on the table's top fell over and crashed to the floor. The lamp blinked on and off like a strobe light as it made its' way down to the ground, filling George's vision with light spots. The lamp settled between the table and bed, remaining on. The bright light aided the surrounding darkness, only allowing George to see silhouettes at best.

Joy reached his hand out, using it to block the light from George's eyes. In the lambent area the details of his pale face was brought into sight. The face was powdered white and a devious smile was painted on. A red foam nose complimented his outfit. Joy said, "Ladies and gentlemen, children of all ages, welcome to the . . ."

Joy shook his head in disapproval and retreated into the darkness. "This'll never work. Nope! There are two things wrong that need fixing! It does!"

Complete silence blanketed the room for several minutes,

leaving George the task of trying to decipher things beyond his view.

Forcefully George was jerked from the floor and his bones responded with a crack. He was dragged backwards; his heels skipped along the floor and collected the soiled laundry that'd been thrown carelessly about. He was forced into a chair and his arms and legs were tied with a cord. Joy's fingers pried George's eyelids open and he held his head straight. This is when I returned, coming through the floor and quickly taking on my physical form.

"Joy?" I questioned, my tone harsh, punishing.

"I haven't been bad," he said, retreating. "Nope!"

"What have you done here? Where is the woman?"

"Bad I did by her. I did! Show you, I will!"

He walked to the bedroom door and opened it. There, strung to the door, hanging upside down was the body of the woman. Thick crimson blood soaked her nightgown that hung over her head. My concern and regret for having left Joy unaccompanied couldn't help her because she was already gone. I turned to George and saw he was leaving too. His heart was failing, and thankfully, he wasn't trying to fight it.

I shook my head in disgust and said, "Ever since you started working under the big top and you started to lure innocent people away from the crowds and began to murder them, I knew you were uncontrollable. You said you were doing it for our Lord's dream. Yes, you are to spread the word of our Lord and the promises of his dream, but you are to have mercy on those that don't share that same vision. I figured when your mortal life ended by the man that shot you when he found you trying to kill his wife, your vicious ways would cease and a calmer, more rational way to deal with things would surface. You serve the cause well at times, but other times you are far too vicious."

"I'm sorry," Joy said. "I won't be bad anymore. Nope!" He leaned towards George and whispered into his ear, "True, that is. I've been bad and I've hurt you and your wife. DemAngel is not happy with me. Nope!"

George's head slumped forward and his soul stepped from his body. Confused, it remained there.

"Come, Joy," I told him. "Though you did a bad thing by killing these soul's vessel, you may not have ruined what we came here to do. I've come up with another plan. We can still lure Travis around for a while and keep him occupied while Navarro tends to his business with the girl Amanda."

"One thing left for me to do. There is!" Joy said, and took off the red nose he wore and placed it on George's nose. He turned to me, and said, "Now it is certain the Spirit will come for us. He will!"

We left the physical realm and retrieved the souls of the Winter parents. Near their lifeless bodies I educated joy on the details of my new plan, knowing for sure the Spirit would come.

Chapter 13

Osiris

Amanda was standing before a cave with her back to the falling veil of water that dumped from the mountaintop inside the Land of Chova. She looked to her left, seeming to want to continue on the path that wraps around to the opposite side of the mountain but found she couldn't go that way. Something invisible keeps everyone, even Divination from going that way. She lit the lantern she carried and entered the cave before her. As she carefully descended into the mouth of the cave towards its belly, I followed cautiously, remaining close to the wall behind her and out of sight.

As she moved onwards in her travels, the lanterns light revealed ancient engravings chiseled into the caves wall. The engravings were identical to the ones depicted in the stained glass windows on the House of Chova, though the pictorials in the cave are more detailed.

Amanda walked slowly, examining each engraving with the utmost curiosity. Befuddled by their meaning, I was sure she was, but interested nevertheless. Beyond the engravings, she came upon a giant closed wooden door. A rope was tied off at the doorknob and hung close to the ground. She pulled the rope and the door slowly swung open, responding with an eerie creak that reverberated disturbingly throughout the fissure. Uneasiness held Amanda in the doorway, left her teetering on the edge of the blackened chamber before her. She held the lantern up high and peered cautiously inside the room. She saw a cobblestone fireplace located on the right side of the room and an exceptionally large wooden table and six chairs that had rocks piled to the height of the seat tops sat in the rooms' center.

Amanda located a loose stone available on the ground by her feet and used it to hold the door ajar. Checking the security of the door before she entered the room, she walked to the table and lit the candles that were on its' top. She placed her lantern down and began to aimlessly explore the room.

On a shelf located above the fireplace, Amanda discovered a small wooden box. She took the box and returned to the table and sat, placing the box before her. She tugged on the rusted lock and saw its strength was far greater than its frail appearance. She chose a palm-sized rock from the pile stacked beside the chair she occupied and struck the lock until it broke open. She dropped the rock back on the pile and brushed the dust from her hands. Anxiously, she removed the lock from the latch.

"What do you think you're doing?" I questioned, unwilling to allow her to go any further.

She jumped in her chair and nervously searched the room. She slid the box across the table and took the lantern in hand. "Nothing. I'll leave, I'm sorry," she said, and stood from the chair. She walked towards the door. I stepped through the doorway and into the shadow of her light. She gasped and covered her mouth. I wasn't sure if it was my sudden appearance that startled her or if it were my physical appearance. Standing barely three feet tall, being bald and having skin as white as snow, I figured it was my appearance. I found her consternation to be flattering.

"A Dezrect?" Amanda asked.

"Osiris," I said, and offered her a formal handshake. She obliged, placing her hand into my own, and allowing a smile to overtake her face. I pumped her hand up and down, and said, "Please, sit. There is no need for you to leave, but please, don't ever open that box. Its contents are dangerous and useless to you."

I escorted her back to the table and she sat. I walked to the opposite side of the table and climbed the rock pile and settled into the chair. I adjusted my silky robe and leaned back, and said, "This was once Divination's lair. He abandoned it when the construction of the House of Chova was completed. But we, the Dezrects, liked it here in the cave and decided to stay. Being Divination is a lot larger than we are, we've had to make a few adjustments to the place. It has been so very long since I told the story about the things I know. Would you like to hear it?"

"Yes," she said with a smile. I was ecstatic.

"My name is Osiris, and I am a part of a clan called the Dezrects and we are from Heaven. God sent us to aide Divination in the protection of the Spirit's bones.

"We are not Angels, no, we are what you would call the workers of Heaven. We aren't very good warriors because of our size, but we will fight if it is necessary. The Angels are the ones who fight the wars, but the Spirits have been created to eventually become Heaven's ultimate warriors.

"Hell's society is set up akin to Heaven's. Navarro the Devil is their god. The one called DemAngel is equal to Divination in every aspect. Other servants of Hell such as Ice and Joy are comparable to Heavens Angels in the sense that they are all devoted warriors. Hells' workers are the tiny demons that cannot leave the spirit realm like us Dezrects. We Dezrects are similar to the demons but we're pure white and the demons are pink like pigs.

"So, you see, in the war between Heaven and Hell God has an unmatched advantage: the Spirits. The longer a Spirit can survive, the stronger he will become. Hell is making their move against the Spirit before it is too late for them. They understand trying to attack the Spirit directly is a fool's mistake. They are using you to get to him and that is why you are here. Now the Spirit has gone to his son to bring him here. All leverage the Devil has will be taken away."

Amanda stood from the chair; a stern look scrunched her brows together. "That's my mother and father you're talking about. I have to go to them!"

"I'm sorry," I said and looked away from her sorrowful gaze, knowing I'd said too much. "It would be unsafe for you to leave here."

Amanda dropped to one knee and firmly grasped my hand. "If you truly are a creature of God then you would understand that I have to go to them. I recently lost someone I loved dearly and I couldn't bear to lose my parents on top of that. Please, have mercy and tell me how to leave this place."

I shook my head, fighting the ache in my heart. "You need to let the Spirit do what he has to without your interference."

"Osiris," she begged. Tears of frustration rolled down her cheek. "I need to see them. I don't know what it is, but I have a terrible feeling about this. I fear I may never get to see them again."

I wiped her tears away and began to blubber in my indecision. "Please, Amanda, don't cry. This is a place of happiness. Don't leave the security of Chova and don't ask me to do what you are asking of me because if anything were to happen to you I wouldn't be able to live with myself. My life is eternal, and that is a long time to suffer for making a decision I know is wrong."

Tears poured down her face and her cheeks glowed bright red from frustration. "How am I ever to be happy again when I am being kept here against my will? I want to see my parents and you're the only one who has the power to help me do so. If anything happens to them and I don't get to see them, I'm going to hold you responsible! I'll never speak to you again, Osiris. Ever!"

I closed my eyes and sighed heavily. Either way I was damned. The girl's feelings and desires were important to me, more important than holding her against her will. "Alright," I said. "But you need to promise me you'll be careful and return as soon as you can."

"I promise," she said, her expression immediately turning joyful.

"I would go with you, but I cannot," I explained. "I fear the other side. You're going to have to take this journey alone." I stood up and walked down the pile of rocks. I took Amanda's hand and led her to the rear of the room where someone had chipped a hole in the wall. "The only way out of Chova without Divination knowing is through here. One of the Dezrects discovered this when he went to make some engravings and pieces of the wall broke away. He learned this is a passageway to your world, and he uses it frequently to watch people. You're going to have to crawl, and a candle cannot go with you because there are gasses inside that are flammable. But there are no other dangers inside, so don't worry yourself. You will come out someplace called New York City. I wish you luck and Godspeed."

"Thank you," she said and kissed my cheek. "You don't know how much this means to me. I won't let you down."

Amanda dropped to her hands and knees and disappeared into the darkness of the tunnel. I returned to the table, grabbed the wooden box and returned it to the shelf while contemplating the decision I'd made concerning Amanda and her departure from Chova. Before I could absorb the severity of my decision, I'd already begun to regret it.

Chapter 14

Spirit

I was looking down at my son's lifeless body and trembling intensely. I'd been working up a scream for an unknown amount of time when I fell to my knees and broke into tears instead. I removed the red foam ball that'd been placed on his nose and closed his still open eyes with a brush from my fingertips. I rested my head on his lap and hugged him around his stiffening waist. "Why!" I moaned. "Why did they have to kill you?"

I cried and cried until the tears didn't flow anymore. I felt guilty for having mourned my loss so quickly and hung my head before my son, and said, "I will avenge the desecration of your body and save your soul from their torment. I will not allow them to do to you as they've done to me!"

I dropped the particles I controlled to create a physical form and quickly entered the spirit realm. The moment my transition was complete, I spotted the demon's Joy and DemAngel holding the souls of my son and his wife. DemAngel smiled at me tauntingly and began to plummet downwards with Joy struggling to stay by his side. I knew I was being lured, and I didn't care either. They couldn't have my son's soul; I would sacrifice my existence to see to that. I dashed downwards and seemed to catch them without much effort. I reached to grab Joy, the slower of the two, and just before I made contact, both DemAngel and Joy released their prisoners, halting my pursuit instantly.

I went to my son and gently took a hold of his hand. I did the same to his wife. Caringly I looked into their eyes and thought of a million things I could say to try and comfort them. But, their confusion broke my heart and paralyzed my tongue. Speechless, I ascended to the light with them and sadly watched them drift into the lights source. When the bright light faded away and took them to a place beyond the one I was in, I morbidly descended and returned to Chova's entrance. I momentarily paused before the void to wipe away the tears that started to streak my face once again. I fought to keep the tears away, to allow the pain to turn to something that would be more useful to me: unabashed anger. The moment would change me forever.

The ground in which I stood upon began to shake as it did some fifty years before when the Angel's invaded Hell. Electric blue sparks lit the tunnel as a rush hour train blasted by me, clanging loudly as its massive weight moved from section to section of uneven track.

I raised my head and stepped into the void. I was sucked within and tossed about and spat into Chova's forest. I rose to my feet and took my time making my way to the House of Chova. "Damned existence," I muttered dozens of times along the way, and before the entranceway of the House, I paused again to rub the tears away that escaped my control.

I pressed onwards and entered the dark hallway, illuminating the way with a dull light that surrounded my fist. When I finally reached Divination's chamber, I let the flame fade from my hand and I dropped to my knees. I fell to my side and rolled to my back.

"Is it possible for me to sleep?" I asked.

"No, Spirit, it is not," Divination said from the platform that held the casket which held my bones. He walked down a few steps and sat. "Sitting is something we can do, but oddly enough it is something I haven't done in a long time. It feels good."

"Well I feel strange Divination. Almost like I could fall asleep right now if I really wanted to."

"Your son and his wife, Spirit, you went for them. Where are they?"

"In the light. It appears they suffered tremendously before they were killed. I can't even think about the chaos that took place in that room before I got there. For some reason my mind won't allow it."

I sighed, rolled to my side and propped myself up with my elbow. Looking to Divination, I said, "When I returned to the spirit realm after I discovered my sons body, I saw DemAngel and Joy. I got the impression they were purposely waiting for me. As soon as I gave chase, they released the souls they held and returned to Hell, confirming my suspicions. I've been mulling over the reasons why they just didn't take them down to Hell before I arrived. And you know something? I can't think of any reason why they wouldn't. I should've continued after them, but I decided not to because I didn't want any stray demon keeping them from the light. There were times before that I gathered a bunch of lost souls and thought to bring them to the light, but some of them had been disoriented and fell away from the group. I left them behind figuring to return for them once I brought everyone else to the light. But, they had been grabbed up by a few demons that'd been waiting patiently for such an opportunity. That costly mistake always remained painfully fresh in the front of my mind. And this day above any I didn't want to make that same mistake again."

"You made the right decision, Spirit."

I thought and smiled in appreciation of his say-so. "Navarro has been using his family to get at me. He's thinking I'll lose my head and go after him on his terms. I won't do that. And now that my only remaining relative is here in the sanctity of Chova, what does he have?"

"The only thing he's ever had, Spirit. His corrupted ways."

Chapter 15

Navarro

When Osiris showed Amanda how to leave Chova, I knew where she would emerge; sometime ago my demons saw a Dezrect emerging into the physical world and quickly came to share the news with me. I thanked them for the information, but commanded their minds to forget they ever had that knowledge. That information would be only for my use; in the wrong hands it could've been dangerous. I know I could've used that secret passage to enter Chova and steal the Spirit's bones but I chose not to. Hell was not prepared for the final war, and destroying Travis was never my intention; I figured to let things play out to see what would happen. That might've been an error on my end, but I would chance it. When I'd first fallen on hard times, I must admit, I thought of accessing that passageway to gather the Spirit's bones. I never did and hoped my restraint would pay. I decided to explore other options I'd left myself.

Amanda was led to believe I was the devil and that I was going to attack her parents. She was desperate to get to them, to save them from my clutches. I can only laugh when I start thinking about this. I can assure you there was never such a plan. But, I know who put that thought into her mind. I won't tell, but will suggest you try and figure this one out on your own.

What I did do was send DemAngel and Joy to Spirit's living siblings house in an attempt to stall the Spirit once he arrived. I needed to get Amanda alone so I could talk to her, explain my intentions. She was a reasonably intelligent girl and knowing this I figured she might listen to me on neutral grounds. I knew my time to act was limited, though, because the Spirit would eventually discover her missing from Chova and would begin to search for her. The first place he would go would be his son's house, and from there he would backtrack. If this assessment was right, my chances of saving my dream might be endangered. DemAngel and Joy's interference would buy me the extra time I needed to set my plan into motion. This was done because the Spirit's cooperation seemed, at times, to be an impossibility, therefore, my recourses to finding a peaceful resolution was running low.

I spotted Amanda hurrying down a sidewalk in a rundown part of the city. On the pothole filled street beside the sidewalk, an approaching taxi caught Amanda's attention. She stepped from the curb and waved to the advancing vehicle. It didn't slow. She jumped up and down in a final attempt to gain the drivers attention, but the cab sped by her. "Shit," she said, and returned to the sidewalk. She put her head down and walked hastily.

I kept watch over her from a nearby rooftop, nervously reciting my plan. A junkie fixed as a regular man was walking towards her and he plowed into her with a stiff shoulder. Amanda went crashing down to the pavement.

"I'm so sorry," the man said sincerely. "Are you hurt?"

He seemed genuine. I let my defenses down.

He helped Amanda to her feet, and Amanda said, "I'm alright." She examined her bare elbow and saw blood surfacing. She brushed away tiny pebbles smashed into the skin and stepped past the man, continuing on the sidewalk.

The man turned and followed her close behind, waiting for the opportune time to strike. Without warning he grabbed her from behind. He covered her mouth with his hands and pulled her backwards and dragged her down an alleyway between two abandoned buildings. Amanda flailed and kicked but couldn't break away from her attacker. His strength was far greater than hers. Down the darkened alleyway the attacker pulled her. He paused before a rusted steel door, and kicked it open. The roar of the attack stirred birds nesting within the empty warehouse. Amanda loved the sound birds made and hung onto it for comfort; it was the only thing available to her.

The attacker dragged Amanda inside the building and tore the shirt from her back. He pushed her to the ground hard, the force of the shove sending Amanda's head crashing into the cement. At that time, I quickly left the building top and ran to Amanda's rescue. But even my reaction wouldn't be quick enough to keep her from the tragedy that was about to happen.

The crazed man tore through her pants and flimsy silk underwear, exposing her genitalia. He became frantic with lust and lowered his pants. Erect, he began the ritual of planting his seed. Amanda tried pushing the man off, but she was dazed and outmatched by both his strength and desire.

"I'm sorry, Osiris," she muttered, knowing she broke her promise to him.

The man continued to thrust himself in and out of Amanda with short steady pumps until his seed spewed into her. Just then I entered the physical realm and pulled the man from her. My anger said to kill him but my mercy for those weaker than me is what spared his insignificant life.

"Leave here," I growled and the man ran from the building. Amanda lay unaware and her body convulsed violently from the trauma. I knelt beside her and placed my hand on her belly, looking to remove her pain. But before I could, I sensed the Spirit was near. Not desiring a confrontation, I moved into the spirit realm and quickly returned to my lair below the earth's surface, immediately beginning to flesh out a new plan to save my dream.

Chapter 16

Spirit

Unable to find any meaning behind DemAngel and Joy's dealings with my son, I left the House of Chova in search of Amanda. Divination directed me to a hidden cave behind a waterfall, and he gave me specific instructions how to arrive there. Immediately I journeyed to the cave, and once inside I briefly studied engravings etched into the rock wall. I instantly noticed their resemblance to the pictures depicted in the stain glass windows on the House of Chova. I ran my hand over the rough surface in attempts to find some hidden clue behind their meaning. One thing was made clear during my examination was that the man with the sun ring around his head was God, and the other man was Navarro. I got the impression the engravings told the story about the day Heaven and Hell were made and how each living creature was divided and forced to choose a side.

"Spirit?" a voice whispered from behind me, frightening me slightly.

I ignited my fist and raised it above my head to spread the light. A bald milk-white man stood barely waist height with his head bowed and his arms folded across his chest. "I am Osiris," he said, yet unwilling to raise his head and make eye contact. "Are you familiar with my kind?"

"No, I'm not," I said.

He raised his head. His eyes were glassy and red, glowing brightly like a mid summer sunset. He'd been troubled and had been crying. "My kind was created to aide Divination in the protection of your bones. We are pale because we're the representation of God's pureness. But I'm not standing here before you to tell you about our history, as I'm sure you didn't come to hear it. I have done something terrible, Spirit. Something I know I never should've done, but I was weak and was convinced otherwise. It'd been so long since I had contact with one of the flesh. They look and act so feebly. The crying and pleading made me soft."

"So what is it you've done, Osiris?"

He hesitated, then said, "I showed the girl Amanda a way out of Chova. Through these caves there is a back door to her world."

I walked before Osiris and knelt before him. I placed a hand on his shoulder and gave it a reassuring squeeze. "I know your intentions were good; I can feel it. What is done is done. What I need you to do is tell me where she was going so I can help her."

"Her parents. She said she needed to see them--that she already lost a loved one and couldn't bear to lose another. Go, help her, Spirit, I have a terrible feeling about this."

"And where is the way she journeyed into her world?"

"It is through that door," he said while pointing behind me. I turned to see a giant wooden door. "But it would be faster for you to exit through the hidden cave beside the House of Chova."

I traveled swiftly from the cave and exited the Land of Chova. I returned to my son's den and knew Amanda hadn't yet arrived; no remnants of her scent were around unlike the fresh scent of death that lingered. I closed my eyes and listened for Amanda's thoughts and discovered through brief visions exactly where she lay alone, quietly hoping someone would find her.

DemAngel

Down on one knee I proudly bowed my head before my Lord,

and said, "Lord, I've come to deliver exciting news!"

He stood from his throne and walked before me. "Please, DemAngel, stand. We're all equals here." He pulled me to my feet. I smiled wide and took hold of his hand, and said, "Joy and I followed the Spirit after he retrieved his son's soul from us. He sent them through the light, as we knew he would, but afterwards he shot downwards, but he didn't go as far down as us. He went into the subway system and began brooding over his son's death. He was so disappointed for not being able to protect his son that he didn't look to see if anyone were around watching him. He stepped forward and moved into a darkened corner where he disappeared before our eyes!"

"Chova!" Navarro declared excitedly.

"Yes, Lord. I left Joy behind to scout the area while I came to tell you."

Navarro was exhilarated. He patted my back, and said, "Gather a mass of demons, the time has come for us to raid the lair and take the Spirit's bones."

I said, "This will be done, my Lord. Once I gather the Spirit's bones, I will come back for you." I stopped a passing demon fluttering through the air, called him over, and whispered into his ear, "Gather the others, we've located the Spirit's bones."

The demon flew away from me, his wings pattering the air, his body floundering grossly. I smiled at Navarro, and said, "Elation, my Lord. That is what I feel. I know without the Spirit in our way we will be able to see your dream finally reach fruition."

I backed away from Navarro and a mass of demons flocked around me, and as a group, we ascended into the subway system. When we came upon the void, I found Joy standing over the body of a female soul lying before his feet.

"The Spirit left, saw him I did!" said Joy. "I saw her hiding in the shadows. When I grabbed her and beat her she admitted she'd been following the Spirit for a long time. She was! She also told me she'd never seen us before and that she wouldn't tell the Spirit about us. She said she didn't even like him. Believe her, I didn't. Nope!"

I looked at the limp body and then back to Joy; her presence had no meaning to the cause or me. I said, "Leave her here, we have no use for her. Come on guys, let's do this."

The demons began pouring into the void. The fluttering of their wings sounded like chaos if it had a voice. Despite the description, it was a pleasing sound; it was the sound of order and power, the sound of excitement and life. Smiling, I turned back to Joy, and said, "Now let's go, we have the Spirit's bones to steal. You did good here, Joy!"

"Good, I did! I thought Joy did bad, but he didn't. Nope!"

Together Joy and I stepped through the void. We were tossed about and we plummeted without control. Moments after we entered the void, we were spit out and dumped in a small clearing inside a forest. Getting to my feet, a demon landed softly on my shoulder and told me which direction to go. I helped Joy stand and I led him through the forest.

Emerging into the clearing before the House, Joy and I paused together unrehearsed. The buildings beauty was captivating, something worthy of admiration. I alone moved forward and climbed the steps before the darkened entranceway. I turned to face all those who followed me, and said, "I know the anticipation to see the Spirit—the impediment of our Lords dream destroyed is great, a moment to be cherished, but you should prepare yourselves for war and focus on what we've come here for. Resistance may come."

I stepped away from the entranceway and pointed into the gloomy opening. The demons poured into the corridor in a frenzy. When the last of them went through, Joy went to follow.

"Hold it," I told him, and grabbed his arm to be sure he obeyed me. I made him wait a few moments, and said, "There. I think we gave them enough time to take control. We can enter, shall we?"

I released his arm, and he immediately started down the hallway. I followed.

"Boo!" Joy yelled playfully in the darkness, and I grew irritated. The moment was to be cherished, experienced to the fullest—not spoiled.

"Now is not the time to play. Okay, Joy?"

"No fun, DemAngel. Nope!"

When we emerged from the hallway, all the demons were in

the far corner of the room. They were confronting someone that wasn't obeying their commands. They began to attack it. I watched and waited fully confident in their abilities.

A single demon broke from the pack, took to flight and approached me. He hovered head height, and said, "It is that scoundrel, Divination. We have him beaten and down."

The demon returned to the corner of the room and I followed. I went up the stairs of the platform and went to the side of the coffin and looked down on the Spirit's bones still dressed in his World War II garb. My body tingled with pleasure and my mouth was misshapen with a satisfied grin. I returned to the steps, and shouted, "Enough!"

The continuing struggle halted and everyone looked to me.

"Bring him to me!" I demanded, and the demons responded with a cheer. They dragged Divination's long limp body that was lost in the cloak her wore. Forced to his knees, Divination was immobilized.

"It has been a long time, hasn't it, Divination?" I asked. I paused long enough to allow him to speak but he chose to remain silent. That was fine with me, the moment was mine. "Remove his cloak, I have use for it!"

The demons attacked Divination and stripped the cloak from his body. One delivered it to me and I opened it up and spread it on the floor before me. I removed Spirit's skeleton piece by piece from the casket and placed it in the center of the cloak. When all the pieces were transferred, I folded in all four ends of the cloak, tied it, and slung the sack over my shoulder.

"On behalf of Navarro and his servants, I'd like to thank you for this generous gift. We could never repay such a kind act."

As I made my leave from the House, the demons piled off Divination and followed me. Joy was standing over Divination's grotesque naked body when he said, "You don't look so good, Divination. Nope! Feel bad for you I do."

Chapter 17

Spirit

In the rundown part of the city, I sat inside an abandoned warehouse in a solid state. Amanda's naked body was slumped in my arms and I rocked her gently back and forth. "Why, why did you leave Chova?" I asked and removed my cloak. I wrapped Amanda's chilly body with it and lifted her from the ground. I stepped into the spirit realm and quickly journeyed back to the Land of Chova.

When I arrived before the void, I tripped over a female soul that lay unaware at my feet. I looked from left to right in wonder of who might've left her there. When I found I was alone, I placed Amanda inside the void and picked up the woman soul and stepped through.

Arriving in the small clearing inside the forest, I stood over Amanda's body as the surrounding cluster of bushes began to shake. "Spirit?" a voice called from the shrubbery.

"Osiris?" I answered unsure.

Osiris stepped out from behind a bush, and said, "Yes, Spirit, it is me. The others are with me too."

A pack of bald pale men stepped out from the cover of the bushes and inquisitively looked to me, to Amanda, and to the female soul lying motionless in my arms. They quickly formed a circle and began to communicate amongst themselves with the strangest, most unexplainable sounds I'd ever heard.

"They are trying to decide who they should take to the House of Chova first," Osiris explained.

"I will take Amanda," I said, and placed the nameless woman down. I swore to protect Amanda and failed to do so once. I would be sure to take special care of her. I picked her up and slung her over my shoulder.

"They were here, Spirit," Osiris said, his tone of voice concerned me.

"Who was?" I asked, and began for the House.

"DemAngel and his demons were."

I paused to look at him. "You're kidding."

"I'm sorry, Spirit, kidding and lying Dezrects cannot do."

I ran with Amanda and the Dezrects followed close behind, using a smaller covered path next to the one I was on. I entered the House, hurried through the hallway and found Divination lying face down on the floor. I placed Amanda on the table and went to Divination's side. Hovering over him, afraid to touch his body, I said, "Divination, it's Spirit. Are you alright?"

His body was covered with patchy red blisters that were moist and oozing. He remained so still I thought he was dead. I gently placed my hands on him and attempted to roll him to his back.

"No!" he shouted. "I don't want you to see my face!"

"But your body . . ."

"Old wounds," Osiris said. "Wounds that won't heal. That's why he wears the cloak."

"Tell me, Divination," I said caring nothing about old wounds. "What happened here?"

"DemAngel and his demons came here for your bones," Divination said. "They've done what I thought was impossible."

Osiris stepped to Divination and took hold of his hand. The care, love and respect between the two was heart warming. "I'm sorry, my friend, we arrived here too late to help you. DemAngel and the others got away."

"For the better," Divination said, his face buried in the floor. "There was so many of them you wouldn't have been able to stop them."

Osiris rubbed the back of Divination's hand, and said, "Rest easy, my friend. I will tell the Spirit what he needs to know now." Osiris turned to me. "Navarro promised God a war long ago and he's been preparing for it since that day. His army is being built from human souls he's enslaved and corrupted. God knows and has known what Navarro has been doing to His people, and in response, He's created a warrior to roam the earth and spread fear into the wicked. This warrior is called the Spirit, and surprisingly enough, it was found they were inexperienced in battle and made from ordinary human souls. God's new warriors ultimate task is to prevent the theft and corruption of the human souls; to slow Navarro's progression while God works on the details of his battle plans.

"Navarro has been obsessed with his lust for revenge since his fall and he doesn't care about the consequences his actions will bring. He knows the destruction of you, Travis, the Spirit, will give him free reign over the earth until another Spirit is chosen. If this were to happen than the slaughtering of millions of humans would commence and surely the apocalypse would begin."

"But I am only one," I said feeling both angry and perplexed by this grand scheme.

"You posses the power of God, Spirit. The power you control is beyond anything you could ever imagine. You must learn to exploit this power, use it to your advantage. Navarro knows if you become educated then his dream will be stalled, possibly for good. But if he can gain control of your bones, then and only then can he gain control of you and the power you control."

"No!" I shouted, suddenly realizing why DemAngel came to the Land of Chova. I ran up the platform and looked into the casket that held my bones. I lowered my head and rested it on the wooden frame. "They've taken my bones," I muttered, partially defeated. "Surely my existence will be coming to an end, and if what you told me holds true, then all of humanity is doomed!"

DemAngel

I tossed the tied cloak containing Spirit's bones to Joy. "Stay here," I said. "Guard that package with your life. I'm going to Navarro to inform him of our accomplishment!"

Joy moved to a headstone and pulled himself onto its top. He put the prize in his lap and pulled his knees to his chest. He hugged his legs, and said, "I won't let anything happen to Spirit's bones, DemAngel. Nope! But hurry back!"

I acknowledged his uneasiness with a smile and told the demons to split into two even groups. I told one group to follow me and the other group to stay with Joy. With my group of demons, I descended into the cavern falsely named Hell and I went before Navarro sitting in his throne. I tried to hold a straight face, to keep the smile of ultimate satisfaction away, but my excitement was to be shared—not to be harbored in jest or any other way. I smiled widely, showing all my teeth. "Lord, the Spirit's bones are above, wrapped like a gift for you!"

Navarro stared at me. He slowly stood from his seat, and said, "You were able to attain his bones?"

I could only smile. He plopped down heavily into his throne and hung his head. "So long," he muttered. "So, so long I've waited for this moment. I am elated, but feel as though my strength has been drained."

I helped him stand again, and while doing so I said, "Come, Lord. Now is the time you should have all the strength in the world. All your years of suffering from His unjust punishment is nearing an end. You rid yourself of the Spirit then we move onto the one true evil being that started this all!"

Navarro passionately looked into my eyes, hugged me, then said, "I feel as though I am dreaming, like this couldn't possibly be true."

I smiled in understanding. "This is real, Lord. Let us go now to the surface without further delay."

He cheerfully agreed and together, arm-in-arm we ascended. Arriving in the cemetery I left Joy in, he hopped from the headstone and held the wrapped cloak out before Navarro. "I told you I would watch them. I didn't let anything happen. Nope!"

Navarro took the tied cloak from Joy and handled it as if the contents were fragile. He knelt to the ground and placed the cloak in front of himself. The bones clunked loudly, sending eager smiles to each face that stood and watched this historical event unfolding before them with anticipation. Without further delay, Navarro untied and folded the ends of the cloak out. Within the center of the cloth were Spirit's bones stacked in a neat pile. Navarro reached into the pile and grabbed the skull bone and held it mere inches from his face. The left side of the face just beneath the eye socket was shattered, remnants of that day his human life ended. Navarro stared into the empty eye sockets and spoke with a sound of sincere regret.

"The Spirit has been a worthy adversary. It is unfortunate he's unwilling to hear our story and share in our dream. But this is war, and in war there are casualties. Let us have a moment of silence and pray for the Spirit."

Everyone bowed their head and prayed in silence.

"Amen," Navarro concluded and everyone repeated. He said, "Our dream has been delayed long enough. It is time we approach the final phase in this endless struggle."

Navarro dropped the skull into the pile before him and wrapped the bones back up. He stood to his feet with the prize in hand and pointed to the ground before him. "It is here we will bury his bones!"

Several demons flew to the chosen location and dug a hole suitable to bury the Spirit's bones in a traditional manner. When they finished preparing the grave, they moved off to the side to allow Navarro access to the hole. Before it he stood, thrusting the wrapped bones in the air above his head. Passionately he scanned the crowd before him as they cheered wildly.

A bright light flashed before Navarro and consumed him. When the light faded, the dirty rags he wore had been replaced with a neatly pressed black suit and his hair was neat and tied in a ponytail. "There," he said in response to his new attire. He looked himself over, and said, "How could I've forgotten the most important part of this outfit?"

He touched the collar of the black button down shirt with his pointer finger and a white clerical appeared. "Now it's official," he proclaimed, looking handsome in his preacher outfit. "Each and every individual here has helped in one way or the other to achieve this level of success in our pursuit to living a life in paradise. You should all be proud of this because I know I am."

Navarro dropped the package into the grave, and said, "Let us prepare!" He hung his head and whispered to the Spirit, "I'm sorry I couldn't convince you to come to my side. I would've been proud to have you fight alongside me. I pray for an ending to this madness and can only hope you're the last casualty it claims."

Navarro kicked dirt into the hole and looked to me. He said, "Have them fill it in."

I called forth some demons and ordered them to fill in the hole. Once it was covered, Navarro stood on the fresh mound of dirt and packed it down with heavy stomps. "It's done," he announced. "Let's go home!"

We all returned to the vast cavern beneath the earth's surface. The mood of Hell's natives was celebratory, but Navarro was self-effacing, disbelieving still that things were finally going our way. He took his rightful place in the throne and requested the soul of Alex be brought before him.

The demons brought him forward, placing a collar around his neck and fastening the chains to the iron rings set in the floor.

"I know you fear me and my companions," Navarro said. "I can't say I blame you either. After all, human myth has taught you that I am the Devil and this place I live in is Hell; a place of torment and suffering. I'm sure my appearance doesn't help my cause any, but it is what He's done to me. It was His way of keeping me from gaining the people's trust.

"You were never a prisoner here. I was only protecting you from the Spirit and his ways of violence and corruption. You are free to go now, Alex. Free to wander the spirit realm as you wish without worry of your safety. We've destroyed the Spirit. If at any time you choose to return here, you're more than welcome."

Navarro nodded his head to the demons standing off to the side. They approached Alex and broke the chains that bound him. He was given an escort to the surface and released.

Chapter 18

Osiris

Spirit stood in the threshold of the hallway inside the House of Chova. His back was to us, and he paused in his departure because of a rare outburst from me.

"Spirit!" I sternly shouted. "Calm yourself and listen to what I have to say!"

Spirit slapped the wall in response, and angrily snarled, "I already told you no, Osiris! They have my bones and I haven't time to waste listening to jabber that won't help my situation. If they're given the opportunity to bury my bones the world will be doomed. I must confront the Devil now!"

Spirit took another few steps into the hallway, his anger driving him.

"Please," I begged, my tone softening. "Just listen to what I have to say!"

Spirit roared so loudly the sound shook the House at its foundation. He fell backwards and hit the ground with a meaty thud.

Amanda screamed in horror, Divination sat up to assess the situation, and I ran to Spirit's side. I placed my hand on his head, listened for thoughts within then turned to Amanda who was hysterical, and said, "Calm yourself! He's alive but unconscious."

Divination dragged Spirit to the center of the room where we gathered around him and awaited his return. Hours dragged by before he finally began to regain consciousness. In the meantime, the female soul had awakened from her unawareness, and Amanda's pain from her trauma had begun to subside enough that she was able to move about freely.

"How are you feeling, Spirit?" Divination asked, fully clothed again.

"Okay, I guess," Spirit groggily muttered. "I remember a sharp pain engulfing the side of my face, inside the part that remains unhealed. I grabbed at it . . ." He touched his fingers to the wound hidden underneath the mask and reared. "Damn. It's tender . . ."

"And it will always be," Divination said. "Just like mine have been since they were inflicted. I'm most positive Navarro has buried the bones he thought were yours. He thinks you're at rest by now and he surely believes he can do as he wishes without having to worry about your interference. Your real bones have been transferred to a tomb located beneath the Dezrects cave, accessible only by a hidden ledge behind the falls."

Spirit sat up. "I should go to him now, before he begins soul robbing."

"No," the woman soul interjected. All eyes turned to her. She had an unusual appearance; pretty, but distinct. She had bright auburn hair and her face was bright white and outlined with clusters of thick brown freckles. Her nose was button like and her lips were as bright red as her hair.

"And why is that?" Spirit inquired, a condescending tone could be detected in his voice.

"My name is Nature," she said and offered her hand to Spirit. He obliged. "I was selected as a Spirit for the war but never matured like you, Spirit. I've been stuck in this form for many, many years."

"Another Spirit?" Travis questioned and turned to Divination with inquisitive eyes. Divination remained silent.

" . . . Would have been, but I never developed," she said. "And for that I was judged by God and was sentenced to live eternity as I am now. In the many centuries I've been living out my punishment, I've learned something that's very useful to you, Spirit."

"And what would that be?" he asked, his patronizing tone unwavering.

"I know where Navarro buried the bones of the last six Spirit's before you. I also learned if we were to exhume these bones from the earth the Spirit's will come back. Before you go to do battle with Navarro, you should consider waking the other Spirit's so they can help you in your quest."

"No time," Spirit said, and stood. "With Navarro thinking I'm at rest, he's sure to be spreading his hate throughout the world as we speak. I need to find him and end this once and for all!"

Spirit walked into the hallway and disappeared into its covering darkness. Everyone remained quiet, dumbfounded by the Spirit's determination to confront the powerful Devil. I could only sit and wonder if what compelled him was stupidity or true heroism.

Chapter 19

Spirit

When I arrived inside Navarro's lair, I was surprised to find it was free of any life. The only activity around was from the boiling river that curved aimlessly throughout the cavern. The rapids swished and swirled and sizzled as it splashed along, bubbling over the bank and evaporated into steam.

Navarro's throne was empty. The iron rings embedded into the ground and walls also sat empty. The hot air was still and thick, restricting my breathing. Moisture built on the ceiling rained down around me and sizzled when it touched the ground.

"Spirit?" a calling voice echoed all around me.

I searched for it, spinning in circles with widened eyes and tensed muscles. Had I walked into an ambush?

"I can tell you why we war. Fighting you is not my intention," the voice said, bouncing around the cavern, confusing my senses because its locality constantly shifted.

I continued to search for the voice, remaining positive it was Navarro who was mocking me with his child's play. "It seems you've buried the wrong bones. A mistake the Devil should be sure never to make," I said. My words were boisterous, but strangely enough, they didn't echo.

"The Devil I am not, Travis," said the voice from behind me. I quickly turned around and found Navarro was sitting in his throne. What sort of being was this I was up against? "If you promise to listen," he continued. "And promise not to fight with me, I will tell you everything you ever wanted to know about yourself, me, and the one you call God. I can tell you why I war with Him and why you've been drawn into this."

I was sickened being so close to the beast that has condemned man, and I didn't want to hide it. "I don't make deals with the Devil!"

Navarro peered into the distance and chuckled. "Spirit, you can play the role of the fool so well! I'm willing to provide you with all the answers to the questions you've been searching for but you would rather allow your unjust hatred of me to guide you and keep you from hearing what I have to say. If you wish to continue this fight with me, then let us fight now . . . then we will never find resolve. But if you listen to what I have to say then you can make an educated decision whether or not you wish to destroy my dream or embrace it. You are free to make your own decisions, aren't you? After you realize my dreams genuineness, I'm confident you will agree to help me see it through. What is it you have to fear, Spirit? Time has no meaning to us here and I've emptied my home of all those who follow me. By listening you suffer no loss and are in no danger of physical harm."

I drew closer to the Devil and pointed at him. "I don't fear you or any of your followers, Navarro! You've raped an innocent girl! You speak of dreams and being given the benefit, but what benefit have you given her, what dreams have you shattered in the name of your quest? I've come to destroy you, Devil, not hear your factitious stories."

"If you came here to fight you would've done so the minute you saw me, Travis. There is something inside you that wants to hear what I have to say, that is enamored by me and my willingness to stand against those I oppose no matter the odds . . . I can sense it. Sit, Spirit, so I can tell you everything from the beginning."

"I'll stand, demon!"

"Very well," he said and sank comfortably low in his throne. "A long time ago I was created by God before there was Heaven. I was His first creation. I was perfect and powerful, as powerful as God Himself but not quite. Like you are, Spirit.

"The instant I came to be I knew what love was. The way God looked at me. The passion His eyes held was deep and compassionate. But as time went on the passion He had for the existence He created began to fade from His eyes and heart. He was bored with me and I didn't know what I could do to entertain Him; I owed Him for what I was and what I had. Then, without much thought, God pointed His finger and nodded His head and there was space, the sun and stars. Amidst these stars there was a place He called Earth. And earth is a place that became the center of our attention. Its beauty was wondrous and breathtaking, and together, we stared in awe at His newest creation.

"I continued to watch this creation from a domain that later became Heaven. But from Heaven, I wondered what the surface of the earth was like and prayed silently I would be able to see it up close. God knew my desires and sought to fulfill them. He created a container or body for me that I could move around freely on the surface of His new world and touch it, breathe its air, experience everything it had to offer.

"I was thrilled by this and explored His creation for a long, long time. I ate its vegetation, swam in its lakes and oceans and slept on its ground beneath its stars. But soon I bored of the place and began to pay no mind to the things around me. I so badly wanted to return back to God's side and feel His love no matter how distant He was. God knew this and brought me back to Heaven. Even more distant He seemed to act around me, losing Himself in the vastness of Heaven. Until the day He came to me and said, 'I've created something new for you in the world below. This will amaze you as it has even me. Go there, observe what I've done so maybe one day you can do it too. I've created you in my own image, Navarro. You are Godlike and you wield infinite power. You can do as you like. Will what you would like to happen and it will happen.'

"I knew what God was telling me. I could feel the power

within, waiting to be released. I left His side at that very moment and willed myself down to the Earth to see the changes. Downwards I descended, blasé by my first accomplishment. It was a small feat, nothing too great. I wanted more.

"Things were quite different on Earth than from my first visit. Other life forms roamed its surface and claimed their own territory. Fish swam in the waters. Animals, rodents and bugs roamed the surface, walking on just a few or many legs. They were all a thrill to watch and they occupied much of my time. But my excitement was nothing compared to what I discovered next. In the far distance I saw a creature walking upright on two legs. I'd been amazed how much this creature had looked like me. Its intelligence far exceeded those around him, though it was far less powerful than I. It was man, and I watched him develop.

"After many years of seeing them learn, grow and reproduce, I became quite fond of them. I saw how each man was unique in his or her own way. Their emotion was genuine and fragile. Quite interesting. I was excited by this and went to my God to share my enthusiasm. But to my surprise, many creatures that looked like man crowded the newly constructed streets of Heaven. I passed them, looking for my Lord's throne and saw them all looking to me like I was the stranger. I was appalled by this.

"Upon approaching my Lord sitting on the pedestal He'd put Himself on, I saw many of the creatures were surrounding Him and showering Him with attention. But the attention I saw was a form of worship rather than love. Yes, I was envious of that attention and I won't deny it. I was His first creation, His most perfect creation and He looked to them for comfort? Words could not express the hurt I felt.

"I cleared my throat, and said, 'Lord, I've returned to your side to share my thoughts with you on the world below.'

"God looked down on me seeming thrown off by my return. Maybe He'd forgotten who I was. He pursed His lips and narrowed His eyes in thought, then said, 'I need no instruction from you! I am aware of everything that goes on there.'

"'I am lonely there, Lord,' I respectively replied. 'I have no one there to act as my companion and I miss you!'

"He smacked His lips and looked away, appearing to be annoyed by my confession. He called forth a great number of creatures and sent them to my side. He said, 'Make yourself a home there, Navarro. Live among the people and create things as you see fit. I've created many things below that would worship you. You just have to be creative enough to find out what they are and take charge of them. Now go. Go back down to your world and return only if things are wrong and unfixable.'

"After those words I was returned to Earth with the group He assigned to me. I didn't agree with God when He said I should live among man and twist things as I saw them. I never did as He suggested and was never tempted to do so. It was the people's world and I was just a visitor in it. I watched the people from afar, never allowing them to see me, and never interfering in their lives.

"As time rolled steadily along, I continued to watch the people of the world from afar and saw some things that frustrated me. I gathered all those who followed me, called a meeting, and explained to them what I was feeling. They too began to explain they were feeling an unfamiliar sensation: sadness. We conversed for hours, going in depth about the things that saddened us. We all saw how the people's disposition was changing. They began to cheat, steal, lie and create weapons of destruction. They continued to create life but also savagely took it away. Sickness, death, famine, floods, murder, rape were becoming part of everyday life on the revolving world. The pain and suffering the people had to endure was never-ending and it took its toll on those who had to witness it. It was something we were ignorant too and found the behavior to be quite disturbing.

"I willed myself unseen by the humans and watched them from a closeness I dared never do before. When I did this, I entered a new place, a spirit realm here on Earth. And with that revelation a new discovery followed. The fleshy shells of a human contained a soul. This soul is the same form you and I hold now. I found once the body could no longer house its soul it would die and the two would separate. The body would turn to dust, but the soul would step into the spirit realm and drift to the light and go to Heaven.

"We pondered this and were angered by it. What was the

purpose behind their life if they were destined to make it into Heaven anyhow? Why make them endure the pain of the world?

"I willed all those who followed me to Heaven, and while we ascended, my followers nominated me to speak to God about the events we witnessed. They all told me they were afraid of Him and feared His wrath. I was taken back by this and questioned their reasoning. They told me He'd changed since I knew Him. They said He was doing awful things just like the humans were. But I dismissed their accusations remembering my God was as I'd been: perfect. After all, God said I was created in His image and I knew for sure evilness wasn't within me.

"When I approached God's throne, I explained all I had witnessed. I asked Him why the creatures on Earth contained the spirits and why they had to suffer down there before coming to Heaven. His eyes opened wide and He thrust Himself forward, coming mere inches from my face. 'You dare question your creator this?' He asked, disdain hardening His voice.

"I kept my composure and didn't back down. I wanted an answer from Him, deserved one. I asked, 'Why do this to your creations, my Lord?'

"'I will amuse you and tell you the answer you so unintelligently seek. But be warned. Once I answer you I'll hear not another word!' God slid back in His throne, a slight smirk overtaking his anger. Proudly He said, 'The souls from the people don't come here when they travel through the light; that is an assumption of your own. The souls are rerouted into new bodies that are waiting for them inside mother's wombs. They live a new life with no recollection of their past one. This process repeats itself over and over again forevermore. Those imperfect souls of that world never make it here. They are neither welcome nor wanted. They are for you and your imperfect place! You may call it a gift from me.'

"Reincarnation. That is what God was speaking about and it appalled me to hear it. I told Him so and also told Him I couldn't return to the Earth to witness the things that was going on. I told Him I feared another twenty years of changes and what it would bring. I said, 'Why do this, my Lord? So you can watch the people suffering while it provides entertainment for you? Those creatures you're turning your back on are precious, freethinking individuals that have all the same emotions as us. We are all your creations, your creatures of light, and we deserve better than what you're giving us! You, the most perfect being, a God, created something imperfect, riddled with flaws as you say. There is only one difference between the souls below and the ones that are standing by your side. They have pain and suffering, something those here will never have or know. They know evilness, embrace it, and like a child they don't understand they need to turn away from it. I want to know why you've done such a thing to precious creatures that came from your imagination! Or is the answer a simple one? Have those creatures been made in the image of what you've become?'

"God's eyes seemed to hold such hatred for me, for my rebellious ways that He actually had a sinister look about Him. He waved His hand to me as if He were merely dismissing me. 'I told you I would hear no more,' He said. 'It seems you've been away from me for far too long. You forget what happens if you disobey my word. Be gone. Go back down and sit in that pathetic world of yours and I will forget this ever happened.'

"'You can do no worse to us,' I said, turning and pointing to those who followed me, who believed in what I was saying, and I continued by saying, 'than what you've done by making us bear witness to the things that are going on down there. I rather you not forget what I said to you and you do something about it!'

"God began to laugh and all His creations began to laugh along with Him. I stood my ground and waited for the silence to come. It did, and that's when God handed His sentence down to all those who followed me to the throne and stood up for humanity.

"'Your chance to leave without punishment was given. You refused to accept my mercy, to hear my word. Now you must pay the price for your insurgent behavior. You will spend eternity witnessing your worlds agonizing destruction. You will be known as the Antichrist, the Devil, and you will be the representation of the people's evil. This will be done and you'll never be able to undo it. The place you will reside in will be known as Hell, Hades, or Sheol. It will be a dark, hot, depressing place, a place of misery and suffering. My domain will keep the name Heaven and it will be known as a blissful place of peace and joy. It will be taught those who are bad, evil or cruel will be sent to you for unbearable punishment. It will be said that those who live their lives in goodness shall come to me to spend a blessed eternity smothered in unworldly riches. If the people look upon you as being evil, Navarro, how could you possibly help them? They are going to fear you, distrust and hate you. This is too simple for me to do—to be able to ruin you. You have not only damned yourself but all those who've followed you here today, you Devil!

"'But now as I sit here and reflect on the reasons why I created you, I guess it would be fair for me to say I didn't fail in my first attempt to create after all. I created you for amusement, and now you're finally doing what I created you for. You're amusing me. Your caring nature has amused us all.'

"God rose to His feet and sent a gusting fiery wind racing towards us. All in Heaven stood around, pointing and laughing as we were consumed with the fire and burned. My appearance and that of my followers changed into what you see it as being before you now. Once His blaze died, our screams continued until we had no strength or voice left. God demanded silence and a hush fell throughout Heaven. He told me I was unworthy of His attention and He promised to send something created in His image that would deal with me and thwart my attempts to exact my revenge. That something He created is you, Spirit.

"God cast us all down to begin our never-ending sentence here on Earth. I soon discovered that I could actually take souls and hold them in my domain. I try to explain to them what is going on, but most souls see me as God promised: evil incarnate. It has been a struggle to try and change that image . . ." Navarro paused and laughed gently. "This whole thing has been a struggle, for us all.

"Shortly after the discovery of my being able to contain the human soul, the Spirit's began to interfere in my growth. There were many before you, Spirit, many that wouldn't have heard me out like you just did.

"My army is close to being ready now, but if I could get one more being to believe in my dream, maybe someone as powerful

114

as you, I could end His evil reign of terror and create a place where we could all live in peace and harmony. I would destroy this world and gather all the souls from it and live with no more death and no more sickness. Only love and harmony would govern. I look upon this world that I once saw as beautiful and just see pain and suffering. I look at the taking of the people's souls as being an act of mercy. I don't look at their death as being a time to mourn as you probably do. I have a dream of a perfect world, Spirit, and I ask you if you would deny all those you ever loved this?"

Navarro shook his head in doubt. Abated he whispered, "I don't think you would ever do that."

I silently agreed with him but there were so many questions yet unanswered, so much confusion dwelling within. I chose the most predominantly disturbing issue in need of a response, and asked, "How is it you're merciful by raping a woman?"

Navarro shifted uncomfortably in his throne, then settled his eyes on me, and said, "If you look inside her mind, Spirit, you'll see it wasn't me. It was an ordinary human man riddled by the evil I've told you about. I only changed the growing fetus to be my own afterwards through touch."

I couldn't believe the things I'd heard. It was too much for me to absorb. "And I'm supposed to accept what you say as being truth, the final word?"

Navarro shook his head back and forth, telling me no. He said, "Divination and the Dezrects were all present during my judgment. Question them and they will tell you what transpired. But pressure them for the answers you seek. Their fear of God may still grip their tongues."

Navarro stood silently and walked away. Pausing, he said, "I always thought if the suffering of myself and a handful of others could save millions of souls from suffering, then everything I've ever gone through would be worth it. I ask if you choose not to help me overthrow God then you leave me alone so I can fulfill my dream. I don't feel my request is unreasonable. I want you to think about it."

He walked away from me and there I was, left alone inside Hell to ponder his words.

Chapter 20

Spirit

I've made some decisions that directly involve you, yeah you with the book in your hand. By the time I depart, everything will be made perfectly clear. But be prepared, this decision I've come up with is going to change your life forever. I'm sorry, I'm not giving you a say in this either.

When I first came to you with my story it was with the intent to prepare you for your existence as the next Spirit of Independence; you were chosen to become my replacement. The tension of the events unraveling around me compelled me to make this decision. I began showing you my way of life to give you an advantage that I was never given.

I can see Navarro's dream and believe the being I called my God is corrupt and evil. Understand this decision wasn't easy to reach, but events throughout my life have played a greater influence than I could ever imagine. I first began to question my faith in God when I was an impressionable young boy. Both my parents were killed in a train derailment accident and I was placed in an orphanage. I lived there until I grew into a strong independent young man that fell in love and married a beautiful young woman named Paige. Following the construction of my new family, I joined the military to build a promising career. This decision would eventually lead me to my death. Every day of my adult life I would grieve the loss of my parent's and blame God for the anguish I'd felt. At times I even found myself hating God for what happened to my mother and father. I couldn't understand His reasoning. How could He allow that to happen to them? They were good people, undeserving of such punishment!

About three years after I'd been freed from Hell, my faith in God came into question again. I'd gone to my son, George, who was a grown man with children of his own. I posed as a close friend of the family separated by time and distance. My son was beautiful, strong and polite. I silently complimented my Paige on the fine job she'd done raising him without me. I sat with him over a cup of coffee that I never drank because my inexperience at creating an artificial body didn't allow me to hold liquid. I asked him many questions pertaining to the family, but clearly, my attention was on his mother. I asked him how she was doing, where she was living. I'd been told she'd died a few years after the war ended. Details of her death were sketchy, but they really weren't needed. I felt it was my sudden departure from her life that was to blame. If I'd been there for her maybe things would've turned out differently. But they were the way they were and I had God to blame for that too. He was a wicked entity for taking me away from her, and her from me. I curse Him for it!

I also recently discovered it was Divination who took my human life and had me transformed into the Spirit. The Spirit before me never selected his replacement, and therefore, Divination was left the chore of choosing his successor. He came to me in human form and took my life without prejudice.

I've handed my bones over to Navarro for burial and I know you have formed an opinion as you listened to our story. I hope you apply it and use it according to the way you are going to operate as the Spirit.

Amanda, Divination, Nature and the Dezrects all await your arrival in Chova. Be sure once your transformation is complete you go straight there. I ask you to look after Amanda for me and keep her safe from anything that may be sent to destroy what she has growing inside of her. Navarro changed the fetus to be his own because if things should go wrong, then what she holds may one day save the soul of millions.

Once you've read these final words in your hands, I'm going to come and kill you. Maybe I'll do it as soon as you read the last word, or maybe a week afterwards. I haven't decided when yet and I'm not going to warn you once I reach that decision either. I know you fear death and I'm not getting any thrills by taking your life; being I'm standing right beside you as you read this, I assure you I can smell your fear. I promise I shall use care in what I do and will make your transition into becoming a Spirit a quick and painless experience. This is what I see as being best for now. After I have taken your life, I will be put to rest for eternity. I wish you luck in whatever it is you've decided to do.

Part 2: The Apocalypse

Introduction

I've been given the privilege to be the first to tell you about the events succeeding Spirit's decision to have himself put to rest. Years have gone by since then and many things have changed rather dramatically. Some events have been tragic, but others have been great beyond comparison of any past event in the world's history. I am excited and look to jump right into the forever after part, but Spirit sees it important I tell you the story from the beginning and not skip anything.

My name is Alex. If you can't remember who I am then think back to the events last shown to you. My human life ended inside Amanda's jewelry store, and immediately following, I was brought down to Hell to experience its functions. Later, Navarro released me to walk the spirit realm in search of the truth and to find my place within the strange new domain. I think my brief role in the crisis I'm about to tell you about proves I am one of good.

°

Chapter 21

Alex

About a month ago human time, my frantic two-year long search for acceptation of Navarro's figuration of the war came to an end by a chance encounter with a woman entity named Nature. I can remember when the petite redheaded woman first approached me. Her pale skin and white eyes clashed terribly with her bright red hair and lips. Even in the realm of souls, Nature had a transparent appearance, as did the flowing silk gown she wore. An odd appearance, yet strangely attractive.

"I've come for you, Alex," she said with caution, remaining a safe distance away from me. "It is important you follow me to a place between the physical and spirit realms."

"And who are you?" I questioned, looking her over. "And what is this place you speak of?"

"I am Nature and the place I speak about is a paradise called Chova. It is a place where humans and souls can interact without the normal complications of being on two separate realms. Its location cannot be spoken aloud. But to you, it can be shown."

"And what is there for me, in this place called Chova?"

"The love of a human woman. She has asked for you and I promised her I wouldn't return without you."

"And who is this woman you speak of?" I asked, tiring quickly of having to speak over such a great distance. I started to approach her.

"The granddaughter of the Spirit of Independence. She goes by the name Amanda."

I was stopped, surprised to hear her name. I had all but given up hope of ever seeing her again. I felt a longing ache grip my heart. I wanted to see her. "Please, Nature, take me to this place you call Chova."

Together we journeyed to the Land of Chova. On the way we spoke of Navarro, the God, the entity I once thought was the devil. We spoke of the infamous Spirit and the two meeting mutually together inside Hell. She told me in vivid detail the content of their conversation, which ultimately led to Spirit sacrificing himself for the betterment of man. Afterwards, the focus of the conversation shifted to Amanda. Nature said, "I've been watching over Amanda since the Spirit gracefully departed. Since your human death, Alex, Amanda has been asking for you. She's been curious to your fate. Out of good will, Navarro told the Spirit he released you into the spirit realm and in turn Spirit transferred this information to Divination. As you can guess, Divination passed this information along to Amanda. Over the years, the two have formed a strong friendship. Ever since the day Amanda told Divination she wished to see you, we've been searching for you. Now that I've found you, I need to tell you that Amanda is pregnant. But this pregnancy is different than any human pregnancy. You see, while Travis and Navarro still warred, an ordinary human male raped Amanda and his seed was planted inside her. At this point of the story things get real complicated. Navarro feared his destruction by the Spirit's hand was imminent and quickly approaching. Moments after the rape happened, Navarro discovered Amanda and knew she'd conceived. He touched her belly and changed the fertilized egg within her body to match his own DNA as if it were his own. This baby has been growing inside Amanda for over two years now and it is ready to come out. The labor she is having is life threatening, and she's scared. Divination asked me to use any means necessary to locate you so you can help Amanda through this—give her hope during a desperate time."

I never wavered; I immediately knew I would accept the challenge and told Nature so. She smiled knowingly and led me to the void. We stepped inside and were thrown about, spinning and twirling without control. Moments later, we were dropped inside a small clearing inside a dense forest. I stood to my feet and looked into the woodland. Unmoving I remained, confused by all the paths that branched out from where I stood.

"This way, Alex," said Nature. I hadn't seen her standing before me. She took hold of my hand, and said, "We must hurry. I'm sure she's already in the process of delivering the baby."

Hurriedly, Nature pulled me through an indistinguishable path and we emerged from the forest. I released Nature's hand and stared in amazement at the castle towering above us. "Come, Alex, we haven't time for this," she said, and grabbed my hand again. She pulled me into the House, through its blackened hallway and into a dimly lit room. When we emerged into the room, we were greeted with a terrifying pain filled groan.

I searched for Amanda and located her in the rear of the room. Her head was cradled in Divination's lap. Divination dabbed sweat beads off her forehead and coached her lovingly. Her legs were spread wide and nothing covered her lower half. Peering from between her legs were two pale bald midgets. Amanda shouted in agony and the two men quickly returned their attention to the task on hand.

"I can see its head, Amanda," one of the little men said. "You're doing great, but I need you to push for me just one more time!"

"I can't!" she screamed and panted and took a moment to settle into Divination's lap.

"You must, Amanda!" Divination coached. "Just push one more time!"

Amanda lifted her head and puffed heavily. She held her breath then pushed. Her teeth showed through strained lips and veins bulged on her forehead from the pressure. I heard a baby cry, and one of the little men said, "It's a boy! You have a baby boy, Amanda!" and he held him up for everyone to see. He was wrinkly and pink, helpless and vulnerable, but precious and cute. The Dezrects began to wrap the baby with a blanket when it began to flail its arms and legs wildly. Kicking free of their grasp and falling to the ground, the baby landed on its feet and stood upright. Before our very eyes the baby began to grow. The layers of human flesh began to peel away, revealing fire red skin coated with a layer of thick snotty liquid. Pointed ears formed on the side of his head and two sharp fang teeth pushed through his gums and hung over his bottom lip. Two spiked horns protruded from the top of his head and a spiked tail waved gracefully behind him.

The two pale men I later learned was Sear and Osiris ran from the atrocity that had instantly grown over six feet tall. Amanda screamed out in horror, and her baby swung its' spiked tail towards her. The disrupted air whistled as it parted. Divination snatched Amanda away as the tail whipped the floor where she lay only moments before, cracking the cement.

I charged the creature, belting out a war scream. He slapped me away with his tail as if I were nothing more than an annoying gnat. "Must flee," the vile creature hissed. Velvety veined wings opened from his back. The wings flapped nimbly, pulling the creature into the air. He crashed through the wall of the House and made his getaway.

Silence blanketed the inside of the House. Everyone was stunned by what they saw, were discounting it, and were unable to find the words to express this. I didn't even try. I watched the sunlight beaming through the massive hole in the wall. Dust particles swirled about, slowly revolving in the spotlight without direction or care. This reminded me of the very first dance I had with Amanda. The dance was slow and intoxicating. We held each other tightly, lovingly, spinning round like a carousel. We were unaware of the world around us; two lovers caught in a timeless moment that was ours and only ours.

"What have I done!" Amanda cried, bringing me back to reality or what passed for it. I looked to her, searching the depths of my mind silently, looking for comforting words to say but she shamefully looked away from me and buried her head in Divination's chest. Some reunion.

"Come, Alex," Nature said from outside the House. The two Dezrects were standing patiently by her side.

"Let us go," Divination whispered to me, nodding towards Amanda. "We should head to a safer place."

Amanda remained quiescent in Divination's arms as he stepped through the gaping hole. I followed. Once we regrouped, we began a journey on a dirt path that seemed to curve endlessly through a forest.

After walking quietly for miles, everyone consumed in their own thoughts, heavy rumbling sounds filled the air and stole our attention. A light mist floated around us and the surrounding trees dripped with moisture. It was a welcomed distraction.

Once we emerged from the forest, a great mountain that seemed to touch the sky created a beautiful backdrop. From the mountaintop water fell white with rage into a lake below, sending violent waves outwards that turned into gentle ripples the further they were pushed towards the shoreline.

We kept on the path and maintained a sullen pace while we traveled up the side of the mountain and across its' center to a cave hidden behind the waterfall. Upon entering the blackened cave, the Dezrects went ahead and lit some candles hanging low on the walls. Explicit engraving covered the walls and Nature explained their meaning to me. I was intrigued, but evenly concerned about Amanda. Everyone pressed on. We came to a giant wooden door that'd been propped open by a rock.

Inside the room, Divination laid Amanda on the floor, and the Dezrects scrambled around looking for a blanket to cover her with. Divination asked us all to settle around the table and we did. Once we were settled, Divination sat, and with a distressful tone to his voice, he said, "I feared this day was going to come."

Concern filled me. If a celestial feared something then I was terrified to death of it. I said, "What, what is it you fear?"

Divination hung his head. "Navarro's first born has the power of a God and his ways are immoral."

Osiris leaned forward and placed his elbows on the table. He cupped his hands together and looked up. "Please, Lord," he said. "Help us through this, we really need you."

Divination slowly raised his head. He paused in deliberation, and said, "Please forgive Osiris and his kind. Ever since the Spirit of Independence decided to step down, they've gone to their old ways of prayer. They saw Travis as the last hope for souls and humans alike. But I don't know why Osiris is praying to God, it doesn't seem to do any good. It hasn't in quite some time."

The Dezrect named Sear stood on his chair, and growled, "How dare you speak about our creator, our God like that, Divination! You've served Him without ever questioning Him before. Why now do you speak ill of Him?"

Divination tried to lose the knowledge that changed him by shaking his head. It seemed as though it was something embedded in his mind forever. Divination said, "I'm starting to feel this God we serve so blindly is evil. He hasn't come for us like He said He would. I feel as though He's forgotten about us, abandoned us like He did Navarro."

The Dezrects faces told me they were troubled by Divination's inner turmoil. "That just isn't true, Divination," Sear said, and sat. "He loves you and me. Us all! He will return someday like He said He would. When that day comes we will return to the Heaven's with Him just like we were promised. You just have to keep the faith."

Divination pounded his fists into the tabletop, startling me. "Faith? I wish to ask you a question about faith, Sear. Why are you led by faith that is blind? God hasn't come for us since He sentenced us to serve Him in this hell!"

The Dezrects stared at Divination scornfully as if such an outburst wasn't within his right. "Stare all you want," Divination said, softening his tone. "I've decided to aide Navarro in his war against God."

The Dezrects both hopped to their feet and shouted at Divination from the chair tops. Sear called Divination's words blasphemous and Osiris told him he was a traitor.

"Sit down, the both of you," Divination commanded. The Dezrects returned to their seats without further objection.

"I suppose I owe an explanation to you all," he said. "At the last minute Spirit changed his mind from allowing Navarro to bury his bones to having Alex do it. Just before this was to be done, the Spirit approached me. He told me all he'd discovered about the war between God and Navarro. He told me how his confusion and his personal beliefs were too deep and it was best for him to find a replacement that could apply all they were taught to make a better decision concerning these issues. Before he left me, he asked me to take all the facts presented to me and to make a just decision as to whether or not I was serving God for the right reasons. I did as the Spirit said and questioned myself this over and over again. I can honestly say I don't believe I have been serving God for the right reasons. As much as I've denied it over the years, I believe in Navarro's dream and my only regret is that I didn't see its genuineness sooner. I know you are all thinking that he takes human souls and holds them against their will. That is true, and the Spirit addressed this issue with him. Navarro answered these issues by saying this: 'If the suffering of a few thousand souls ensured a permanent euphoria and the happiness of billions of souls, then such a sacrifice would be a small price to pay.'

"I truly believe this and I have to base decisions off of what I believe."

Divination moved his gaze around the table slowly, first to the Dezrects, then to Nature, and lastly to myself. "Spirit gave the ultimate sacrifice for his belief in Navarro's dream. I need to ask how many sitting here in this room would do the same?"

Again, Divination moved his gaze to each one of us, stopping momentarily to add emphasis. He continued. "Navarro's dream of unity is pure and needs to be brought to fruition. Our God has forgotten us, abandoned us, and I feel we're being left to play the fools. I cannot accept that position anymore--I refuse. You two go to the others and tell them what I've told you. Return once everyone has made a decision whether to help Navarro's cause or not. Now go, I have things I need to discuss with Alex."

The Dezrects stood and descended the pile of rocks. They began conversing in their strange language, moving out of the room quickly. I followed them with my eyes as they removed the rock and closed the door behind them.

Divination looked from the closed door to me. He pulled back his hood and revealed his disfigured face to me. The skin was red and riddled with blisters. Thick slow moving puss rolled down his face, reminding me of wax melted by flame.

"I was one of the first to pay the price of this war," he said, and pulled his hood back over his head. "It happened immediately after God sentenced Navarro to this world. I was sent after him so I could aide the Spirit's in the war that was yet to come. I'd gone down to Navarro's Hell to beg him to stop his foolish up rise. But Navarro wouldn't hear my plea and he demanded I leave him. I ignored his request and pressed him even harder, lashing out with words of conviction and anger. I despised him for what he was doing and I let him know it.

Navarro said he could no longer listen to my whining and he walked away from me, going to the rivers edge to see if he could spot a Surefire fish, a fishlike creature that lived inside the boiling river. But when I went to his side and continued to press him, something terrible happened, something that I can remember like it happened only yesterday . . .

"'Navarro, have you gone completely mad!' I said. 'Stop with this adolescent behavior before you get yourself and all those who followed you destroyed!'

"Navarro refused to look at me. He said, 'Quiet, Divination. I said my peace to Him and I meant everything I said. I needn't apologize for it either. Leave here at once, I can't take your badgering any longer!'

"That was it? He would just try and brush me aside? I felt as if my plea meant nothing to him and this enraged me, intensified my hostility towards him. I pressed him even harder, making sure he heard my warning. I said, 'He has created His first Spirit, Navarro. This is the being He promised would come for you. I've been sent here to aide the Spirit's. I ask you not to do this to me, to Heaven. Go back and tell Him you see things differently now, that you made a mistake. It is not too late to beg for His forgiveness.'

"'I will not,' he shouted with anger, his teeth showing through tautened lips. 'What I've seen is appalling! Unforgivable! He's the one who should be asking us for forgiveness! I will ask you one last time to take your leave, Divination. I have all but run out of patience for you and your insulting accusations.'

"I allowed my anger to get the best of me. I stepped to him with clenched fists, and said, 'Swallow your pride, you Devil!'

"Navarro turned to me with a look of betrayal teased with anger. Unexpectedly, he pushed me, sending me stumbling backwards. He turned away from me and began walking away, unaware the momentum of his shove carried me into the boiling river. At first I was frozen with pain as the rough waters carried me away. But soon I embraced the pain and didn't fight it. I allowed it to carry me along until I was able to grab hold of the riverbank to pull myself free of the mighty rivers fiery touch. My condition was much worse than what you see now. Thousands of years have gone by since then, allowing my wounds to heal somewhat. The sting has long since subsided although the grotesque melted flesh remains and probably will for the remainder of my existence."

A moment of silence fell between Divination and me. I was fidgety and squeamish from seeing his skin and hearing his stories. I wanted to leave.

"Now," Divination said. "I need to know where you've buried the Spirit's remains."

"What?" I asked even though I heard what he'd said. His request imposed a different type of anxiety on me.

"Travis Winters bones, where have you buried them?"

"By the Spirit's orders I am not to reveal that. I was told to uncover his bones only if the Spirit that has been chosen as his replacement has been destroyed." I really wanted to leave, but, nervously leaned back in my chair and chewed my nail instead. Would he dare harm me if I wasn't willing to give him what he wanted?

Divination leaned forward. I was intimidated but tried not to show it. I kept my gaze locked into the blackness of his hood while he spoke. "That thing Amanda gave birth to represents the third antichrist mentioned within the prophecies of the book of Revelations," Divination said. "He is the creature that will usher in the apocalypse here on earth. The Spirit that has been chosen to take Travis's place is weak and inexperienced. I don't think he could handle a situation such as this. Travis can destroy him but before he can we need to wake him first. Let us not delay in doing so, we need to deal with this problem before the creatures powers fully manifest."

"I understand what you're telling me, Divination. I do, but the Spirit has chosen his replacement. We need to make contact with him, not Travis. The new Spirit should be given the chance to deal with this."

Divination shook his head. "I can only see things turning worse. This new Spirit has been carefully chosen and has been shown what his responsibility is to be. He hasn't been to Chova yet and it has been over two years since he assumed the responsibility. Does this not cause any concern to you?"

"It does, but the Spirit came to me out of trust. His wishes I respect and will obey. We will locate this new Spirit ourselves and we will tell him of the events that have transpired and what his destiny is now to become."

"And if he proves to be the failure I expect him to be? Then will you agree that we must wake Travis?"

"Agreed," I said.

"Very well, Alex. I need to prepare for the absolute worst and bring this new Spirit's bones with me. This will enable us to observe him from afar, and if he is trouble like I suspect, then we can bury his bones and pull him from existence."

A slow steady creaking sound came from behind me. I turned in the seat and saw Osiris entering the room with a bulky satchel slung over his shoulder. "Here are the Spirit's bones, Divination," said Osiris. He climbed the rock pile next to the chair and plopped the satchel on the tabletop; the bones within clunked loudly. "The Dezrects have finished the meeting."

"And?" Divination asked impatiently.

Osiris turned away. "I'm afraid the news isn't very good at all," he said. "It seems the Dezrects believe they should still serve our Lord above. I, as an individual, believe in you and the Spirit, Divination. I am only one and couldn't convince the others. I have stepped down as the Berusht, their leader, and I left Sear to guide them the rest of the way."

Divination walked to Osiris, gave him a hug and took a step

back.

"Thank you, friend. I need you to remain here and keep watch over Amanda. Wish us luck."

A nervous chill crawled through my spine and I couldn't understand why. The Spirit was hand picked by Travis. This meant he was good. Right?

I got up from my chair, watched Divination take the satchel and head out the door. Unexplainably reluctant to meet the new Spirit, I followed Divination.

Chapter 22

Alex

When we left Chova, Divination and I paused so he could search for the Spirit and learn his location by using the power of his mind. Once that task was complete, we quickly journeyed to the Spirit's location. During the journey Divination seemed troubled but never said so. I allowed him to have his thoughts without invading. If his ascertainment needed my attention, I was sure he would say so.

Divination led me to a quaint house in a quiet middleclass suburb. Before the house we paused. Divination said, "Searching for someone with your mind is a difficult task. It is even more difficult to learn their mental state. I sensed something troubling but I can't place exactly what it is. Prepare yourself for anything."

Divination turned the sack over to me, and said, "If trouble ensues you're to bury these immediately."

I took the sack and squeezed it until my knuckles were white. At the first sign of trouble, I would bury the bones and be done with the Spirit. We entered the house through a rear wall and found ourselves inside the master bedroom. Divination thrust out his hand, signaling me to be still. I immediately froze and listened for the slightest indication the Spirit was in the house. I heard nothing.

"There is no one here, Divination. What are you listening for?" Divination patted the air with his hand. "Hush, Alex. The Spirit is here! Be silent for a moment so I can locate him."

I stood quietly and Divination bowed his head and listened to the silent house. A whaling scream filled with terror erupted from the opposite end of the house in which we stood. Divination took off running, fading through walls at a speed that was impossible for me to keep up with.

"Enough Spirit!" Divination shouted as I was entering the room. The sight inside the room was daunting. Two humans were in the room along with the Spirit. A female human was on her knees crying hysterically. Her long hair was wrapped in the Spirit's hand, rendered immobile. A young man was lying in the rooms' center, naked and his legs spread. His crotch was covered in blood. His hands and feet were pierced with wooden stakes driven into the floor. A leather strap was wrapped tightly around his neck and his face was dark purple under the choking pressure of the strap. His eyes stared into nothingness, glossy and lifeless.

I looked to the Spirit and a bright flash coming from his side caught my eye. In the opposite hand he'd held the woman's hair with, the Spirit wielded a steak knife that gleamed red from the blood that covered it. I immediately turned and ran for the outside with the intention of burying the Spirit's bones. Unexpectedly, I was attacked by a group of souls I'd overlooked. I was smacked around, thrown to the ground and held down. I was stripped of the satchel and completely immobilized.

"Is that what Travis chose you for?" Divination angrily shouted, his attention on the Spirit.

The Spirit released the woman from his grasp and stepped towards Divination. "She's a cheating bitch! I've searched for her for over a year only to find her fucking this piece of shit!"

"Dismemberment and murder is not what you were created for. You're a supreme entity now, Spirit. Sex is something you're no longer a slave to. You are needed, come with us."

"No," he said, taking possession of the woman's hair again. "I told her what I'd read. I told her what the Spirit said he was going to do to me. She didn't believe me; she thought the book was a work of fiction. I couldn't convince her I never bought the book. The damn thing was just there, in my house. I started to read it and I don't even like to read. I was scared shitless of it but kept reading. I told her, and do you know how she reacted? She hugged me and told me she loved me. With a promising smile she said if anything was to happen to me that she would never have anybody else take my place. She lied to me! For her dishonesty I made her watch her man die a slow death. That leather strap was wet, and it dried, it strangled him. Now that he is gone, she is next! I keep good on my promises."

The Spirit pushed the woman to the floor and stomped down on her neck. Something inside her body cracked loudly. He turned to the lost soul that had taken the satchel from me and demanded he bring the sack to him. The lost soul headed to the crazed Spirit when Divination placed himself between the two. He said, "What were you promised, lost one?"

The lost soul stopped walking, and said, "The light. He told me he would take me to the light if I served him."

"He can, lost one, but he won't! He's sick with his own power and he'll use you without ever fulfilling his promises. I can show you the way to the light. Bring the satchel to me."

The lost soul stood confused, looking from Divination to the Spirit undecidedly.

"I told you to come to me, you fool" shouted the Spirit. "Bring the damn sack to me! Whoever brings the sack to me will be brought to the light!"

The souls that held me to the ground released me and charged the confused soul that held the satchel. Souls that seemed to come from everywhere joined in the frenzy for the sack. The Spirit began chuckling madly.

"Alex!" Divination said without speaking. He sounded like he was in my head. "These souls shouldn't be here. Navarro's demons should've taken them to Hell where they would try and sway them to join his cause. Something is not right here!"

In the chaotic scuffle for control over the satchel, it dropped from the center of the rioting souls to the ground. Together Divination and the Spirit scrambled for the sack, as did the numerous souls that fought like a pack of starving wolves over a fresh kill. I stood and eagerly waited to see who would emerge with the prize.

The pile of souls was thrown about the room as if they were lying on an exploding bomb. The Spirit stood, dusted himself off and held the satchel up high to show all he was the one who recovered it. The Spirit laughed and the souls began to melt away like ice cream basking in the sun. They moaned in agony and some pleaded to the Spirit for mercy, but in his madness, the Spirit laughed even louder.

"You are corrupted, Spirit! I will see you destroyed," Divination growled from his position on the floor.

"If I didn't know any better, Divination, I'd say you're angry with me," said the Spirit. He was sarcastic. Over confident.

"Not as angry as I am saddened. You've failed your task."

"Shut up, you deformed inferior. You are here to serve me!"

"I'd never serve you. But Travis I would serve proudly. He had mercy on those who were weaker than himself. He carried love in his heart, but you, you carry hatred and destruction. Travis sacrificed his own needs for the bettering of others. But you kill others because you're unhappy. So tell me, Spirit, what have you done that deserves my service?"

"My say so!" said the Spirit. He reached down and grabbed Divination by his cloak and pulled him to his feet. "I'm going to hurt you real bad and I'm going to take my time doing it!"

A sense-shattering boom filled the room and caused me to stumble drunkenly backwards. By the time I recovered, Divination was struggling to stand, and the Spirit that held him was gone, the satchel containing his bones left on the ground where he once stood. Divination took notice to the satchel by his feet. He picked it up and tossed it to me saying, "Bury it, Alex, and hurry!"

I caught the sack and immediately ran for the outside. My progression was abruptly halted when I collided with the redheaded entity named Nature. I fell to the ground, and unmoved, she looked down on me. She pulled me to my feet, and said, "Hurry and bury those bones while Travis is able to thwart off the other Spirit!"

I bolted outside and gave the Spirit's bones the proper burial in an inconspicuous location. I returned to the house, and inside, Travis Winter, the Spirit of Independence stood with Nature and Divination. How was that possible?

"You've done well," the Spirit told me. "I knew I could count on you . . . all of you."

"How?" I said aloud, openly expressing my confusion.

He smiled, and said, "Nature woke me. She knew where you buried my bones."

I shook my head, denying such an event could be possible. "She didn't know where I buried your bones. Nobody did."

Nature giggled, and said, "He knows you didn't tell me, Alex. When Divination told the Dezrects he was going to aide Navarro in his war, I knew that was going to cause tension. I used that distraction to slip out of the cave unnoticed by you or any of the others. I went into the physical realm and headed straight to the location you chose to bury Travis's bones in. With haste I dug up the Spirit's bones. A fine mist seeped from the bullet hole beneath his eye socket. The mist was colorful and it swirled in a counterclockwise motion that picked up great speed and formed a funnel. Then, a forceful eruption coming from the funnel's center blasted the mist outwards, and as you see the Spirit before you now, is how the Spirit stood before me. Unfazed by his resurrection, Spirit told me of the danger you and Divination were in from the Spirit he'd chosen as his replacement. He took hold of his bones, grabbed my hand and quickly brought us here."

"But how? I never told you or anyone for that matter where I buried Spirit's bones!"

"And I never told you or anyone else that I followed you the day Spirit came to you and told you to bury his bones. I watched your every move from as close as I am to you now!"

"Impossible," I muttered, shaking my head in disbelief. "I was careful, making sure I wasn't being followed or watched the whole time."

"I know. I saw how you took the long way to where you had to go. I also saw you looking around, trying to find anything from the ordinary. But one thing I know how to do is sneak around undetected."

"No matter, Alex," Spirit said. "It was for the better anyhow. When I distracted the Spirit with the noise I produced upon my arrival, it gave me the opportunity to pull him through the ground and stall him long enough for you to bury his bones. He is in the essence of his bones now, in a place I call Limbo. This Limbo is where I've spent my time since my bones were buried. It's a place of complete nothingness. Consuming blackness. But strangely enough, while I was there, images were being played in my mind of the surrounding world. The images came constantly and all at once, confusing me and driving me into madness. Imagine every person's thoughts and actions flooding into your mind all at once.

"I quickly learned how to separate and choose events I wanted to see. Two events I witnessed were disturbing. I know you were all witnesses to one of the visions I had: the birth of Amanda's demonic baby. I saw this happen from the births' beginning to the baby's transformation into a vile creature that escape from Chova. My second vision was of Navarro preparing to leave Hell to storm Heaven's gate and overthrow God. I never saw this visions conclusion, but I did see explicit moments of the war. Casualties were high for both sides. I am frightened by this vision and need to leave now. Alex is going to accompany me. I have to convince Navarro not to leave, to wait until he is better prepared. I need both of you, Divination and Nature, to help the souls here, and when you're done with them, return to Chova and wait for my return."

Nature and Divination agreed with Spirit's requests and began to aide the surviving souls. I had no time to react to my new quest. The Spirit took hold of my hand and started to descend through the earth, bringing me to a place I still thought of as being Hell.

Chapter 23

Osiris

Not too long after Divination and Alex departed from Chova to search for the new Spirit, Amanda woke. She moaned and cradled her abdomen as she rolled on the floor. I sat next to her, trying to comfort her. Hours passed and her condition never changed. I couldn't bear to hear her struggling anymore and looked to take her pain away. I placed my hands on her belly and searched her insides with my touch. I'd discovered a lot of her reproductive organs had been mangled badly by the beast that grew inside her. I didn't want to tell her, but the beast actually ate pieces off of her uterus wall. It was amazing she wasn't dead. I worked long and hard to correct the damage as best I could, and I removed all the pain from her body.

Once the process was complete, Amanda moved to the table and I followed.

"Do you still hurt?" I asked her.

"Only in my heart, Osiris. I'm ashamed of that thing I'd given life to. For two long years it was inside me. The thought of that makes me sick."

"What you gave birth to was beyond your control, Amanda. You have nothing to feel shame for. Divination has gone to get the new Spirit so they can destroy the beast."

"I heard some of the things Divination said about God, about Navarro, and about the devil I gave birth to. He thought I was sleeping but I was really awake."

"Some things aren't meant for your ears, Amanda. They are beyond your understanding."

"I should've killed myself by jumping from the ledge and into the waterfall. I thought about it so many times during my pregnancy. When the baby kicked or moved I could sense things weren't right."

"Amanda . . ."

"Please, Osiris! Let me finish. I also can't understand how you, Spirit, Divination, Nature, and Alex can believe Navarro is virtuous. His essence is evil and he lies to hide it. His seed has produced an offspring that hasn't yet learnt how to hide its sinful nature, but you'll see, in time it will learn and it'll be able to fool all of you like Navarro has."

"Amanda, if only you could understand. When the child was born there were two very important factors that made it become what it was: a human side and a supreme spiritual side. Navarro passed his vast powers to the creature, making him godlike. You passed on the evil seed that makes up human nature. This is what gave him his undesired physical and personal attributes."

"My seed?" Amanda questioned. She was outraged by what I was saying, but it was the truth. "You're telling me it was my seed that created this devil?"

"Truthfully? Yes. And this is one of the reasons Navarro wars with God. He feels the evil seed that has been placed inside the human body and the unnecessary circumstances that surrounds the life and death of a person is wrong. Navarro wants unity, a place of peace and harmony. A place where the evil seed cannot survive."

The door behind us creaked and Divination and Nature entered the room and joined us at the table. Divination told us that Travis had returned and this excited Amanda and me. But our mood was quick to change when Divination shared bad news with us. He said, "Yes, Spirit's return is something to celebrate, but there is disheartening news I must share with you both. The human that

Travis selected as his replacement was consumed with hate and he killed two people before our eyes. He also manipulated some human souls for his own gain and destroyed them when he had no more use for them."

"That's impossible!" I disputed. "A Spirit cannot contain such evil! An impure human cannot accept the Spirit seed; their bodies would outright reject it."

"That is what I thought, Osiris. But the evil seed within this Spirit is not something that could be denied."

"Damn," I said with certain dismay. "This may very well be the beginning of the end. The devil has begun to spread the seed of corruption throughout the spirit realm. And if his corruption is enough to contaminate a Spirit, then it could quite possibly become an epidemic."

Chapter 24

Alex

When Spirit pulled me through the Earth, the sights that filled my eyes were astounding. The vivid details of the Earth's inner layers: the squirming worms, the snaking tree roots searching for nutrition, and the biggest of rocks to the tinniest grains of sand were captivating and intriguing. It was a pulsating spectrum that glowed passionately. Enchanting.

On the journey downward, Spirit held onto me to mitigate any fears I may've had of falling. "It is beautiful, I know, Alex," Spirit said; I didn't realize my mouth was hanging open. I shut it. "It's something that you will never get accustomed to. I want you to know you can will yourself here anytime you wish."

I was confused by his words, not realizing at the time how ignorant I was to the potential of the mind once it was free of a body. I asked, "What do you mean?"

Spirit's voice never faltered and always remained strong and supportive. He told me, "When I left you with the responsibility of burying my bones, I taught you how to walk between the spirit and physical realms. Now I feel you're ready to learn how to go places, to do things with a silent command from your mind. Just will what you wish for and it will happen."

"Just will it," I repeated.

Just then, we arrived inside Navarro's lair. It was barren, left as though it had been abandoned for years. The air was steamy hot and still, burning my lungs with each breath. The chains that were connected to the rings embedded into the walls and floor sat eerily empty. Navarro's throne was unoccupied, the image of his face engraved in the top portion of the backrest that seemed to follow my every move. The two cement bowls located behind Navarro's throne ceaselessly burned Hell's flame though it was low and weak. Dying.

"It seems we're too late," Spirit said in a shout. I barely heard his words over the noisy sounds of the boiling rivers' choppy rapids. He neared me, and said, "When I told you and the others about my vision inside limbo, I only told half the story. Now I feel I should share the rest of the story."

"Spirit?" I questioned, detecting something amiss in his tone. He looked to Navarro's throne then back to me.

"The visions I was getting while I was in Limbo were disturbing. So disturbing I called on Divination to find you so you could wake me. If I would've known where you buried me I would've told Divination so he could've exhumed my remains himself . . ."

". . . Spirit," I interrupted, feeling ashamed. "Divination had Nature find me and she brought me back to Chova. Divination tried to get me to resurrect you but I refused him. I told him that was against your wishes."

Spirit walked to a long chain that'd been discarded on the ground. He bent at the knees and picked it up. One end of the chain had a collar that was open, and the other end of the chain had a snapped link. He examined it from one end to the other. He said, "That still doesn't mean he heard my call." He held the chain out for me to see. "Do you remember being bound in one of these things?"

I thought his question over for only a second. I got goose bumps and my neck began to itch where the collar once fit snug. "Yes, Spirit, I remember like it were yesterday."

Spirit dropped the chain to the ground and smacked his hands together, cleaning the dirt from his palms. He looked around the cave, spinning himself around completely. "Without God sending His Angels amongst the humans to spread the myth of the Devil, this place alone would've been enough to frighten even the bravest soul to death. And those damn chains and collars . . ."

Spirit bent down and retrieved the chain. He bunched it together and tossed it towards the river. He was agitated. "If Navarro is so godlike, why does he use such cruel tactics to get the things he wants? Something about this just doesn't make sense to me."

I followed the chain as it sailed through the air and hit the water. No sound could be heard as it unnoticeably disrupted the swishing rapids to sink to the unknown depth of the river.

"If they would've just let me live out my life like a normal person," Spirit growled angrily, "I wouldn't have affected so many lives with the confusion that surrounds me. I always wondered, out of all the millions of people in the world Divination could've chosen, why choose me? What was it I had that nobody else had?"

Spirit put his head down and paused for a moment. He walked to Navarro's throne and sat. He looked to me, and said, "Do you realize how hard it is for me to sit in this chair?"

Spirit held his eyes on me and I could see the anger seething within. His line of questioning was rhetorical. I remained silent but attentive. I was willing to listen to what he had to say; it was what he needed.

"Every fiber of my body is pulling me to move away from this place. What a pathetic existence this is. I've been created to battle a god and I struggle with something so simple as emotions."

Spirit stood and walked to me. He placed his hand gently on my shoulder. "We need to return to the surface. I want you to will it, Alex, and it shall happen. Let's ascend slowly so I can continue to explain the things I need to."

Spirit started for the surface, floating upwards. I gave a mighty jump in the air to impress Travis how quickly I could learn. Disappointingly, I landed back on the ground.

"Will it," Spirit said from behind me, scaring me. Last I saw him, he was heading to the surface and I didn't hear nor see him return. I turned myself around and looked at him.

"Will it," he said again. I nodded my head in understanding. "Good," he said satisfied, building my confidence with his unabashed trust. Spirit started for the surface again. I closed my eyes and willed myself to the surface as the Spirit instructed. My body began to rise and it felt as if it were being lifted by something invisible. I opened my eyes and began to panic from the unfamiliar sensation. I began to drift downwards. I didn't want to disappoint Spirit, so I willed myself up again and was able to maintain control over my fears as my slow steady ascent started.

I caught up to the waiting Spirit in no time at all. Spirit looked to me and appraised me for my new accomplishment. He said, "You learn fast, Alex. Now, allow me to explain the reasons why I brought you to Navarro's lair without further delay. Like I said when I returned, I saw the events of Amanda's baby being born and Navarro's raid on Heaven. I saw both events happening simultaneously and no matter how I tried, I couldn't receive any other visions after this. It was as if I was being shown those images on purpose, and whoever was doing it, they wanted to leave a lasting impression. Something tells me those two events will lead to the destruction of the earth, and ultimately, to the apocalypse. I came here to see if the events were from the future or if they were actually happening as I was seeing them."

We hit the surface where I stopped and stood silent in thought. I was terrified. I wanted to say something, anything, but the feeling of impending doom gripped my soul.

"Let us go back to Chova, Alex. We're going to tell Nature and Divination about our findings in Hell and how that coincides with my visions in Limbo."

Spirit turned his attention from me and continued onwards, making his way to Chova. I watched him extend the distance between us as I tried to absorb the realization that the end of the world was a possibility. It was strange, the way I started to think. When I was a human my worst fear was death. Not just the actual act but the whole thing that would lead up to it and the unknown of what would come after it. I used to make myself sick with those thoughts. And at this moment, it was happening again. I was making myself sick worrying about the unknown. I was already dead; I'd already faced the unknown once and survived. But I was about to face it again and wondered what was to come.

In my internal fear I became oblivious as to what was going on around me. Demons, a pack of a dozen or more attacked me without my sensing their nearness. The souls hissed and tore into my flesh with sudden fierce strikes from their razor-sharp claws. By the time I gathered enough thought to realize what was happening to me, I was on my back, trying desperately to push the demons off me. Thankfully, Spirit heard the commotion and returned to aide me. He pulled the crazed beasts off me and gathered them. Ascending with them into the sky where he disposed of them.

When the Spirit returned, with urgency, he said, "Things have gotten bad and seem to be worsening with each passing minute. Come, let us return to Chova immediately."

Obliging with the Spirit's request and understanding its importance, I did my best to keep up with him. "Did you send the demons through the light?" I asked.

Spirit glanced back at me. I think he realized I didn't fully understand the things that were going on and the severity of it. He said, "Those weren't demons, Alex. They were human souls. I brought them to the light and questioned each one before I sent them through. The evil seed has tainted them all, and it has altered their appearances. Some were so contaminated with this seed it actually made them incoherent. Those were the first I sent through the light. The souls that weren't completely riddled with the seed told me of a red skinned creature that influenced them to stray from their pure ways. It was the creature Amanda gave birth to. I saw it while I was in Limbo and the souls described him perfectly. This devil has developed and influenced a change within the spirit realm way faster than I ever anticipated."

When we arrived inside Chova, we immediately went to the cave hidden behind the waterfall. Nature, Divination, Osiris and Amanda were gathered around the table, awaiting our return. All of them looked sick with worry, and I could only wonder how our news would affect them. They knew there was something more.

They studied me and Spirit, trying to see if something we wore, whether it was an expression or an article of clothing, would recite our experiences in Hell. If they only knew what we found there was only part of it . . .

I quietly found a seat and retreated for a moment to my own concerns. There was so much on my mind, where was it I should begin?

Spirit called Osiris forward and requested he get the rest of the Dezrects so they could hear what he had to say. Osiris rushed out of the room.

Chapter 25

Spirit

I can see the way I left you when last we spoke was unfair and somewhat cruel of me. I know I told you I chose you as my replacement and I never came for you. The reason behind this is because I chose several other people and randomly picked one person and used him as my replacement. But it seems my judgment was in error. I should've chosen you. I've taken a certain liking to you and see it important I keep you informed of recent events. I feel as though I may need your services after all. Each day that passes is another day I learn of the dangers surrounding my existence. Something big is happening here, but I don't know exactly what it is.

When Alex and I returned to the cave inside Chova, I asked Osiris to get the rest of the Dezrects so I could share the news I had with everyone. The few moments Osiris was gone, I was left to feel the tension and compete with everyone's accusing glances.

When Osiris returned with all the other Dezrects, I felt somewhat relieved to get on with the meeting and took my place at the head of the table and to my left, going clockwise around the table, Nature sat. Next to her was Sear and Osiris sharing the same chair. Divination sat at the foot of the table, and Alex and Amanda sat to my right. The group of Dezrects were scattered about, encircling the table. When everyone was settled, I was feeling too distressed to remain seated. I stood, and immediately broke into my rehearsed speech. I said, "Some of us have been around before man ever established themselves on this world. Other of us has always been without a physical body while others are new to the vessel used to maneuver around in the afterlife. We even have a human amongst us. No matter what form we are in, what I have to say affects each one of us equally."

I carefully peered into everyone's eyes, keeping a firm look about my expression to assert the severity of my words. "I brought Alex with me to Navarro's lair in hopes of finding it busy with activity of Heaven's rebels holding human souls against their will. But when we descended into the depths of the earth, the barren sight of Navarro's lair terrified me. I need you all to be patient while I explain why this is so.

"As you all know, when I stepped down as the Spirit, I had Alex put my bones to rest. When I left this world to enter the state of eternal sleep, things weren't exactly like I expected them to be. There was no rest and I remained completely aware of the world around me. I could see the human I chose as my replacement and his abrasive behavior. I also saw horrible glimpses into a future that seemed like a warning at first, but now that I've investigated the circumstances surrounding them, I see the events were foreordained. These visions were clear and they frequently invaded my non-sleep. I saw the birth of the demonic baby and Navarro's preparation to raid Heaven. Succeeding these two events, I saw the earth consumed in battle, leading to worldwide destruction. Death riddled the world, and the apocalypse had begun!"

The people in the room reacted to my shared experience. The Dezrects began communicating in their cryptic language. Divination and Nature muttered their concern, and Alex rested his elbows on the table and cradled his chin in his hands. Amanda began to sob. They were all scared, and as horrible as I felt about that, there was goodness to it. They would be invaluable to my plans and its success, and I could use the fear to guide them. I continued to speak again and an immediate hush fell throughout the room. "I believe Navarro's raid on Heaven and the birth of the devil were visions into the future. But I think the future is only hours ahead of our own. I believe I've made a connection between the two visions and the apocalypse to come.

"When Alex and I were returning from Navarro's lair, he was attacked by several lost souls that had been disfigured by the evil that consumed them. I took those souls to the light, but before I sent them through, I questioned them. The soul's that were coherent enough to hear me told me of a vile creature that radiated with hatred and anger. This entity they spoke of had the same characteristics as Amanda's demonic baby.

"As we all know, when a soul steps into the spirit realm, the evil it once knew when it was inside a body is left behind. The relief of being away from the evil is only temporary, lasting only until they enter another human body where it will learn corruption again. But now, the human souls aren't getting the relief from evil they all knew and harbored as a human. An example to this point is necessary:

"Suppose I have a glass of water sitting right here before me. I will use that glass of water to represent every human soul that enters the spirit realm. If you inspected the water, you'd see it was clear, free of contaminants. Now, suppose I had some black ink that represented Amanda's offspring. Imagine now if I were to put a single drop of ink, the Devil's corruption, into that clear, pure water. You would see the water becoming tainted. That is what I believe has happened to the souls inside the spirit realm.

"So, now you see, the two visions I've foreseen have come to pass, those visions being the birth of the devil and Navarro's raid on Heaven. Now only the destruction of the earth remains. I feel Navarro's raid on Heaven will be devastating for both sides. I also believe Navarro and God's demise will be within the wars mass casualties. The death of the two Godlike entities leaves only one godlike entity remaining: the devil. If it is not stopped, the Devil's corruption will spread wildly. I believe within days the contamination of the spirit realm will ultimately cause the Earth's destruction. Within the visions I saw while I was in Limbo, I saw humans and spirits rioting. But this wasn't human versus human and spirit versus spirit. It was a combining of both realms. You see, without Navarro or God there is no balance, and without balance everything erupts and collides."

"You, Spirit!" Alex called out. "You have ultimate power. You can defeat this Devil, you can be this worlds god!"

"A god?" I laughed at the notion. It was inconceivable. "A god I am not and could never be. I'm just a human soul whose life was interrupted by something that is much bigger than he could ever hope to be. I was created for amusement by a corrupted God!"

"Wait a minute!" Sear interjected. "How could you stand there and tell us you were created for amusement? Stop speaking ill of our creator before your soul is damned!"

I walked behind the chair Sear sat in and I placed a hand on his shoulder, and said, "Look at what I've gone through, Sear. My soul has been damned since this cursed existence began. I need your help, Sear. I need everyone's help to stop the coming apocalypse. "

"I don't think so," Sear growled and batted my hand from his shoulder. He stood on the chair top and went nose to nose with me. He pointed his finger into my face, and said, "We already gave our answer to Divination when he asked us to aide him in Navarro's unholy war against God."

I backed away from Sear, staying far enough away so he couldn't reach. I remained composed, and said, "I hope the others you lead don't follow by example, Sear. Everything I told you means much more than some damn belief you know doesn't hold substance anymore. Everyone needs to listen to what we must do to stop what has begun. This is going to have to be a combined effort if we hope to avoid the day of reckoning."

"Bah, Spirit, we refuse! This was decided long before you returned. I would like you to know I speak for all the Dezrects," said Sear. He buckled his lips and narrowed his stare, lowering it to Osiris. "I speak for everyone except for this traitorous imp sitting next to me."

"Ignore him, Osiris," I said. There were bigger wars to fight. "I won't allow this to become a debate, Sear. You will help us! Besides, if you decide not to, where will you go? In case you didn't hear what I was saying, your Gods' kingdom may not even exist any longer."

"I will not betray my God nor will any of the Dezrects that follow me. Unless, of course, you attempt to use your power to force us to do so."

Sear smiled slyly, provoking my control. "I will not play this game of scorching words, Sear. Yes, I could force you to help, but I won't. But I will not allow you to speak for the others now that they've heard what is at stake."

I turned my attention to the crowd of Dezrects that moved together into a tight group. The candles light enhanced their white glassy eyes, giving them the appearance of the mirrored reflection of the bright moonlight shining atop the surface of a still lake. Enchanting creatures.

"Everyone here is free to make their own choice," I said to them. "Sear will not be forced to do anything against his will or will he have any punishment for his decision not to, just like all of you. Now that you've heard what's at stake, I'll ask you what Divination already has. Will you help me avert the coming apocalypse?"

The Dezrects retreated to the rear of the room and discussed my words with serious deliberation. The meeting lasted only briefly; the circle disband and one from the group approached me.

"I am Barnabous," he said. "I speak for all in the group. We've come to a decision and that is to help you in your quest, Spirit."

Sear rose to his feet and began to yell. "You too will turn your backs on our creator? You have all bought into the Devil's deceit and surely God will punish you for it!"

Sear stomped down the rock pile and exited the cave. As he disappeared into the darkness, I shouted out to him, asking him not to leave. He ignored my request and never returned. I went to the seat at the head of the table and took a moment to regain my composure.

"Sear has made his decision," I said. "I only see it as being fair we allow it without judgment. Let us move beyond this moment and face the worldwide catastrophe before it's too late."

All agreed with my words with nods from their heads and

whispered yes's. "Very well," I said. "I'm going to need to assign tasks. Each task has a great reason behind it. Once they have been completed, I will explain what we are to do next. Is this agreeable?"

"Agreed," everyone said at once, and the word echoed around the hollow room.

"Good," I said, revealing a slight delighted grin. "Nature?"

Her attention became undivided. "Yes, Spirit?"

"I remember you telling me before my burial that you knew of six Spirit's previous to me and their resting spots. Do you still possess this knowledge?"

"Yes, Spirit, I do."

"Good. Being you can freely walk between the realms, I'll need you to exhume those Spirits' bones." I scanned the room, searching for Barnabous. Spotting him within the group of Dezrects, I called him forward.

"Yes, Spirit?" the small pale creature said as he came before me. I knelt to one knee, and asked him, "You and the rest of the Dezrects are familiar with all the Spirit's before me. Am I right in assuming this?"

Barnabous reached to my ear and whispered, "May I have one minute?"

Though pressed for time, I sensed the importance of his request in his tone and agreed. Barnabous turned away from me and gave his attention to Osiris. The two began conversing in their cryptic language. Osiris stood on the chairs top, climbed down the pile of rocks and he walked before Barnabous. The two exchanged smiles. Barnabous turned and walked to the pack of Dezrects and blended into the sea of white faces.

"Barnabous told me the Dezrects want me back as the Berusht, the leader," Osiris said. "And they insist I immediately begin to speak for the group again. I told Barnabous I would be proud to have that honor once again."

I smiled in approval and patted Osiris's back, offering him my congratulations. "Osiris," I said. "The Dezrects are familiar with the Spirit's before me. Is this correct?"

"Correct, Spirit," Osiris said.

"Great! I'm going to need all the Dezrects to accompany Nature to the Spirit's resting spot. I'll need two Dezrects to stay with each newly resurrected Spirit. The two that are assigned to each Spirit is to stay with them and teach them current events. Also, I want them informed that they will be meeting other Spirit's here along with me.

"Nature, don't wait for each Spirit to recover from their awakening. Wake one, then leave the two Dezrects behind and make your way to the next."

Nature acknowledged my instruction by nodding her head.

I stood and approached Divination at the foot of the table. "Your mission is as important as everyone else's. I need you to keep watch as Nature and the Dezrects make their way through the spirit realm. I don't know how much the realm has been contaminated by the devil, so I need you to assure their safety. If you're confronted by any soul tainted by the evil seed, bring it to the light without delay. Can you do that for me?"

"I have faith in whatever it is you have planned to stop these terrible events you've foreseen from happening. I would walk to the end of the world for you."

"I thank you, Divination. You are truly a friend." I turned to Osiris, and said, "I need you to stay here in Chova with Amanda."

Osiris hurriedly climbed up the rocks and onto the chair, then hopped on the tabletop. He sat down in front of Amanda with his feet dangling over the table's edge. "I would love to do that, Spirit. We can talk about anything she wants." Osiris smiled and placed his hand into Amanda's.

"Perfect. As soon as you have all completed your part of the mission, return here right away. Remember to move quickly, there is a lot at stake. Alex and I are going to Heaven to see what's going on there."

Chapter 26

Osiris

I closed the giant wooden door as the last of the group filed out of the room. I returned to the table and climbed on its' top, sitting Indian style before Amanda. "Are you feeling okay?" I asked.

"Just fine," she said irritably and shifted uncomfortably around in her seat. "I don't want to sit. I don't want to stand. I don't even want to breathe anymore!"

She jumped to her feet and crossed her arms over her chest.

"It's okay," I said. "I understand you're going through a difficult time."

She puffed and looked away from me. She turned her back to me and pulled her shirt over her exposed stomach.

"I should be losing weight being I haven't eaten' a damn thing since all of this shit started! But I guess I'm destined to be fat my whole life!"

Amanda hurried to the table and sat. She purposely kept her eyes from me. She tucked her head between her knees and covered her face with her hands. She began to sob. I went to her, placed a reassuring hand on her shoulder, and said, "I'm sorry, Amanda, I wish things weren't so grim."

She sat up, distorted her face wet by tears, and screamed,

"Grandfather—Spirit—Travis . . . whatever his name is, he treats me like I were the ghost and not him! I hate it here!"

I said nothing in response. Amanda studied me, her expression turning neutral. Aware of her outburst and its potential to hurt, she sympathetically said, "My god, Osiris, I'm so sorry for saying that!" She took my hand into her hand and wiped her tears with her free hand.

"I know you are," I said, really believing she was. I could feel the care she had for others. This woman was special, she meant a lot to me. "Let us take a walk, Amanda. We can go to the lake. The fresh air might do us some good."

Amanda agreed, and I patted the back of her hand in approval. I jumped from the tabletop and hurried to hold the wooden door open for her. When she saw this, she smiled and thanked me, hurrying through the door. I followed her out the mouth of the cave and into the bright sunlight piercing the sparkling veil of water.

Amanda led the way, descending the rocky path on the mountainside. The mist drifting away from the waterfall held the sunlight, casting a giant rainbow that stretched from the mountaintop to the lake below. Amanda pointed it out, thrilled by its presence. I smiled, delighted to see her mood improving.

Once at the shoreline of the lake, Amanda kicked off her shoes, rolled her pant legs up and stepped into the water ankle deep. "Oh, this feels good! Is there fish in here?" she asked, shouting because of the thunderous roar the falls produced.

"No," I shouted in response.

"Good," she said. "Because I'm afraid of them. They're slimy and smelly."

I chuckled heartily and watched her walk from the water and stand next to me. She began to disrobe.

"Amanda!" I said assertively, unsure how much she was planning to take off. "Please, put your clothes back on." When I saw her standing in nothing but her underwear and bra, I turned around and closed my eyes.

"Why!" she stated rather than ask. "I need to bathe and the clothing I have on my back is the only thing I have to wear. I can't stand sitting in wet clothes."

She draped her bra and underwear over my head, and I heard her skipping into the water. I turned to catch her sinking below the surface of the water. When she came up, she pushed her long blonde hair away from her face and wiped the water from her eyes. "Come on in, Osiris! The water is so refreshing!"

"No, thank you, Amanda. I'm just fine where I am."

"Please, Osiris!" she begged.

I hated when she spoke like that. I was soft to it, and whenever I gave into it, somehow trouble followed. Forgetting the warning, I said, "Okay, but only for a little while."

I pulled the red silky robe I was wearing from my body and walked ankle deep into the lake. "Osiris?" Amanda shouted and stared, bobbing in the choppy water. She swam to the shore and stood before me. "Where is your thing?"

"Excuse me?"

"Your penis . . . Where is it? I can't tell by looking at you. Are you male or female?"

I turned from her gaze that was fixated between my legs. I hurried from the water to put my robe back on. Amanda ran up behind me, and said, "I'm sorry, Osiris, I didn't mean to embarrass you. It's just I never saw anything like that before."

"I'm not embarrassed," I said. "All of the Dezrects, the Spirit, Divination, and Nature are all without the reproductive organs you are familiar with as a human. But this does not mean we are not of man or woman, because we are. Only the Gods are capable of carrying such a heavy burden of being able to reproduce. We are never tempted with the constant desire to mate or to fight the desire to relieve sexual tension. To be the slave of the hormone is a liability the people of the world have to face. You'll understand this more once your souls parts from the body it's in. You should get dressed as well. Spirit and everyone else will be returning soon."

"I'm sorry . . ."

"Don't be. If you don't ask, how will you ever know?"

Amanda gathered her clothes that were scattered on the ground, and she dressed. Together we returned to the cave beneath the falls and Amanda lay on the floor and wrapped herself in the blanket we'd found her when she first arrived. I sat at the table.

Pushing herself onto an elbow, she asked, "If I die, what's going to happen to me?"

"Your body and soul will separate and you'll be brought to the light. Once you're there, you will return again into another human body without memory of this life. This goes on forever unless Navarro is given the chance to change this."

"My, parents," she said, looking at me definitively, her sad eyes returning. "I have no chance of ever seeing them again. They were both brought to the light. Now they could already be inside the body of an infant, oblivious to the worlds' corruption and disappointments. Or, maybe they could still be sitting somewhere where it is cold and dark, waiting for their new human body, worrying about me. What does it mean when they say you should live your life being the best person you can when there is no payoff in the end? There is no unity in the afterlife, no joyous celebration or congratulations for making it through. Just misery. It can't be. I don't believe it!"

I hung my head in understanding of her frustration. Things were complicated and they needed to be simplified. "I wish things weren't this way too, Amanda. I'm hoping Navarro and the Spirit can change it."

"When we first met," she said, sitting up. "I was sitting at that table looking to open a wooden box. Do you remember that?"

"Yes, Amanda, I do," I recalled fondly. I said, "You were sitting in the chair next to the head chair. I can still picture you being there. You were so curious to know what was inside that box."

She nodded towards the shelf above the fireplace where the box still remained. "Is that the same one that's there?"

Cautiously, I said, "Yes, it is."

"Tell me, Osiris, what is inside the box?"

I shook my head in dispute. "I can't tell you that. It's forbidden."

"That's okay," she said, lying back down. Rolling over and facing her back to me, she said, "Because I already know what's inside. Please, wake me when everyone returns. I'm tired and need a nap."

Chapter 27

Spirit

When Alex and I journeyed from Chova to Heaven, we discovered the infection of corrupted human souls had begun to spread throughout the spirit realm. From all around us they came, snarling like feral animals and swiping the air with their razor sharp claws, snapping their fang teeth in an attempt to fend me off as I approached them. I always remained close to Alex in case any of the monstrosities saw him as easy prey and thought to attack him. I could protect him, would protect him. As with Amanda, it was my duty. I gathered as many of the infected souls as I could and brought them to the light where the evil seed within them would die. Knowing they could begin life anew gave me piece of mind, though only a minuscule piece.

When we reached the blackened void high above the clouds, I stopped Alex and gave him a stern warning. I said, "Once we step through this void, we will be whisked to Heaven. I don't know what looms within the domain so I want you to remain close by my side."

Alex nodded in understanding.

I looked down on the world below me. It was beautiful—a mere lighted speck active with precious creations. I would save them no matter the cost. I looked to Alex, and said, "Take my hand, we must do this now."

His hand trembled and it steadied in my firm grip. Acting fearless, I pulled him into the void. The journey was similar to the void used to access Chova. Darkness covered us, and we plummeted, like we were descending on a slide, although this ride was smooth. Abruptly we were pinched from the darkness and placed on our feet inside a land so gorgeous, yet so defiled I could barely believe what I saw. In fact, I outright denied it and dug at my eyes with the heels of my hands to smear away the mirage.

Opening me eyes I scanned the landscape. Nothing had changed. Standing at the bottom of a hill and in the middle of a street paved with gold so pure it was clear like glass, I gawked at the endless echelon of unique mansions constructed from rare stones lining either side of the street, and stretched beyond the hilltop. Just beyond the mansions on either side of the street, the River of Life flowed with gentle grace, splashing melodically. The street forked before me, giving passage to an island center with a golden sidewalk. On this island beside the sidewalk, two heliodor fountains made from beryl spewed a constant stream of water. Beyond the fountains and further up the walkway was an elaborate altar protected by a giant ornate marble canopy supported by thick stanchions. Beyond the altar, at the islands center, was a tree bearing a wide variety of ripe fruits. I could find no sun or light source even though Heaven was brightly lit.

Within the sacred land, mangled bodies lay mounded and askew, bleeding their lifeblood on the streets. Faint moans of agony and torment rolled from the distorted mounds of torn bodies. I began to tread my way through the dead so I could aide those who still clung onto life. I waved Alex on, requesting he follow. Stepping where I had stepped moments before, he followed me to the side of a soul still with life, but beyond my saving. His wounds were bad, deep and gushing, exposing vivid colors of unidentifiable organs that hung out of his body. He drew shallow breaths and struggled to draw more; he cringed in pain every time his chest rose and fell.

"What happened here?" I asked the soul, quiet in my query,

not wanting to disturb the dead.

"It was that foul Devil, Navarro!" the soul coughed, struggling to speak.

"It's okay," I told. "Everything is going to be just fine."

"No, it won't," he said. "Because the antichrist struck without warning, thousands of his evil followers raided our peaceful domain and have killed all of Heaven's children. By my Lords honor, I fought as hard as I could. But there were just too many of them. Now I lay here without reason in a pool of my own blood waiting for my second death."

I quieted my lips, not wanting to upset the soul any more than I already had. I sat there with the soul and comforted him as best I could until his struggle to breathe seized. "Come, Alex," I said saddened. "Let us move onwards."

Together we continued to sift through the piles of dead for those still with life. A handful of those I found alive were committed to Heaven and all told me the exact story as the first soul I'd stumbled on. Each one cursed Navarro and wept for their fallen God and fellow servants until their dying breath. But the souls from Navarro's fallen multitude told a much different story. They all acknowledged me right away and thanked me for the glorious day that betided. They spoke with passion in their weakened voices about the destruction of the evil God that cursed them so long ago. They were excited knowing under their own assessment that Navarro's dream could reach fruition. I never told any of the dying souls that their god named Navarro also seemed to be a casualty of the war. I thought it necessary to allow them some peace before they departed. It was the least I could do for their sacrifices.

A fortunate break came when we stumbled on the badly pulverized body of DemAngel. His limbs were askew within the mound of bodies that were stacked on top of him.

"Spirit," DemAngel muttered barely loud enough for me to hear as I walked him by. I searched the pile and could see only his face, smiling in either relief or fear, I couldn't tell. "I don't think there are any of us left," DemAngel said. "But our sacrifices have been worth it; the God we sought to destroy is now gone. I saw

Him perish by fire when battling Navarro. I am content with the outcome, Spirit. But, before I go, I need to share something with you. As I laid here and listened to the moans of those suffering, I came up with something that could bring some sense to the madness around me. Suppose God was all knowing, that He knew He was sick with power and He sought a way to end the madness within His mind. Do you think He chose you knowing you were the one that would find truth to Navarro's dream and help him make a stand against God because of it? Maybe He was like a man who was aware of His terminal illness, and He was paralyzed, unable to stop the pain Himself. You were His relief of the pain, Travis! You pulled the plug on the life-support. It is the only plausible explanation I could come up with. He has called you to glory, Spirit, and your celebration should begin on this day!"

"No," I said dolefully. "No celebration or glory. Just chaos and misery."

"Leave me be, Spirit. Let my remaining moments be peaceful ones. I know you have the power to heal me, but I beg you not to. I ask you to go to Navarro and give him back his strength so he can see his dream reach fulfillment. Use your power on him, because above anyone, he deserves it."

"I'm afraid I can't do that," I said saddened by the loss. "I think Navarro has perished. I've searched the mounds of bodies and you are the last."

"He is there," DemAngel said, looking beyond me to the canopy above the altar. I followed with my eyes. "His battle with God was up there, I witnessed the whole thing."

"Thank you, DemAngel."

"No, I thank you. Now go."

Without delay, Alex and I climbed the piles of bodies to reach Navarro as quickly as possible. Grabbing Alex's hand, I ascended to the canopies top. The surface of the precious stone was stained with blood and soot. Navarro's thin body was sprawled and torn up badly. I went to him and checked his life signs. He was breathing, but only barely. The battle with God must've been a fierce one.

I gathered some life energy into my right hand that I could use to sustain Navarro's life with. I placed my hand on his chest and pushed the energy inside. I said, "This is all I can give you for now without endangering myself."

"I did it," Navarro said weakly, his eyes barely able to open. "He's gone! I wish you could've seen our battle. It was glorious! My followers fought for the dream with honor and pride. I will never forget them. Ever!"

"Save your energy," I said. "You're dying from your wounds, and I don't know if I can save you."

"No matter, Spirit. I am comfortable knowing I have you to carry on my dream."

"Me?" I said with refusal. "I am no god and this is your dream. You've come this far, you will see it through!"

"I feel weak, like my life energy has been completely drained. I can hardly feel my body. I know I am beyond your saving. You need to kill the devil that's running free inside the spirit realm before you can build Heaven like we spoke about."

"No," I said sternly. "I will return to heal your wounds so you can destroy the devil and build Heaven. I gave you enough of my energy to keep you alive until I return. Be strong, Navarro."

Together, Alex and I exited Heaven and began our descent towards the Earth's surface. During our journey I filled the time explaining to Alex what I'd done to keep Navarro alive.

"We are all made up of energy," I said. "And everyone has a limited supply. Navarro has depleted his supply in his battle with God to a dangerously low level. I pulled some energy from my own body and pushed it into his. I had to be careful not to give him too much of my energy because if I did, then I could be left drained and defenseless. Sometimes, like in Navarro's case, if the energy level becomes too low, it leaves you so weak you are unable to replenish the supply that was lost. But, don't confuse the energy I grab from the air with the energy I'm speaking about now. Life energy and basic energy are two very different things. To replenish life energy, you need to drain it from someone else."

Unexpectedly, I was barraged by a snarling group of contaminated souls that were hiding within the shadows shadow. I was being pulled away from Alex who stood and stared in disbelief. I saw a separate pack sneak up and attack him from behind. They bit him and swiped at him with their sharpened claws. He batted some away only to have them return with an enraged bloodlust. I tried to break free of those who clung to me, but their numbers were great and overwhelming. I struggled, desperate to break free.

I saw the souls grab Alex's limbs and begin to pull in all different directions. From where I was being held, I could hear his muscles and tendons tearing. His arms were being ripped from his body. Alex screamed in agony, I roared from rage. I was released, and the souls scrambled away. I darted to Alex's side and hooked one of my arms behind his knees and the other behind his neck. I lifted him from the ground and he told me he couldn't feel his hands.

"You're fine, Alex. You're alright," I said, ignoring his arms that'd been chewed and discarded some distance away from where he lay. I quickly headed to Chova, and during the journey, Alex lost consciousness and didn't wake until several hours later.

Osiris and Amanda were inside the cave with me watching over him when he finally began to stir. I asked them to leave and when the giant wooden door tapped shut, I shook Alex lightly and asked him how he felt.

"I hurt, Spirit, real bad!" he said.

"I've stopped the bleeding, but I couldn't save your arms. I'm sorry."

He didn't respond with words. His bottom lip quivered and tears rolled from his eyes.

"I was weakened from the energy I'd given to Navarro," I explained. "There was so many of them, Alex. The condition of the spirit realm is worsening with every second that passes. I'll send Osiris in to help you with the pain."

I morbidly shuffled away from Alex's side to get Osiris.

Chapter 28

Divination

The resurrection of a Spirit named Constantine

Nature led the way to the first of the six Spirit's burial sights. Together, Nature and I walked side by side while the Dezrects remained separate, following us close behind.

"Tell me, Nature," I said. "How come I never heard of a woman entity that was to become a Spirit? I'm curious to know, were you once human or a celestial sent down from the Heavens?"

"Whether I was a human or a spiritual entity before my judgment day, I just couldn't tell you. Certain portions of my memory have holes in it. But I can remember the day I stood before God like it were yesterday.

"I was inside the spirit realm and had some lost souls following me, looking for me to guide them to the light. I myself was lost, given powers and tasks I didn't understand. I aimlessly wandered around unable to accomplish any of the jobs I'd been instituted to do.

"'Come to me and I'll show you the way,' said a soothing, powerful voice from behind me.

"I turned to see the source and found myself awe struck by a majestic creature. His hypnotizing blue eyes looked like blown glass skating around the group of lost souls. Long flowing hair that dropped lazily over each muscular shoulder blew gently off his tight skin. Giant feathered wings sat closed behind his back. His chest was free of any covering and its definition was perfect. Nothing so perfect could be natural. He was molded. Black pants clung tightly to his legs and stopped in the center of his calves. His feet were bare and clean; the nails on both his hands and feet were well manicured. The souls that surrounded me encircled the Angel and gave him a hopeful look.

"'Do you all wish to leave here?' the Angel asked, his voice twanging like a finely tuned harp. The souls began to float around excitedly. The Angel looked to me with a smile. I smiled back. His pearly white wings opened wide and flapped gracefully back and forth. 'Follow me and I'll show you the way,' he said, then looked to me, and said, 'Remain here, Nature, I'll be back in a moments time.'

"He flew into the sky, and with care he guided the souls. Moments later he returned and landed gently on his feet before me. He folded his wings behind his back and politely introduced himself.

"'I am Michael,' he said and offered me his hand. I kissed it.

"DemAngel," I interjected, excited hearing his name from a time long gone.

"Yes, Michael is DemAngel," she confirmed. "That was him many years before he was sent to rescue Travis Winter. So, after Michael introduced himself to me, he explained he'd been sent by God above to bring me to Heaven. The Angel took my hand and brought me through Heaven's gate. I was completely engulfed by its opulence, its smell, and by its invisible comfort. I couldn't remember why at the time, but I missed it and was glad to be back there. But my return wasn't meant to be permanent. I was led to a giant mansion atop a soaring hill, and within, I was brought before God. He was sitting in a throne covered with plush red velvet. His feet were being soaked in a bucket of steaming water and servants that surrounded Him massaged His shoulders and fed Him grapes.

"'Leave us,' God commanded, and His servants quickly

dispersed. I watched them depart, their movement desperate, fearful. A deep voice cracking like thunder commanded me by saying, 'Humble yourself, child! Pay no mind to anything but me while I'm here! You should find yourself lucky to be in my presence!'

"He startled me. The tone of His voice was hostile and His demeanor was as sordid as He made Navarro appear with His lies. I turned and looked into eyes that weren't really eyes. His eyebrows were narrowed and His mouth was cracked open deviously.

"'I've created you to be perfect,' God said. 'Perfect enough to serve my cause without confusion and or question. I haven't any use for you or anyone like you. Reject! As punishment for your incompetence, I'm forced to revoke your powers and title you've been given by my right.'

"I shivered, my knees banging loudly together. 'Please, my Lord,' I begged. 'If you can spare me some time . . .'

"'Time?' He questioned and thrust Himself forward. 'Time is something you've run out of, my dear. Your destruction would be most pleasurable as well as amusing, but fortunately for you I've been amused by Navarro every day. Amusement is something I don't need more of.'

"God reached forward and touched my forehead. I couldn't move away from His touch. An unseen force paralyzed me, held me still before Him. God smiled at His small accomplishment and slid back into His throne satisfied, and said, 'There, your punishment is done. The memory of your past has been taken from you. You will leave here with nothing, not even with the knowledge of yesterday's events. You will never remember who you are or where you came from, only what you could have been. Leave me now, failure, I've already grown tired of you.'

"The Angel returned for me and took me from Heaven and back to the Earth. He placed me on the ground, and confused by the day's events, I asked him what had happened. He told me to hush, that he was forbidden to converse with the damned. He said he feared if he uttered a word, he too would face a disgraceful ousting as I did.

"Now, Divination, it is time to place the stories of the past to the side for the moment because we've arrived at the first Spirit's resting spot."

A tense hush fell throughout the group and Nature laughed playfully, spinning herself round and round freely. "There's nothing to worry about," she said, continuing to dance like a refined ballerina. "I promise!" She settled and pointed into the group of Dezrects, and said, "Beyur and Tiy, you two will be the first to confront and stay with the Spirit. Your part comes in when Divination and I dig up the Spirit's bones and lure him back here."

Nature pulled an empty satchel from the folds of her flowing gown, and said, "Are you ready, Divination?"

"Yes," I said confidently. "I'm ready."

Together we entered the physical realm. We arrived inside a room that'd been constructed from outcroppings of rock. The floor was dirt, and before us was a life-sized statue of a man in a position of authority. The stone man was standing upright and was carved from the stone that made up the wall.

"Where are we?" I questioned, my bearings off.

"Egypt. We're in the Valley of Kings across from the Nile River from Luxor. This particular sight has been buried by rubble and has been unknown to man for nearly a thousand years. But recently, human excavators discovered the sight. They haven't yet begun to dig it out, but I fear they soon will. If this happens there is a chance they could stumble on the Spirit's bones. I can tell you this: if that was to happen that would be a catastrophic moment for those scientists. In his daze you never know if the Spirit would take the people's presence as a threat."

Nature pointed to the statue I noticed when we first arrived in the room, and said, "See that man?"

"Of course," I said. "It's someone they worshipped. A God maybe."

She chuckled. "Yes, it's someone they worshipped. But who?"

I thought for a moment and studied the timeworn rock face. I was at a loss. "I can't tell," I said. "Half of its face is missing."

She giggled. "Time will do that to anything on this side of reality. That's the Egyptians interpretations of our Osiris. You know, the Dezrect. Dig here," she said while stomping the section of ground she wanted me to dig.

"Funny," I admitted. "Osiris looks nothing like that."

I began to turn the stiff soil.

"Osiris played with the humans that had sight into our world," Nature said. "Those he communicated with interpreted him as that statue. It is what they thought him to look like. Osiris was looked upon as a god of the afterlife."

"A god?" I chuckled and looked to Nature in disbelief. Imagine that, Osiris the Dezrect, a god! I paused in my work. "This work is tedious, Nature. Instead of digging into this packed dirt, I wish we could wiggle our noses and cast some sort of spell to exhume these bones."

Knowing that wasn't possible, I dug some more. I bent down into the hole I'd made and picked up a satchel filled with bones. I held them up. "Look at what I've found!"

"Hurry, Divination, the Spirit will awaken soon!" Nature shouted. "We need to lure him into the spirit realm so the two Dezrects we've appointed can take over. We don't want the groggy Spirit to attack us in his dazed state, especially one that's been sleeping for four hundred years!"

Nature quickly fizzled from the chamber and I followed, taking the sack with me. When I came into the spirit realm, the two Dezrects stood ready, awaiting the Spirit's arrival. The Spirit fizzled in. Unsure he looked to everyone in the room. He was perplexed. The two Dezrects, Beyur and Tiy, took the Spirit's hand and led him away. Satisfied with the success of our first objective, Nature and I gathered the remaining Dezrects and journeyed to our next destination.

The resurrection of a Spirit named John

"This Spirit we're about to resurrect has been at rest for nearly seven hundred and fifty years," Nature explained. "His name is John Harris, and he was the best next to Travis. His commitment to fighting Navarro's cause ended unexpectedly when Navarro's demons gained control of his bones and handed them to Navarro for burial."

"Yes, I remember John well," I recalled fondly, falling into silence. I'd come to know and love many of the Spirit's. The time I was allowed to spend with them was memorable ones. It would be good to see them all again.

Nature twirled and faced everyone. She enthusiastically announced that we'd arrived at the second Spirit's resting spot. She then she called forth the next two Dezrects to care for the Spirit, and they came forward. Nature and I immediately departed for the physical realm and arrived inside a small-boxed room that had a hardened clay ceiling and packed dirt walls and floor. I stood with a bend in my lower back and a tilt to my neck to keep my head from hitting the low ceiling.

"Where are we, Nature, I am most uncomfortable and have barely enough room to maneuver?"

"We're just north of Beijing China inside a section of the Great Wall of China that Navarro hollowed out. The wall was built from earth and rubble and faced with masonry, making it the ideal location to preserve the Spirit's bones where he would likely rest undisturbed forever, that is if it weren't for my interference. Navarro chose this particular area of the Wall for its popularity. He knew it had the best chance of remaining intact because the care the people put into it."

I could only wonder how she could follow Navarro, a god in his own right, without being detected. Her stories seemed flimsy, unbelievable. I couldn't help but question this. "And how was it you found these burial sights without anyone knowing?"

"Well, I used to follow Navarro around," she said without thought. "Just like I did Alex when he went to bury Travis' bones. I entered this particular burial site just a moment after Navarro departed. I saw the fresh dirt that'd been recently packed down with his feet, and smelled the foul lingering odor of Hell that was and is plainly identifiable to a minion of the underworld. It was quite a sight to see and a smell to wiff."

Either she was prepared for my line of questioning or she was telling me the truth. Either way I couldn't tell with a brief inspection of her mind. I realized I would have to accept her stories as being truthful until I was given reason to believe otherwise. "Where do you want me to dig?" I asked.

She pointed to the ground at my feet, and said, "Being it is so cramped in here I'm going to return to the spirit realm so you have room to work. Please, grab the Spirit's bones and come through as quickly as you can. The Dezrects and I will be waiting for your safe return."

She handed me an empty sack and disappeared. I began to turn up the soil until I uncovered portions of bone that broke free of the burlap sack they'd been buried in. By hand, I gathered the scattered remains and placed them inside the sack. I went to fizzle, but before I could, I was grabbed from behind and was forcefully shoved into the wall that began to crumble.

"Why have you come for me?" the angered Spirit growled and pulled me out of the collapsing wall. I quickly spun in the Spirit's tight grasp and stood upright only to have my head meet the hard ceiling. I groaned. The Spirit grabbed me and started shouting, "Tell me, what year this is?"

"2001," I said, and tried to ignore the throbbing sensation on top of my head. The Spirit lashed out, grabbing hold of my cloak. He jerked me forward, painfully cracking my neck from the force, and then he suddenly shoved me backwards. The force of his shove sent me through the wall. Outside the wall I flopped to the ground and landed heavily on my back. With widened eyes and my defenses jumbled I could only watch the Spirit following up with his attack, charging me from his 750-year-old tomb. He grabbed me by my cloak and began shaking me violently. His eyes jutted and a large vein bulged on his forehead.

"Where is that Devil, Navarro!" the Spirit shouted. "I see he's so bold to have sent one of his demons after me!"

Desperate to calm the Spirit in his frenzied mental state, I reached up and pulled the hood of my cloak back, revealing my face. The Spirit released his hold, my presence baffling him.

"Divination," he muttered and backed away. "I'm sorry, I didn't know."

"You couldn't have known," I said and pulled the hood back over my head. "Please, help me stand then follow me. The Dezrects are on the other side waiting for your arrival. I would explain what was going on, but I haven't the time. The Dezrects will answer any questions you may have."

The Spirit offered me his hand. I took it, and he pulled me to my feet. I quickly fizzled into the spirit realm, and the Spirit followed. The two Dezrects assigned to care for him took charge and I handed the sack containing the Spirit's bones to Nature. She slung the sack over her shoulder, and with the dwindling pack of Dezrects, we moved onwards in our journey to resurrect the third Spirit.

The resurrection of a Spirit named Zacharius

As we moved through the spirit realm, Nature unexpectedly stumbled and struggled to regain her footing. I casually looked to the ground we traveled to try and find what may've caused her folly. I found nothing, not a lump in the ground or debris floating about that could tangle her feet. I turned to face her to find a single contaminated soul wrenching on one of the satchels containing the Spirit's bones. Nature was on her knees, wrestling for the sack that was slipping from her shoulder.

I quickly approached the crazed soul and stomped down on the back of his head, thrusting him forcefully into the ground. The soul released his hold on the sack and yelped like a dog. He retreated and growled at me from afar. While I watched the soul untrustingly, I went to Nature to check her condition. She was fine but shaken. I helped her up, and was relieved when I saw the soul retreating.

"Are you okay?" I asked.

"I'm fine," she said, and appeared to be. She pushed the sack back over her shoulder and reassured me with a smile. "I was caught off guard and I'm embarrassed by it. I was daydreaming about the day we would get to live in Navarro's euphoric Heaven."

"Pleasant thoughts are good, Nature, even if the contents are dreamlike. Don't ever let anyone take that from you."

Silence befell, and we moved onwards. Without intent, the formation of the group tightened, and the composition was apprehensive; the reality of another attack on everyone's mind was very real and very frightening.

By Nature's knowledge, once we arrived at the next burial site, the next two Dezrects to serve the Spirit's were called forth. They came forward, and Nature asked for a moment and fizzled. I wondered what she was assessing and why it required her to go alone.

She returned, and with insistence, she grabbed my hand and pulled me, saying, "Now is the time, Divination."

I didn't resist; I allowed her to pull me into the physical realm. Coming in before a human war soldier frozen like a statue, a massive block of white marble situated next to him caught my attention. It was engraved with a message and I read it. It read: HERE RESTS AN HONORED AMERICAN SOLDIER . . . KNOWN BUT TO GOD.

"Shush," Nature said in response to my reading. "We don't want to be heard, Divination. I could only temporarily freeze the humans immediately surrounding the Tomb. We need to do this quietly and swiftly so we don't attract anyone. Let's get a move on; we're tight on time. Lift the slab so I can retrieve those old bones."

"Very well," I whispered and looked into the eyes of the oblivious man. He was prestigious, elegant, and organized. But mostly I saw how precious he was. Well worth the fight. I moved past him, and said to Nature, "What Spirit has been buried here?"

"Zacharius Alexander. He's been at rest for over 1200 years."

"Impossible," I disputed knowing the calculations were all off. "The Tomb of the Unknown Soldier hasn't been around that long." Nature smiled. "Navarro moved the Spirit's around as he saw necessary. He exhumed Zacharius from his former resting place deep within the Amazon Rain Forest because humans began to strip the rich land bare for its resources. Navarro strategically moved the bones to a military cemetery located in France. On Memorial Day, 1921, four unknowns were exhumed from four different World War I cemeteries. U.S. Army Sergeant, Edward F. Younger selected one from the four men placed in identical caskets at city hall in Chalors-sur-Marne, France. Sgt. Younger's choice just so happened to be the casket that Zacharius's bones were in. The chosen Unknown was transported here to rest eternally complete with 24-hour guards to make sure his rest goes undisturbed.

"Now, let us get this over with, the tradition of the Changing of the Guards will commence again any moment. Lift the top—eighty tons is much too heavy for me to lift in my physical form let alone my spiritual one."

I grabbed hold of the massive marble slab that covered the Tomb and began to lift it slowly. The tinny sound of marble scratching marble filled the early evening, panicking me that we could be discovered. I thought to drop it and run, but Nature's expression showed no concern. She appeared to be concentrated on the task, her composure calming me.

"Changing of the Guards, what does that mean?" I asked whispered.

"The Tomb is guarded by soldiers from a nearby military base called Fort Meyer. The base assigns a guard to watch over the Tomb, and they change every hour or half hour depending on the season. It is an elaborate and precise military ritual."

I began to struggle beneath the massive weight of the slab. "Can you reach the bones?" I whined.

"A little higher," Nature said, her voice muffled coming out from the underside of the slab. "I can't reach them."

I lifted the slab with one last mighty heave, and moaned, "Now, Nature, I can't hold it any longer!"

My limbs began to shake violently. I fought desperately against the compulsive thought and strenuous whine in my muscles that screamed at me to drop the slab. Just when I thought to release the slab, Nature popped out from beneath the Tomb, and said, "I've got them, Divination. Hurry!"

I quickly but carefully let the slab down and fizzled into the spirit realm before the newly exhumed Spirit could manifest. The Spirit soon came looking confused and sluggish. The two Dezrects immediately went to the woozy Spirit as did the others before him.

"Dezrects?" the Spirit questioned, and dug his eyes with his fists.

The Dezrects took his hand and began to walk with him.

Nature reassembled the few remaining Dezrects, and without rest, we moved onwards.

The resurrection of a Spirit named Kane.

I scanned the vast landscape in which we traveled and took notice to how lifeless it was. I couldn't help but mention this observation to Nature. I said, "Do you think it odd there isn't a soul in sight?"

Nature shook her head in response, saying, "No, not really. The land we're traveling through has been a desolate place for as long as I can remember. Very few humans come here and even fewer souls would ever venture to such a location. The California desert otherwise known as Death Valley can reach scorching temperatures in the day of over 100 degrees. The hottest day I recall was in 1913. It reached a blistering 134 degrees; almost as hot as the boiling river you swam in. These conditions play a major role in keeping life, both humans and souls, from the area."

I continued to gape the barren land and noted how every knoll we passed over seemed identical to the one before. This observation I couldn't keep to myself either. I said, "I can tell the Spirit's bones were never in any danger of being found while here. Everything looks exactly the same to me. How are we ever going to locate his bones?"

"Easy. I hid behind a small knoll the day I observed Navarro burying this Spirit's bones. Cover was tough to obtain in such a vast flat place, but it was a must with a being as powerful as Navarro. His senses are heightened and sharp. Once I reach this knoll that I am familiar with, I can count out 100 paces to the north and there is where we will find the Spirit's bones. But I totally disagree with your statement about how the Spirit's bones were in no danger of being found. In the mid to late 1800's, Forty-niners were followed by successive invasions of prospectors and miners that sought to exploit deposits of silver and other precious metals inside the valley. If such a discovery were to occur near the Spirit's burial site the entire surrounding the area would've been mined. In this case, the risk of his bones being found was probable and as with any Spirit, potentially dangerous."

Nature stopped. "One hundred paces from here, Divination." I stopped and searched for the knoll she spoke of and couldn't find anything—not even Nature. She'd disappeared. "Nature," I shouted and listened to my voice being carried around the valley.

"Right here," I heard her respond seemingly from beneath my feet. I looked to the ground and saw her there, well-hidden, laying flat and face up. Her red hair was golden brown to match the earth, as was the rest of her body.

"Now do you see how I could keep from Navarro and Alex's sight?" she asked, and before my eyes her hairs' original color returned, and her flesh became pallid. "I was right here and I was watching Navarro throwing his last shovel-full of dirt on top of the Spirit's new resting place. Thinking he were alone, he spoke aloud to the Spirit. His voice quaked and his eyes welled with tears.

"'I know we could coexist in my world of euphoric harmony. Unfortunately we've been pitted against each other for reasons I cannot fully understand or accept. Once I finally achieve the task of bringing my dream to reality, I promise you, I will bring you back so you can enjoy your life forever, in peace and understanding of each other as we were all meant to do.'"

I drifted into private thought, thinking about Navarro's final promise to the Spirit. I could see him looking down on the freshly packed grave he'd prepared, weeping because of the senseless battles and destruction his ludicrous dream seemed to cause. He would bunch his fists into balls and damn the world and his feelings. Why did he have such a soft heart? I could see him falling to his knees and pounding the ground from frustration. A promise is whispered to make up for any wrong in trying to make right: "I'll return for you," I could hear him utter. He was sincere in his anguish and promise. He would return to his lair deep beneath the Earth's surface and there he would try and push his pain aside. So strong he would try and appear to those who believed in him, and those who didn't.

". . . 99 . . . 100! We're here, Divination, at the Spirit's burial site! Are you ready?"

I looked up, barely understanding what she was doing. I saw two Dezrects standing before us then understood perfectly. I said,

"Yes, I'm ready to resurrect this Spirit." And I fizzled for the deserts night.

Nature showed the exact location of the Spirit's bones and that is where I dug. After several stabs into the Earth, I came upon an old decaying burlap satchel that had long ago released its contents into the ground. I gathered the scattered pieces of bone and placed them into a sack Nature provided for me.

Hurriedly, Nature and I returned to the spirit realm and waited for the Spirit to come. Seconds ticked away into minutes with no sign of the Spirit. I didn't think he was coming.

"I don't think he's coming," Nature said, matching my thoughts. I smiled and agreed with a nod, saying, "I'll be right back."

I stepped into the physical realm and stood motionless for a moment, believing the Spirit was still going to manifest. A cool warm breeze greeted me, and disappointingly left. It whipped by to invisibly explore the desert plain. I let my defenses down and put aside everything that troubled me about the world I lived in. I panned the landscape trying to look at things differently than I did before. I noticed the mountains in the far distance and wondered how I could've overlooked them earlier. Ah, the world had a mesmerizing beauty from its fullest gardens to its flattest most barren desert. Death Valley was proof of that. And for the moment, I was able to enjoy that.

I jumped into the hole I'd dug before and began to rake through the dirt with my fingers. I slowly sifted, carefully searched the dirt, and soon found two rib bones and a thighbone. I plucked the bones from the soil, pulled the hood off my head to avoid a confrontation, and sat on the rim of the hole to relax. The Spirit's form rippled before me; the air muddled. The flickering image of the Spirit taking to form slowed as he took on a more solid state.

The Spirit stood before me looking blankly down upon me, and I looked to him. He was gigantic, like a house. He wore a white shirt with puffy sleeves and a black sleeveless coat that split into tails and stopped just before it touched the ground. His pants were red velvet and fit snug. He had tight olive skin that made him appear ten years younger than he actually was.

"Divination, is that really you?" he asked, his eyes squinted and barely able to focus.

"Yes, Kane, it is Divination."

He dropped to his knees and clamped his eyes shut. "What years is this?"

"2001," I said.

He looked to me with eyes that questioned my response. He asked, "What year did you say this was?"

"I know it is hard for you to imagine so much time has gone by, but it is the year 2001."

The Spirit shook his head. "The last I remember it was the year 1823 . . . No, 1828 . . ."

"Specifics are unimportant, Spirit. The spirit realm has changed rather dramatically since you last protected it. Please, Spirit, come with me, your services are needed once again."

I covered my head and pushed myself to my feet. They ached terribly. I returned to the spirit realm, regrouped with Nature and the remaining Dezrects and moved onwards.

The resurrection of a Spirit named Germaine

"It's been a little over 1900 years since this Spirit's burial. His existence was the shortest of any Spirit before or after him—so short in fact you knew him for just under a human hour."

"Yes, Nature, I remember that well. Though it is a tragic story, it is something interesting to hear, especially during such a lengthy journey. Why don't you tell me it as if I never knew it before?"

"Very well," she said. "I enjoy telling a good story as much as you like hearing one. This story begins when your search for a replacement Spirit ended just east of Jerusalem. A tall man whose intelligence far exceeded those who served him caught your attention. He was confident and maybe even somewhat arrogant. He was an architect that became a King to his people. A great King he was with respect and love from the people who followed him proudly. King Germaine led his people to find refuge in the terrace between the cliffs and the Dead Sea as the Jews revolted against the Romans.

"In this terrace eleven caves were dug and made as home to the people. King Germaine named the place the Qumran site. He occupied his own cave and had two guards stationed outside his quarters at all times while he slept. He feared the Romans would come while he rested, but it wasn't the Romans that would come to get him. It was you, Divination that would come to take his human life while he slept. A broken neck?"

"Yes," I answered regretfully, hearing the cracking of his bones within the confines of my own mind.

"Quick and painless," Nature added, "as you always made it when you were left with the ungodly task of having to choose a human to replace a fallen Spirit. After his death you tore his soul from his body and brought it back to Chova where he began his painful transformation into becoming the mighty servant of Heaven. But, you made one grave mistake when you killed King Germaine, and this was a mistake you would never make again. You left the King's body behind, and unbeknownst to you, Navarro was hot on your trail as he always was when he found you were looking to create a new Spirit. He came into King Germaine's living quarters not long after you left to discover the lifeless body of your new Spirit. The guards outside the King's door were alert to unfamiliar sounds coming from within their Kings living quarters. Bravely they entered the cave to discover Navarro within. They ran from the cave, screaming in their native tongue, 'The Devil has come for our King!'

"The guards outburst woke the entire populace, and all those in the small fearful community arose to investigate their King's cave. They'd thought the Romans had found their safe haven and began their attack. Driven by fear and desperation, the people hurried along, gathering rocks and sticks along the way. Insignificant weapons, really. Navarro stood to his feet as the unsuspecting humans entered the cave to find the Devil standing over their King's body. As the first wave of humans inside the cave caught a glimpse of Navarro, real terror consumed them, propelled them to flee, and they tried pushing their way out of the cave. But, the people outside the cave weren't fully aware of what was going on inside. Believing a few Roman soldiers were trapped inside the cave, they tried pushing their way in so they could kill the enemy while they had them cornered. The men inside the cave shouted it was the Devil within, to flee while they had the chance, but still, the people outside unknowingly pushed forward. Navarro tried to calm the populace so he could explain it wasn't he who was the Devil, and that he wasn't responsible for the death of their King. But, you see, his appearance alone was enough for those people to think that he was the Devil, let alone having the lifeless body of their King at his feet.

"'You Devil!' they all shouted. They threw their weapons but Navarro was unaffected by them and this frightened the people so, that they ran from the cave and jumped from the cliffs to plummet to their death on the rocks below. Their entire society was wiped out in a matter of minutes. Navarro's demons took the souls of the people to Hell where they explained Navarro's dream of peace and harmony. Some actually willingly served his cause and others that weren't so willing were sent through the light to start life anew. After Navarro's demons gathered the souls, he put the Kings body to rest right where you left it. The burial of the Spirit's human body that you so carelessly left behind is what ended your Spirit's existence just as it began. But this story doesn't end here. In his despair, Navarro wrote eleven scrolled documents on papyrus paper. These scrolls contained the history of Judaism, the details why Heaven and Hell battled, and the ultimate destiny of the human soul if Navarro's dream should ever reach fruition or simply end in failure.

"Navarro placed the scrolls inside glass jars and placed a jar into each one of the eleven caves. The discovery of the scrolls wouldn't take place until the year of 1947; around nineteen centuries later, found accidentally by Bedouin Shepherds in the now barren hills. Today interest in the scrolls has intensified and scholars have deciphered some of the scrolls contents written in Hebrew and Aramaic languages. But time has taken its toll and crumbled most of the scrolls' writings. But, the one scroll that contained the factual circumstances surrounding the war between Heaven and Hell and the true meaning behind man's existence is the one and only scroll unaffected by time. It is also the only scroll

Navarro wrote diversely. To this day, it is the only scroll that has remained indecipherable. If only man could crack the code of the language used, their discovery would be great, possibly a tool they could use to save their souls.

"I'd returned to the Dead Sea caves many years after that tragic day and I read each and every scroll. My findings were that Navarro had written that one diverse scroll in a language called Ishua. It is a language that has been lost with the death of the people from the Dead Sea Society. And sadly, I believe the people's chances of ever unlocking the scrolls' contents is forever gone."

We came upon the barren hills surrounding the Dead Sea, and Nature said, "This is it, we are near the Spirit's resting spot."

Dead trees were thick and almost impassable. Giant rocks that weren't quite large enough to be classified as boulders were partially sunk into the earth and were scattered about. We slowly made our way to a hidden cave and entered it. Nature called forth two of the four Dezrects remaining, and we fizzled for the physical realm.

The recovery of the Spirit's bones went smoothly and without incident. Comparable to the previous resurrections, the Dezrects appointed took charge of the baffled inexperienced Spirit, and our group consisting of four individuals moved onwards to our next and final destination.

The resurrection of a Spirit named Julius

"This Spirit is one of the oldest I am aware of. He's been resting for nearly 4,000 years and he fought rigorously against Navarro for over 300 years. He answered to the name Julius, and he carried no last name."

I chuckled aloud as the fond memories of the Spirit named Julius came back to me. "He fought like no other," I said. "I still remember the first time I witnessed the two engaging in battle. They were like two rams butting heads."

"I witnessed Julius's final battle with Navarro," Nature said proudly, as if her recollection of the conflict were a blessing.

I shook my head in ancient bewilderment. I never understood Julius's behavior. I said, "I told him it was my duty to watch over his bones while he was out protecting the spirit realm. But he wouldn't listen to me; either that or he didn't trust me. His fear of Navarro finding Chova worried him constantly and it eventually cost him his existence. After all, Julius would engage in battle while he carried his bones. Not very smart."

"No," Nature said, "not very smart at all."

Silence befell, our discouraging conversation lingering like a black cloud. "You know," Nature said. "The next burial site was constructed by Navarro to gain man's attention, and to this very day man is still drawn to the spectacle. I consider what he had made to be a masterpiece even though what's left today is in ruins. Some of the formation he'd built has fallen or has been removed. For years humans have speculated the formation was once a temple for ancient deities, and at times, it has even been called an astronomical site for significant events on a prehistoric calendar. It has also been suggested it was once a sacred burial site for high-ranking citizens from societies of long ago. It's too bad the speculators never suggested it to be the burial site for a high-ranking official chosen by Heaven to protect the human soul in the afterlife."

Nature summoned the two remaining Dezrects, and they stood on either side of us before we fizzled.

"Welcome to Stonehenge, Divination!" Nature exclaimed. Enormous stone structures stood vertically, and giant slabs were placed across their tops horizontally; timeless defiance of gravity and technology.

"Notice how the formations look like massive doorways?" asked Nature. "That was just another way for Navarro to invite the humans into his world, to give them a chance to discover the true meaning behind their existence. If you were to look at the formations from above, it would be apparent it forms a perfect circle. This circle is similar to a bull's eye, and the center is where the Spirit is buried."

After we exhumed the sixth and final Spirit, we led him into the spirit realm where the Dezrects took over. Together, we all began our long journey back to Chova.

Chapter 29

Spirit

Five of the six Spirits had returned to Chova, and as they arrived, I sat each one of them around the table. I had Amanda, Alex and the Dezrects stand in the rear of the room, and I paced the floor nervous in anticipation. It felt we were waiting an eternity for Divination, Nature, and the two remaining Dezrects to arrive with the last Spirit.

The giant wooden door whined as it slowly swung open. The group we'd been waiting for entered the room. All the Dezrects in the room began to jump up and down in excitement and they all charged the Spirit named Julius. Although the Dezrects communicate with an indecipherable high-pitched squeaking tone, the chant of Julius was easy to understand. They latched onto his leg and began dancing around him.

"Yes, my friends, it has been a long time," Julius told them, curtsying and brushing their heads with his hands. "I missed you all very much and we will reacquaint ourselves after my duties are done."

"Please, take a seat," I said and showed him to the remaining empty chair at the table's head. When Julius settled, I remained standing at the table's head and paced the floor behind his chair. I explained my visions of the apocalypse from its beginning to its most frightening end. Everyone listened intently as I explained the true reasons why Navarro warred with God, and why we, the Spirits were created. I told them about the birth of the true Devil, and how he was responsible for the contamination of the spirit realm that was inevitably going to overflow into the physical realm. I then went on to explain how this disastrous vision was possible for us to avoid if we would combine our powers to destroy the Devil and send all the contaminated souls into the light. I felt I ended my discourse strongly and left little room for any of the Spirits to walk away from what was asked of them. I finalized everything by saying: "Now you all know the truth behind our God, our creator. You are all aware of the danger Navarro's offspring has presented and that I ask you all to help me destroy it. If anyone has doubts about the severity of this threat, then all I ask is that you hear the plan I have drawn up to destroy the Devil, then come along with me to Heaven. I know once you see the influence this beast has you will all instinctively want to destroy it. The world is facing inevitable destruction unless you all agree to help stop what has begun. I ask you all to take what I had to say here before you as something very serious. Do not to delay in making your decision."

The room was still and eerily silent as everyone pondered my words. The Spirit named Zacharius was the first to express his feelings. He looked to me and chuckled, shook his head, and said, "I find this all a little hard to believe! I've seen Navarro holding human souls against their will with my very own eyes. How do you account for that behavior?"

"Travis already explained that," Divination interjected to my relief. "Those souls were crying out because they were scared. How would you expect them to react when they've been taught through their entire life to think someone looking like Navarro is the Devil? I myself have learned a lot about Navarro's struggle, and at times, I still question what I know. I believe that is only natural knowing how our fear and anger towards him has been instilled within our psyche. It has been two years now since Travis has presented the disturbing facts to me surrounding his intentions, and after denying what I thought impossible, I have accepted what is and has been. Search within and you will find as I have. I have aided each and every one of you here in your quest against Navarro and I've served you honorably. You've all entrusted me to care for your bones which was the key to your survival. If you don't trust Travis's words, then I ask you to trust in mine. What he says is the truth. I wish I could tell you otherwise, but I cannot."

"How can I trust you when you never served me?" the Spirit Germaine said bitterly. "And where is our God above now?"

"It appeared to me He'd been destroyed by Navarro," I said. "Torn bodies litter Heaven's golden streets. I know this because I was there. Few remain alive and one of them is Navarro, but he barely clings to life."

"Let him die!" Germaine groaned, stood and pressed his palms on the tabletop. "What is really going on here?" Germaine asked, and leaned on his hands to move himself closer to me.

"And that has already been explained to you," Divination interceded again.

"Was I talking to you?" the Spirit snickered.

"Regardless," Divination said unmoved. "You may not like what you hear, but you've been given the truth and now it's your responsibility as a Spirit to face up to it."

The Spirit turned away from Divination, and muttered, "I don't recall asking you what my responsibilities were."

"Why can't you listen to what he's saying!" Alex shouted from the back of the room. He came forward, looking to the Spirit with anger and disbelief. Knowing the severity of the situation could've changed anyone's belief.

"And now I should listen to you, a crippled soul?"

"Yes, Damnit, you should! For your own good and everyone else's. I've seen these corrupted souls with my own eyes. They tore my arms from my body in an unexpected attack as we were leaving Heaven. If you were there and you could see how the evil consumed them, changed them, then you wouldn't be sitting there ignorantly doubting what you're being told. Lower your nose and face the truth. It is time to do what is right!"

Germaine slowly sat and looked away from Alex. Had he been

humbled? There was no time to contemplate something so meaningless. Julius stood, and said, "I'm in, who else is with us?"

"I'm in," the Spirit named Kane said.

Divination walked behind Kane and patted his back. "I knew you'd be Kane. Anyone else?"

"Me too," said Julius. The Spirit named Constantine was the next to raise his hand and join our fight. John Harris and Zacharius followed. All the Spirits turned their attention expectantly to Germaine and waited for his answer.

"Ahh, the hell with it," Germaine muttered. "This better be the right thing. I'm in."

"It's settled then, everyone is in," Divination said with relief.

"Great!" I cheered. "Now we need to prepare. You all will need to learn how to manipulate energy. That very well may be our only defense against the Devil. Once you are all able to do what I teach you, we will seek the Devil out and destroy him. This Devil is the essence of evil. I don't want anyone getting a false sense of bravado. We do this as a team, it will be the only way."

I walked to the door and pushed it open. "We have much work to do. Let us not waste another moment."

Chapter 30

Osiris

I was left behind to be the caretaker of Amanda. Her humanity made her vulnerable around the violence but also valuable in such an event that Spirit's mission should've failed. If this were to be the case, I was told a fertile male counterpart would be chosen and brought back to Chova where they would remain hidden and protected. Inside Chova is where the human race would begin anew.

"I can't stand the waiting," Amanda barked only hours after the group left to destroy the Devil. She paced the table's round. "It feels like they've been gone for days!"

She stopped before a chair and plopped heavily into its' seat.

"But this is it, child," I said. "Once this is over you can begin to rebuild your life. You'll be able to see your old friends, get a job, and maybe even a boyfriend. How about children, have you thought about them? How many would you like?"

Amanda shook her head in disagreement. She moved her sad eyes to meet mine, and said, "No kids and friends for me ever again."

I was appalled. How could she say such a thing and with such finality? "I think it's important you begin to look forward to these things again. I think you'd be missing out if . . ."

"Stop it!" she shouted, silencing me instantly. Taken back, all I could do was stare. She bowed her head, and said, "I know you mean well, but stop it. I just don't want to hear it."

Amanda's gaze wandered aimlessly. I climbed onto the tabletop and positioned myself in front of her. I reached and took her hand and said, "I promise you this will all be over soon. Your grandfather is seeing to that."

"Yeah," she muttered incisively. "My grandfather the ghost."

"Yes, Amanda, he is the ghost you say he is. He cares for you and he's doing the best he can to protect you, to assure you can live your life normally after this day."

She pulled her hand from mine, and said, "I miss my parents, Osiris. And knowing I'll never be able to see them again hurts me. It tears me up inside." She brought her right hand up to the left side of her chest, and muttered, "Breaking what is inside here."

I felt ashamed for not considering her feelings, how this whole thing has affected her. I could never truly understand, and knowing this, I said, "I'm sorry, Amanda."

She took my hand, and said, "I know you are, Osiris. And I know if there was anything you could do to take my pain away you would. I know I am the only one that can change the way I feel."

I perked; her desire to persevere was encouraging. "The best cure is time."

"No," she said, the passion evident. "I don't think you understand what I'm saying. I don't have anyone to be human for. I have no family remaining. I fear death almost as much as I do living the way I am now. But, I think I've discovered a way to live forever, a way to keep myself from going through the light. Unfortunately I understand death is the only way for me to achieve this, and that is what I've come to accept. Try and understand for my sake, Osiris, that this may be my only chance to join my only remaining family member."

"Why are you talking like this, Amanda? I don't like it one bit, it scares me!"

She laughed and scooted to the edge of her seat. "I really like you, Osiris, and I trust you with my life. That is why I've decided to do this while it is only you and I. May I ask you something?"

"Of course, Amanda, anything at all."

Amanda stood from the chair and walked to the rear of the room. She bent down and shuffled through some of her belongings, and said, "When I die, will you be brave enough to use the contents that are inside the wooden box on me?"

My confusion and concern brought me to my feet. My voice was raised when I said, "Why do you keep talking about dying? You have plenty of life left in you."

Amanda turned slowly, facing me with a neutral look. Was it the peace she'd found? She said, "Not inside this body, I don't! Tell grandfather to forgive me if this doesn't work."

She shoved a shiny silver object into her mouth, and simultaneously, a capping bang filled the room. Amanda's blood splattered the wall behind her, and she limply fell to the ground. I jumped from the tabletop and ran to her side. "What have you done!" I shouted and repeated as I absentmindedly ran to the fireplace and retrieved the wooden box from the shelf. Quickly I returned to her side and removed the boxes contents, clenched it in my fist and punched down as hard as I could on Amanda's chest. I released the seed inside her and stepped away, unknowing the results to come. Thankfully she began to calm.

I dropped to my knees and hugged her mangled cranium. "What have you done, Amanda? Why?"

She gurgled as she tried to speak through her torn throat. She tensed, convulsed and moaned in agony.

I let her head down and fearfully backed away from her, and said, "There is nothing more I can do for you, Amanda, I'm sorry."

"The seed?" she barely managed, and struggled to complete her next words. "Heal me?"

I was addled; the entire ordeal made no sense to me. I didn't know why Amanda did what she'd done and why the seed wasn't working. I could only hope the Spirit would return soon.

Chapter 31

Spirit

I journeyed high into the sky with the group I departed from Chova with. The tension was thick, keeping everyone silent. When we arrived before the entranceway of Heaven, I stepped to the side of the gaping void to allow the other Spirits to enter first. Once inside, Divination followed, and then the Dezrects. I nodded to Nature and took Alex by the waist and stepped to the void.

Alex looked past his feet and he spotted Nature descending towards the Earth. He said, "Nature, she's . . ."

"I know," I whispered, silencing him. "She's got her own part to play in this war. Say nothing to anyone. Let us go so we don't draw suspicion from the others."

I pulled him through the void and held onto him firmly. Gently we were whisked through the dark duct and placed on our feet in the center of Heaven's golden street at the hill's bottom. The Spirits were all standing shoulder to shoulder, and Divination remained behind them. All were entranced by the awesome landscape that'd been rearranged for battle. Blood stains that had dried tinted the golden streets, and the casualties of Navarro's war had been moved off to either side of the street, stacked like a wall to cordon off the playing area.

"You're much earlier than expected, Travis," a scratchy penetrating voice echoed from somewhere atop the hill. Everyone searched the battlefield to locate the body behind the voice.

"Look!" Kane said and pointed to the island center. "Under the tree!"

The Devil was there, sitting on his hind with his back against the Tree of Knowledge, eating the forbidden fruit. The Devil chomped away, his mouth hanging open sloppily, spittle flying from his lips. He twirled the fruit in his hand, studied it. "I wanted to taste the fruit that tempted man and gave him sin and suffering. You'd be surprised all that I've learned since my birth. Perhaps you'd like to take a bite, Travis?"

The Devil stood and discarded the fruit core over his shoulder. He catapulted himself atop the marble canopy above the altar. He was as red as blood and his spiked tail waved gracefully back and forth like that of a cats tail. His wings suddenly opened wide and they flapped back and forth. The air whooshed as the enormous wings brought the beast off his feet. He took to the air and circled beyond our reach and landed on the canopy again.

"Oh, the knowledge," the Devil said joyfully. "Do you know what the fruit from the Tree told me? Perhaps it better I show you?"

A petite plainly cute brunette woman appearing identical to my wife stepped from behind the Devil. "Paige," I whispered, denying what I was seeing. "It can't be!"

Paige extended her hands to me, trying desperately to grab me from so far away. "Come for me, Travis," she whined. "Take my pain away!"

The Devil laughed tauntingly and stepped in front of her. "Because if you don't, I will! Maybe you should take a bite of the forbidden fruit, Travis. You may learn some things that have been missing from your life. Maybe it'll tell you where your wife is . . . it has already told me!"

"No!" I shouted and became frantic with rage. I marched beyond the other Spirits with the intention of confronting the Devil myself. But Julius grabbed me and shook me. Angered by his intervention I turned to him, and thrust my nose into his face.

"What is it you're seeing?" Julius asked.

I looked back to the canopy and saw the Devil standing alone. Where had Paige gone?

"Look upon your God," the Devil said. "And tell me if this is how the myth goes." He pointed down from where he stood and there, Navarro was, nailed to a wooden cross. His arms were spread wide and his legs were together with one foot on top of the other. His head was slumped forward and his body was naked.

"That son of a bitch!' Germaine shouted.

"Let us stick to the plans," I said, refocusing.

"Screw your plans, Travis!" Germaine scourged. "I'll not stand for this for another second!"

Adne belted out a war scream and bulleted through the air towards the Devil. Together, Julius and I shouted for the Spirit to stop but he continued to rocket towards the Devil headlong. When the Spirit made contact with the Devil, the Devil grabbed hold of the Spirit, expanded his wings and flapped them quickly, taking the Spirit into the air. He hurled the Spirit onto the canopies hard surface and descended upon him. Picking him up again, he pulled the Spirit down onto the pointy razor sharp horns that protruded from his head. The Spirit kicked and screamed as the horns slowly slid inside him. One horn pierced the center of his chest and the other went through his forearm. The Devil continued to pull the Spirit downwards and thrashed his head wildly like a shark would do to rend a hunk of meat within its jaws. The horn ripped through the Spirit's chest, and tore his arm off at the elbow. The Devil's spiked tail whipped over the top of his own head and slammed the Spirit on the top of his head. The Spirit went limp and the Devil shook him violently. Tiring of him, he tossed him from the canopy. The Spirit plummeted to the sidewalk below, bouncing sickly.

The Devil cackled aloud and the Spirit's arm dangled from his horn, flapping lazily. He pointed to the cross Navarro was nailed to and it erupted in flames. He turned to us and sent a puff of fire our way. Everyone scrambled out of the scorching flames path and the Devil took a running leap from the canopy. His wings snapped open and he glided through the air, heading straight towards us all.

"Remember the plan!" I shouted.

All the Spirits immediately ran for their assigned positions. Constantine and Zacharius ran beside the canopy. John and Kane ran to my right, and Julius went left. I stood still remaining strong within the path of the Devil's dive-bomb.

The Devil forcefully crashed into me with his head down and his horns forward, aimed at the center of my chest. I stepped to the side but not quickly enough. He hit me with his shoulder, knocking me to the ground. I reached up with both hands and grabbed onto his long trailing spiked tail as he began his ascent. My shoulders popped as the sudden jolt of his changed direction whipped me violently and nearly tore my arms from their sockets. Sudden sharp pain consumed me and forced me to release my hold. I fell to the ground and bounced. The Devil swooped around and landed back on the canopy.

I searched desperately for some energy I could use to heal my wounds, and I chose to take it from Alex. I extracted some of his life energy and it weakened him so his knees buckled and he teetered. Divination caught him before he hit the floor and began to care for him.

All the Spirits' fists began to glow, and together, they threw the artificial energy towards the Devil. He jumped from the canopy, starting a second headlong dive-bomb towards me.

I scrambled to my feet and readied myself for impact. But this time I was prepared, knowing what type of force to expect once contact was made. The Spirits started running towards me. This was it. Everything I taught them would be tested this moment. The Devil and I collided with a force so fierce, the street beneath my feet cracked. I wrestled the Devil to the ground and we began fighting for an advantage like two wild animals. Somehow I'd gotten the better of him and wound up on top. I immediately began draining his energy into myself and yelled out to the other Spirits in desperation, "Now!"

All the Spirits placed a hand on the Devil. The snotty liquid that coated his body was flung through the air as he flailed underneath the intensity of our assault. Each one of the Spirits began to disappear, flickering like a dying florescent bulb.

Suddenly my vision was filled with a radiant light and I possessed power beyond. I took control of the powerful light, bunched it up into a ball and threw it towards the burning cross. I followed the ball of light with my eyes until it hit the flames and exploded. The room was filled with a blinding whiteness that took everything from my sight.

I lay on the ground exhausted and out of breath. I watched Navarro's burning body slump from the cross and Divination run to him. I could only wonder if we'd failed in our attempts to save him. I searched the land for the Devil and couldn't find him. The Spirits lay on the floor around me, unmoving but alive.

Partial success.

"Now, Nature," I called with my mind.

One by one the newly resurrected Spirits began to disappear. Germaine was first. Then Zacharius, Kane, and lastly Constantine. Julius fought his way to his feet and stumbled towards Heaven's exit.

"You knew, didn't you?" I asked in my feeble state.

"Yes, Travis, I did," he panted. "I knew once the Devil was destroyed you made arrangements to have Nature return to Chova so she could retrieve our bones for burial. I have the satchel containing mine; it was taken while no one was looking. I don't know why you fear us, Travis, because we are no different than you . . ."

I watched him part without saying a word; he earned his leave. The pattering sound of bare feet slapping the ground stole my attention. I turned to see Navarro approaching with Divination standing by his side. "You!" I said in disbelief. "You're alive!"

"More than alive, Spirit!" Navarro exclaimed.

"Good Lord, it worked!" I professed, the wind coming from my lungs so quickly that I had to stop speaking. I was weak, dying. Navarro knelt beside me and placed his hands on my back. "I can only wonder how you did it," he said and pumped some of his life energy into my body.

When I felt strong enough to sit up, I did so, and said, "I had the Spirits before me resurrected and I taught them to manipulate energy. When I battled the Devil, I held him down so the Spirits could drain his life energy and push it into me. I balled up the energy and threw it at you." I held my hand out, and asked, "Can you help me stand?"

Navarro pulled me to my feet and held onto me. I checked my foundation, and when I felt confident enough to stand on my own, I said, "I'm okay now."

Navarro let me go and he stepped away from me. For the first time since his return I looked at him with cloudless eyes. His eyes were as blue as a summer sky. His hair was neat, bouncy and fluffy. His skin was peach colored and not a blemish marked him. I took a step back and studied him, trying to figure what about him was missing. Suddenly, it came to me. I waved my hand in the air and white sparkles popped before him. When the flickering energy faded, Navarro was dressed in a pure white full-length robe. A thin gold trim outlined the bottom of the robe and the lapel.

"Absolutely amazing," I said.

Navarro smiled. His teeth were perfectly straight and white, his breath like peppermint. "You've saved my life and my dream," he said, his voice like a whisper being carried along by the breeze. "I can never repay you for that. But I can move forward with my dream now. I still need you to help me, Travis. I need you to continue sending souls through the light."

"The light?" I questioned instantly outraged. "The light is for reincarnation!"

"No, Travis," Navarro said, laughing freely. "Let us walk together while we talk."

I agreed to his request, and we started walking up the hill.

"The light will be the way into Heaven now," he explained. "Once the souls travel through the light, an Angel will be there to welcome them. My Angels, I was hoping, would be your friends."

Divination stopped and pulled the hood from his head. The Dezrects began to dance joyously, and Alex stepped forward and asked, "Angels?"

"Angels," Navarro confirmed. "Messengers of Heaven."

"An Angel," Divination said cognitively. "After all I've done to you, Navarro, you'd make me your Angel?"

"You're worthy, Divination. When you fight for a cause you

believe in, you fight heart and soul. Your service would be a commodity."

"What of Osiris, Nature and Amanda?" I asked.

"They too have been chosen to be my Angels."

I smiled and paused in relief. I'd met with success and it was intoxicating. After all the sorrow that surrounded me, the moment was bittersweet. We'd walked to the hilltop, and from there, I looked to the next hilltop beyond us. From where I stood the streets continued on, sparkling in the daylight. The mansions grew larger the higher up the hill they were. I turned to the group and said, "I must leave to bring Osiris, Amanda and Nature back here. I wish to take Alex with me."

Navarro nodded in approval. "If that is what you wish."

"It is," I said. "We will see ourselves out."

Together, Alex and I descended the hill, and when we reached the bottom, I casually shot a glance back up the hill to see where the others were. They were all out of sight, probably on the opposite side of the hill heading into the city beyond the suburbs. I picked a single piece of fruit from the Tree of Knowledge and whispered to Alex that he was never to tell anyone what he saw me do and that he was never to taste the fruit, it was absolutely forbidden. He agreed.

Once we arrived inside Chova's forest, I went to the House and asked Alex to wait outside for me. Quickly, I went inside and placed the fruit inside the empty coffin that was once used to hold my bones. I covered it with a blanket, and hurried outside. I led Alex to the path behind the House and followed it to the lake. From there we went to the path that ascended the mountainside, which brought us to the cave behind the falls. Inside the mouth we stepped. A murderous scream erupted so loud it could be heard over the rumbling sound of the falls. I inquisitively looked to Alex and he looked to me. Unsure I really heard anything at all, I waited for verification. The scream came again and I ran for the meeting room. I pulled the giant wooden door open and panned the room.

"Spirit!" Osiris said, running to me. He was sweating, his eyes red. "You've got to help her!"

"Who!" I shouted knowingly, and Osiris ran to the rear of the room. I followed him and saw Amanda on the floor face up, thrashing in a pool of her own blood. I dropped to my knees beside her, cradled her stiffening body in my arms and rocked her gently. "No! No! No!" I muttered barely able to maintain my composure. I looked to Osiris and shouted, "Who did this to her?"

"She did," Osiris said, fearful of my rage. He backed himself against the wall and hid his face in his hands.

"Tell me, Osiris, tell me how it was done!"

"With a gun," he said, his words muttered and hard to decipher. "I tried saving her but it didn't work!"

"The seed, Osiris! Tell me you didn't use the Spirit seed on her!"

Amanda thrashed in my arms and gurgled. She was trying to speak. I lowered my ear to her blood filled mouth and listened intently.

"No one to love," she managed. "No one to love me back."

I could no longer contain my sorrow. I cried and held her close. "I was the one to love you," I said, and gently rested her on the floor.

"The seed!" I said to Osiris. "You put it inside her, didn't you?"

"I did," he said. "I was trying to save her."

"Damn," I said, and sat at the table. I could find no anger for him; he always tried to do what was best.

Osiris came over to me, reluctant to get too close, and asked, "Why didn't it work?"

"It did work," I said disappointed. "There is a rule that must be followed in order for the seed to work as intended. The recipient must be chosen. She wasn't. As a price for her suicide, she'll forever carry the pain and wound of this day around with her. Eternal suffering."

"Oh, God!" Osiris cried. "What have I done!"

He ran from the room, and I asked Alex to see after him. I returned to Amanda's side and plunged my hand deep into her chest. I felt around for her soul. It was still within, trapped. I grabbed hold of it and gave it a mighty yank, pulling it free of her body. Blankly she looked at me, her wound disfigured her face.

The pain would surely return and never leave.

"This is the only thing I can do for you now," I said. "I'm sorry." And I took her from the cave.

Chapter 32

Alex

It is to my understanding that when Spirit led Amanda out of the cave he immediately brought her to the light for reincarnation. In agreement with Navarro, she was the last to be sent through using the old God's system. Spirit did this because he knew Amanda would never get the chance to live a normal life again. He wished more than anything that he could've established a relationship with her now that things have finally calmed. Unfortunately, her decision to take her own life left Spirit with little option and he's dispirited because of it.

While the Spirit was taking Amanda to the light, I asked Osiris to wait in the cave in case Nature returned from her responsibility of laying to rest all the Spirit's bones while both the Spirit and myself were absent. I took Amanda's mangled human body to the physical realm and gave it the proper burial, paying my last respects to her; the memory of our time together is something I'll always cherish.

When I returned to the cave Nature had been sitting with Osiris at the table. The expression on her face told me she'd been fully informed about Amanda. In silence all three of us waited for the Spirit to return. When the disheartened Spirit reappeared, he escorted us all to the light where Navarro awaited our arrival.

"Welcome!" he cheered. "To euphoria!"

He stepped to the side to proudly show us the obvious changes that began to transform Heaven from its battered state to a more amiable place. The Dezrects were flying about, soaring through the air like eagles. They'd all been turned into Cherubs—rosy-cheeked baby boy Angels. Divination was a beautiful Angel too; he hadn't a blemish on his muscular body. Wings that were full with white feathers carried him gracefully through the air.

Navarro waved his hand in front of us and a dazzling crackling light popped before us and began to alter our appearances. Unexpectedly, wings sprouted from my back and my skin tightened around muscles that began to take shape. I opened and closed my hands, stretching the muscles that were becoming tense. I felt that same tenseness in my back. I pushed my shoulders forward to try and loosen the tension and my own pair of giant white wings opened wide. I looked to either side of myself and saw the stately wings beyond my grasp. I pulled them to me, wrapping them round my body. They were soft to the touch, like silk, and with the slightest movement they pushed the air with a forceful whoosh. I opened them wide, and began flapping them. They moved with gentle gracefulness, and seemingly without effort I was lifted from the ground. I soared through the air, bubbling with pleasure. Navarro watched us joyfully, announcing, "Alex, Divination, and Nature, you three are my Seraphim Angels now, the Highest of my Order!"

Since that day, I have been here, inside Heaven. I've been preparing the landscape to the way Navarro has envisioned it to be for the sake of any human soul that comes here to live forever in peace and harmony.

Before the Spirit brought me through the light, he asked me to contact you and tell you about the final events. I promised him I would do so and have now satisfied that favor. I can say he still has plans for you though I'm not allowed to share any of the details. For now, I know he wants to leave you in your human form. And in that state, he wants you to protect his bones as Divination did before you. Within the next couple of days, I'm going to bring you a satchel while you sleep. I am using this method because it is important I don't allow you to see me while I am in this form; it could be the death of you.

You know what will be inside the satchel once you find it, and by now you should know how to care for the contents. I wish you luck; Spirit is counting on you.

Part 3: Animation

Introduction

Spirit

It has been some time since I made any attempt to contact you. I know you may feel as though I've forgotten about you. With all the time that has passed, I can't say I blame you for feeling that way. I have plans for you but the events that unexpectedly unravel around me causes dramatic changes in my existence, therefore, it causes dramatic changes in yours. I figured now would be the best time to share recent events in my existence with you.

Some unresolved events that had taken place in my past have finally found resolution. The spiritual realm has undergone more dramatic changes that are both good and bad. But I suppose it would make more sense to you if I started from the beginning rather than the end.

But, before I move along any further, I would like to take a moment to thank you for keeping my bones safe. I placed my existence in your hands, and you didn't fail me.

Chapter 33

Last Alex told you I'd left everyone behind in Heaven to try and resolve personal matters. That is a true statement, but unknown to anyone, Navarro and I met one time privately. He asked me to join him and the others inside his euphoric domain promising me love and eternal happiness. I knew if I was to go there things would be better than any dream I could ever muster from my imagination. But, I wanted time to search myself, to come to terms with my losses under my own resolve. I wanted to take some time to do the things I hadn't time to do since my human execution.

Only a year ago the House of Chova was completely wrapped with vines, the beauty beneath the growth well hidden. I cleared away all obstructions and made much-needed repairs. The stained glass windows that held the images from the meeting where Navarro confronted God are now gone.

I've taken a certain liking to the balcony on the House and I stand on it for many hours during the day, watching the luxuriant scenery that is Chova and its inescapable beauty.

It had been a year since the first day Navarro stood as God, and I was standing on the balcony looking out on the tree covered Land, reflecting in my past when I heard the sounds of branches snapping deep from within the forest. Unmoved, I watched the forests edge for the wanderer that had been the first to stumble inside my domain since the reformation of Heaven.

"Travis," someone bellowed, their voice echoing through the Land. "Spirit, are you here?"

Silently I tried to fit the voice to someone I knew, but one year worth the being alone tarnished all things well-known to me. Silent I remained, still trying to guess my unseen visitors identity.

"Spirit!" the voice called from the forests edge. "You are here! Why didn't you reply to my summoning?"

A tall heavenly creature that seemed to radiate with confidence walked to the opening beyond the forest. Brilliant white wings opened from his back and began to flap gracefully, pulling him from the ground. He stopped his ascent, hovering before me. "Don't you recognize me?" he asked, and smiled.

"I'm afraid not," I answered, still relaxed and leaning on the railing with my forearms. He posed no threat. "Should I?" I watched his wings work back and forth.

"It is me, Travis, it is Divination!"

He landed on the balcony and didn't produce a sound doing so. I turned to him and embraced him with a hug. It had been so long since I last saw him. I'd missed him and the others terribly but forced myself to deny it, to not face the loneliness I felt inside. I'd dealt with a lifetime of pain, and I promised myself I would use the time I had to heal. Last I saw Divination he was skinny without muscle and flesh, wearing a loose fitting garb to conceal the blisters on his body. But that was the past as was the corruption inside the spirit realm. He was beautiful as was the spiritual realm.

"It is good to see you," I said.

"And you," he said. "It has been much too long for old friends."

"Yes, Divination, it has been."

He surveyed the Land of Chova, then turned his back to me. "I see a lot has changed here since I left. I like it."

"Thank you," I said and meant it. "How is everything above?"

He smiled and leaned against the rail, keeping his gaze over the forest. "It's been busy. We all miss you, Spirit, and we all want to know if your time is finished here. Will you return to Heaven with me?"

I drew in a deep breath and slowly exhaled. "I'm thankful for the invitation, Divination, but I like what I have here. And for the moment, I can't see myself leaving it. This is my Heaven, Divination."

"No, Spirit, this place is nothing like Heaven. I think it is time you stop trying to hold onto your humanity because that is what continues to cloud your judgment."

"But you don't understand. This is the only thing I can actually call my own since my human execution," I said, and Divination shamefully turned away. "I didn't say that to harp on memories you'd rather forget. I know you were doing what you had to. It is just that I'm not ready to turn away from those who still need me. Believe me, there are many souls that still can't find their way to the light."

Divination shook his head knowingly. "Is there anything I could do or say to convince you to come to Heaven?"

I shook my head back and forth, "I belong here, and the people need me. Please, I ask you to try and understand that."

"Strangely enough, I do. What shall I tell the others?"

"Tell them that I miss them all very much. Tell them I think of them each day that passes that I am away."

He smiled and brushed his soft fingertips over the top of my hand. "Okay, Spirit, I'll tell them," he said and scanned the distant puff of trees. "The mysteries Chova holds are great. There are many things about this place yet undiscovered. I've always wondered why I could never journey to the opposite side of the mountain and what it was exactly that stops anyone from continuing on the path." He shook his head in frustration. "Maybe I'll never know. Have you been to the cave at all?"

"No, I haven't, Divination. I haven't been there since Amanda's suicide."

"I'm sorry," Divination said. "I know you cared for her."

"I do. Deeply. I miss my son too."

"Are you sure you won't reconsider returning with me?"

"Yes, I'm sure."

"Very well. I should go. If you need anything, you know where you can find us."

"Thank you, Divination."

He smiled and kissed my cheek. He leapt from the balcony and began to plummet. His wings snapped open and he glided to the ground, landing softly. He folded his wings behind his back and glanced back to me, waving before he disappeared into the cover of the forest.

"Travis, you're needed," said a voice. It was a man's voice, and it sounded as if it were coming from behind me, inches away. I quickly turned to search the immediate area.

"Go where?" I answered to find no one there to respond. I looked back to the forest and saw no one. I left the balcony, descending the spiral staircase, and going to the main floor. I searched the entire lower level of the House, and again, I couldn't find anyone. I left Chova and headed to a cemetery located on Long Island. I fizzled into the physical realm and stood before a headstone that read:

HERE LIES TAMMY WINTER—BELOVED MOTHER
GEORGE WINTER—BELOVED FATHER
THE LORD WATCHES OVER THEE

It had been the first time I'd visited my son and daughter-in-law's resting site since their deaths. Still having difficulty accepting their fate, I spoke aloud, saying, "I can only hope you are both living somewhere happily. I would give anything to have either of you back, but I above any know that's impossible. I know neither of you can hear my words, but it helps me through the horrible memories of your last days. I miss you, my son."

"Travis," the voice called again like a passing breeze blowing through the treetops. "It's about to happen again!"

I frantically searched the surrounding area and could find no one. I quickly stepped into the spirit realm and searched there. No one was around.

I shook my head in an attempt to try and clear my mind. I sat and closed my eyes. I assumed I was hearing conversations of the people like I did when I was in limbo. I needed to shut them out before it drove me mad.

"Can you help me?" a passive young voice asked. I opened my eyes to find a single human soul standing before me. I was relieved to know I wasn't going crazy. The soul's life energy was drained and his dimmed aura was proof of that. Standing to my feet, I approached him cautiously like one would an unfamiliar dog.

"I can help," I said. "I am Travis Winter, the Spirit of Independence."

He stepped towards me. "You mean, you're the Spirit of Independence?"

"Have you heard of me?" I brushed the top of his head with my hand to see what was within his mind. When his human life ended he was no older than eight years.

"I have," the boy said. "After we died, I got separated from them. Others like myself told me if I could find you, you could help me find them again. Can you?"

"Find who, your mommy and daddy?"

"Yes, and my sister too."

I knelt before him. "Can you tell me what happened?"

"We were going to the store in daddy's car. I heard skidding and loud noises, like crashes. The next memory I have is being like I am now and everyone else was gone. I was told I was dead, is that true?"

"Life is just beginning for you. I need you to tell me who said you were dead."

"It was other people that look the same way I do. They told me they were lost and they were searching for you."

Instinctively I knew where these people were. I needed to help them. I said to the boy, "Would you like to see your parents and sister right now?"

"Yes, Mr. Spirit, I would."

"Take my hand, and don't be afraid."

"I'm not afraid," he said and took my hand.

"You're very brave. You're going to be just fine." I lifted him from the ground and ascended to the light. Once before the light I paused. I said, "This is where your family is. Go through and enjoy your life with them."

"In there?" he asked while pointing to the light.

"Yes. Go ahead, they're waiting for you."

I stood there and watched him enter the light. At the end of the lights source, I saw the faintest image of an Angel who awaited the new arrival. Once he reached the Angel, they both turned and waved to me until the light gradually dimmed and blinked off.

I immediately began my descent to a particular area on the surface that seemed to collect lost souls from both the spiritual and physical realms: New York's intricate subway system.

Chapter 34

When I arrived on the Earth's surface, the sun was beginning to rise, fighting desperately against the frigid air that blanketed the city that never sleeps. I quickly descended into the complex tunnel system below street level to start my search for the lost souls the young boy told me about. Minutes into my search, I stumbled upon a small group of souls that had been searching for a way out of the giant underground maze.

"Come with me," I said. "I can show you the way out."

The group paused and turned their attention to me—the stranger approaching from the darkened distance. I counted five of them: four men and one woman. All were middle-aged and all had faint auras.

"How can you help us?" the woman soul asked, her voice trembling with fear. She backed behind the male souls. "We've been trying to find our way out of here for many days, but everything looks the same to us."

I walked to them, all standoffish, wary of my nearness. I said, "I can show you to the light. All I ask for is your trust in my say so."

One of the male entities backed away and shook his head. "Nuh uh. Only the Spirit can help us out of here."

Knowing I was unable to convince them with words, I began

to grab energy from the air and I concentrated it into my fist. I began juggling the energy, slamming the particles together to create a spark. A dazzling flame engulfed my fist. The group of souls backed away. I smiled inwardly. The tunnel around us was lit brightly.

The female entity stepped before the souls she traveled with, turned to them, and said, "It is him! It is the Spirit!"

I looked down on her young face that had suddenly become filled with hope and I showed her the smile I concealed. She was precious. Delicate. Scared. Knowing I could provide her with some comfort gladdened me.

"I am the Spirit," I said. "Please, follow me to the light. Your days of suffering are now over."

I turned from them and began to lead them from the tunnel. Keeping my hand lit and held high to spread the radiance, I was satisfied doing so knowing it would make them feel that much more secure.

"Death in St. Rudes church . . ."

I stopped walking and faced the group. I asked, "What?"

None answered. They all exchanged inquisitive glances with one another. I stepped to them, meeting the eyes of each. "The church," I said. "Who said something about death in a church?"

Again, each exchanged glances, the confusion apparent.

Again, I questioned, "Who said something about a church? I want an answer!"

"Nobody did," the woman soul said and I knew she wasn't lying. Her fear was returning, overtaking. I turned around, and said, "Forget it. Follow me."

I escorted them to the surface and extinguished the flame from my hand. One at a time I began bringing them to the light and sending them through. Each one was grateful and thanked me before they left this world to embrace the comforts of Heaven. But, before I sent the female soul through, she hugged me, and said, "There is another soul lost in the tunnels. He is just a young boy. We told him about you and about the great things you've done. We told him to stay with us until we found you, but he insisted going off on his own to find you."

I smiled. "He found me. I sent him through the light already. I'm sure he's been reunited with his family by now."

"I've heard so much about your kindness, about the changes you've made. I thank you for them. There is another who's been around the tunnel that said he was a Spirit. We didn't believe him or his tricks. Something about him didn't feel right so we ran from him. He introduced himself as Julius."

"You should go," I said at his names mention. I nodded my head towards the light, and said, "They're waiting for you."

She looked to the light and saw the silhouette of a winged man waiting for her arrival. She turned her gaze to me; her eyes lazy, blinking slowly. "How beautiful!"

I watched her enter the light, but before it dissolved, I began my decent to the earth's surface feeling excited knowing Julius was near and was actively looking to guide souls to the light. To Chova I headed, passing the evening commuters in the subway station that were receding, moving along like a herd of cattle to their homes until first light called them out to do it all again. Believing my passing was a swooping wind racing from the street above, the people would shutter and fasten the buttons on their coats. Amused by this I laughed and hurried along.

Once before the void, I stepped inside allowing the forceful wind to take me along and drop me inside Chova's forest. Standing to my feet and brushing the earth's droppings from my clothes, I walked through the thickening path to the House. Inside I unexplainably walked to the casket and picked up the fruit I'd hidden there over a year before. It was as shiny and red as the day I picked it. I exposed my teeth and brought the apple to my mouth. Biting the fruit, it crunched and squirted its juices, soaking my chin and filling my mouth. I anxiously chewed the fruit, disappointed there was no flavor, and swallowed it. Feeling the lump sliding down my throat and hitting my stomach, I braced myself for total awareness to consume me. But it never came. I continued to wait.

Suddenly images played through my mind; a movie designed specifically for me. Julius was holding the soul of a human that was still inside its healthy body. He yanked the soul and it popped away from the body. The soul moaned in agony, I moved myself closer and Julius took notice to me. He dashed away before I could react.

"Don't trust him or any of the other Spirits," a voice told me. It sounded like Navarro. "He'll try and wake them," the voice continued. "If he does, misfortune will come to you."

I turned to find him. He was somewhere but nowhere. A second vision came, replacing the concerns from the first. My son, George decided to place his mother, my wife, into a nursing home some twenty years after my death. She'd become violent and suicidal, making claims she was being visited by evil creatures that told her that her husband hadn't really died in the war. Her violence stemmed from the people around her denying her visions. Why couldn't they understand she was telling the truth? After falling into deep depression, she made two suicide attempts and developed a severe schizophrenic disorder. For many years she remained unresponsive to anyone and anything around her, and she became most impossible to care for. George decided to place her in a home where she could be better cared. He visited his mother often at first, but his visitations became less frequent as her condition worsened until he eventually stopped going to see her altogether. Whenever he was asked about her, he'd bow his head and mutter, "She passed on."

For over thirty years my wife had been in that home, and there she remained that very moment of my awareness. I ran off the platform and excitedly stripped off my cloak. I manipulated energy from within the room I stood, meticulously constructing myself a human body that would fool all. I made sure not too overdue any of my features, in certitude, I made myself exactly as I'd looked when I were human. My hair sandy blonde, short and parted to the side. My eyes were deep blue and my face of a distinguished man. My skin had a light olive complexion, and I stood around five-foot-ten. I dressed myself in black jeans and wore a maroon button down shirt I'd tucked in my pants. Settling on brown leather shoes, I realized the frigid night air would penetrate the false shell I created. A brown leather bomber jacket would keep me plenty warm. Once I was satisfied with my transformation, I left Chova and headed for the physical realm to partake in the life I'd left behind so long ago. Deep inside my mind I knew I'd soon get the nerve to visit my wife, Paige.

Nighttime had fallen over the city. The bright lights and giant flickering amber billboards captivated me. I looked up at the giant buildings that appeared to lean and I wondered how they just didn't topple over. My gaze fell to the busy streets. Cars filled the roadway that raced against a clock that was faster there than anywhere else in the world. I stood silent, taking in everything around me. So overwhelming. I exhaled my first breath and watched the air swirl before me. Rolling. A passing stranger whisked by, brushing away the puff of smoke. I watched her walk on and quickly lost interest. I scanned my surroundings. Everything seemed fast and for a moment I felt that if I were to stand still for too long, I'd be left behind with no chance of ever being able to catch up.

A stiff shoulder knocked me. "Why don't you stand right in the middle of the sidewalk, asshole!" that passing stranger roared. I watched his feet pound the pavement, his long quickened strides taking him further away from the spot we'd collided in.

I began to walk, trying to hold pace with the other pedestrians that cluttered the sidewalk. Walk I did. Block after block I shuffled onwards, becoming comfortable with my new legs. A local street vendor selling warm pretzels and hotdogs from a rolling cart with a red and white umbrella caught my attention. I went to the vendor and asked for a hotdog with ketchup and relish. Nodding his head in response, the vendor flipped a lid open on the cart and fished a hotdog from steaming water and placed it on a pre-sliced bun. He squirted some ketchup on it and painted the top with relish. I reached into my pocket and manifested three dollars I used to pay him with. I took the food and walked away.

The hotdog was piping hot, steaming the air like my breath did, and it was irresistible. It was plump and juices seeped from its pores. The bread was cheap and began to crumble in my hand. I delayed no longer and took a barbarous bite. My taste buds savored the flavor of the rubbery meat stick and sweetened condiments that burst with flavor. I packed the dog into my mouth, forcing my cheeks outwards to make room. I chuckled aloud at the sheer joy of being able to taste the food with my artificial tongue. I was delighted how I had been able to masterfully recreate everything on the body, even the tinniest details like the blinking of the eyes.

"Spirit," a pleading voice called. I looked around the heavy flow of people and no one paid any mind to me. I hung my head and listened, using my experience inside Limbo to block out the consuming sounds of the city. I searched for the voice that summoned me.

"Please, go to Saint Rudes church," it said, the lips sounding like they were pressed against my ears. I decided to remain in my human form and hurry along to the church that was near.

Chapter 35

It had been about 10:00 pm and the freezing rain suddenly started coming down at such an odd angle it soaked my face even though I'd tucked my chin in the collar of my jacket. The street traffic immediately lightened, and most of the pedestrians scurried for shelter. I felt the stare of the people I passed as I continued along without pause to the church the voice conjured me to.

After a twenty-block journey, I saw the towering church. It reminded me of the House of Chova with little differences. Two spires holding crosses extended from the roof, and beside the churches walkway were two bushes that were cut into the shape of crosses.

The church had fifteen police cars and five ambulances parked in front of it. Yellow tape was strung around the property of the church and the street was closed off to vehicles and pedestrians. Ducking beneath the yellow tape, I ran towards the church. An officer hurried to me, grabbing my shoulders and spinning me around. He pulled me back where I came from, saying, "You can't go in there!"

The form I was in slipped my mind; I had to shake it. Spinning from his grasp, I turned and faced him. "You don't understand . . ."

"No! You don't understand. You cannot go in there!"

I shoved the officer aside, running for the church. "I must," I declared. He caught up to me, grabbed me and jerked me backwards. "Now you're going to jail."

I shook off the energy I gathered and bit-by-bit it began to break away. The officer released me and backed away, swearing as he watched my body melt before his eyes. Once my transformation was complete, I saw some souls with their backs to me gathered in front of the church door, peering inside secretively. I hurried to them, and asked, "Can you tell me what has happened?"

All moaned from surprise and they dispersed, running in different directions. I zeroed in on one and followed. I caught up to her, a woman in her late fifties, and asked, "Why are you running from me?"

My pursuit and nearness startled her a second time, sending her indecisively into a new direction. I continued my chase, and again, asked, "Why are you running from me?" She fell to the ground and began to pray aloud. I went to her and tried pulling her to her feet but she refused to cooperate, going limp.

"What has happened?" I asked, frustrated. She didn't respond. I released her and searched for another.

I found a male soul in his sixties who'd gotten only as far as a block away from the church by the time I caught up to him. "I know you're frightened," I said. "I just need you to talk to me."

The man stopped running. With winded lungs, he said, "I couldn't run any further if I tried."

"Why is everyone running from me?" I asked, keeping my distance to gain his trust.

The man panted, bent over and grabbed his knees. "I thought you were the guy that took some of the others away and had returned for me."

"Others?"

"The others that were in church for the eight o'clock mass. Things were carrying on as usual when suddenly I felt a hard tugging on my body. Without pain, I found myself standing over my body. I couldn't see who did this, it was all just a blur. But whoever it was, they kept apologizing to me. They sounded very sad. Many of the other people that came to the mass were standing outside their bodies, and others just disappeared without explanation. Then, a man much larger than yourself who introduced himself as Julius began rounding up groups of people. Those he held in his arms were lifted upwards with him through the ceiling of the church. Moments later, Julius would return empty handed and he would gather more people and leave with them. We didn't know what he was doing, so we all split up and left the church. I stayed within a small group that hid together for a while. We returned to the church a short time later to see if Julius had left, but we only got a glimpse inside the church because you showed, scaring everyone away."

I didn't dare attempt to bring the man to the light after what he'd been through. I offered him my thanks and returned to the church. Police and rescue workers were carting bodies zipped in body bags to waiting trucks. I stuck my head inside a passing bag and examined the body within. It had been unscathed; its soul had abandoned its shell seemingly without reason. I wondered if any of the souls I'd scared away earlier had once been housed inside that body.

I entered the church and saw fifty or more bodies littering the pews. All had been abandoned by its host and had already begun to stiffen. I looked around, and discovered on the stage above the giant cross that hung on the wall a message scrolled in red paint that read:

MERCY TO THE PEOPLE WHO WOULD BE BROUGHT BEFORE THE DEVIL

I stared at the message for a long hard moment, watching the dry paint reflect the dancing candlelight. Feet skimming the ground somewhere behind me grabbed my attention. I turned to see Julius standing in the threshold of the doorway. He turned and bolted; this is what the fruit showed me. "Julius!" I screamed, my voice loud enough that the people on the physical realm looked to one another in question. My rage became instant and intense. How dare he harm those I fought so hard to protect. I ran from the stage, bolting outside. Julius was long gone. Had he fled using the spirit realm or did he enter the physical realm and take on a human form, blending himself in with the crowd around? Either way I couldn't detect his presence. He was a powerful individual, maybe more powerful than myself.

I left the church uncertain of the events that unfolded around me. The deniable reality of Julius doing something so heinous boggled my mind. What reasons could there be for doing something so terrible? And the voice that summoned me—who and where was it from? Was it an effect of the fruit? I hadn't any inclination and my head pounded as I tried to give myself one. I retired my uncertain resolve for answers when I reached Chova and unconsciously drifted to my comfort spot on the balcony. There my thoughts drifted elsewhere.

I was a twenty-year-old young man and my wife was a mere eighteen years. Paige had been five month's pregnant with George and barely showing when I left to fight in the war. I told her not to cry as I embraced her one last time before I left. I kissed her cheek and made a promise that I would see her again. At that very moment I knew I could still keep that promise to her.

I shed my clothes and formed another human body for myself. Once dressed and content, I left for the streets of the city again.

Chapter 36

I was standing taut before two doors that slid open for me when I came before them. My mind was commanding my legs to move forward, but they held still, resisting the order. I was nervous, unable to get myself to do what I thought I was so ready for when I left Chova. My being there was a mistake. I felt I should leave.

"Move out of the way!" a doctor running in front of a stretcher shouted at me. Another doctor was running behind the cart and was pounding the chest of the patient that was near death. He was in full cardiac arrest. His aura was tinted yellow—a tell tale sign that the patient wasn't going to recover. When he stepped from his body, if he couldn't find his way to the light, I would be sure to guide him.

I jumped through the doors and stepped to the side, allowing them passage without pause. Sprinting by me without even a glance, the doctors continued on down the hall without seizing their efforts to save the man.

I moved onwards, the excitement of the moment stealing my fears; I followed signs posted about each hallway of the hospital that directed me to the psyche ward. I was led down a long isolated hallway that brought me to a single elevator. I pressed the call button on the wall and waited patiently for the elevator to come for me. When it did, I stepped inside and pressed the corresponding floor number that would bring me to my ultimate destination. The lighted panel dinged, signaling my arrival, and the doors slowly slid open. A nurse's station was located directly across from the elevator, and the woman behind the counter gave me a forced smile. I approached her, and said, "I would like to see Paige Winter."

She studied me. "Are you family or something? She hasn't had a visitor in years."

I nodded my head. "I guess you can say that. I just found out she was alive. I was told she'd passed away years ago."

She pointed, and said, "Down the hall, make a left, and you'll find her in the third room on the left. She your grandmother?"

"Something like that . . ."

I followed the nurse's directions and soon found myself standing before Paige's room that had no door. My artificial heart began to race, my hands became clammy and my tongue dried, sticking to the roof of my mouth. This was the moment I'd been waiting for since the day of my death. I took a deep breath and stepped inside the room, but only one step. My nerves made me hesitate. I could almost see her lying in the bed covered with heavy blankets. She was within the mound of fabric somewhere.

I tried convincing myself I could do this. I was the stronger one of us two and needed to do it for our sake.

I slowly approached the side of her bed and immediately noted her aura was tinted yellow. She had three days to live at best; cancer riddled her body. It really didn't matter now that I was there. I concentrated some energy into the palm of my hand and created a flower seed. I squeezed the seed and a flower began to grow. Once it was full, I placed the bouquet in a vase that was readily available on the table beside her bed. The flowers seemed to add some color to her whitened face. I pulled up a chair and sat close to her bedside.

"Paige?" I called gently. She was unresponsive, maybe sleeping. I called her again, saying, "Paige? It is Travis, I've returned to you like I promised I would."

Her eyes opened slowly and her head rolled to the side. Looking at me she swallowed hard. She moistened her frail cracked lips with her tongue and spoke subtly. "It has been years since I last saw the like of you. Leave me; you've already broken my rationality."

"I am no demon that has come to torment you," I said. "Try and look at me without clouded eyes. It is really me, Travis, your husband!"

She rolled her eyes and let out a hard sigh. "I'm much too tired for such nonsense. I know what you are. The damn devil has sent you to me like he has so many times before. Travis was a good man. He's with God, and I know I'll see him there. You have no place here, demon, leave me."

"But I am who I claim to be, Paige. Look at my eyes and tell me you don't see the love we shared within."

She peered at me through a heavy disbelieving squint. Her forehead wrinkled, mounding her old skin across the bridge of her nose.

"I'm no demon," I continued. "And there is no devil that has sent me to you. I've come to you out of love. And I do this out of mercy. I want to help end your suffering."

I took her frail hand into my own and I released the energy I held to become human. Holding on to her aura, her life energy, I gently pulled on it until enough was separated from her body that her soul could step through to the spiritual side. She stood next to me confused but pain free. Looking into the room around us she saw doctors and nurses rushing to her body. They began working on it.

"Come, Paige. They won't be able to revive you," I said.

"No!" she shouted, her voice cracking terribly. She tried to run on her feeble legs and tumbled to the ground. I stood over her, pulling a seed from my chest and clenching it in my fist. I plunged my hand into her chest and released the seed inside her. She convulsed and began foaming at the mouth, her painful transformation into the Spirit just beginning. I knew the process would take some time to reach completion, so I scooped her into my arms and brought her to Chova. Inside the House I gently placed her on the floor in the center of the room. She continued to writhe during the transformation. I bent and kissed her forehead, saying, "This will all be over soon. I'll return for you in a little while."

I left Chova and returned to the hospital I'd separated her body from soul in and I retrieved her wrapped body that'd been moved to the morgue. I pulled the body into the spirit realm and moved hastily to Pine Lawn cemeteries located on Long Island. I located the plot Paige and I bought when we first married and I entered the physical realm. I placed her stiffened body on the ground and returned to the spirit realm. I descended eight feet into the earth and solidified my arms. I pushed the dirt around, creating a one foot hollow and returned to the physical realm. I unwrapped Paige's body and gathered some energy available around me, concentrating it in my fist. My fist glowed from the intense smoldering heat I'd created, and I lowered it inches away from her body. The heat burned away the flesh and muscle, leaving only her bones. I released the energy from my hand and gathered her bones, placed them in the center of the sheet that wrapped her body, and tied it up. I returned to the spirit realm with her wrapped bones and descended eight feet down. I placed her bones inside the hollow I'd created. Satisfied with her bones untraditional burial, I began my journey back to Chova.

During the journey, I pondered with elation my wife's return into my life, anticipating the coming reunion. Her transformation should've been complete by the time I returned, and some of her strength leaving her well enough to finally begin to care for herself. I paid no mind to my surroundings and its activities as I began walking through the subway station towards the void.

"Destiny, Spirit, I know yours," said a male voice.

I stopped and scanned the darkened tunnel before me, behind me and even above me. "Julius?" I called, my voice reverberating dully.

"No, Spirit, not Julius." Sane laughter echoed. "I can see what you refuse to. Our destiny is already set in stone."

I stopped, turned to the train platform and searched the faces of the few people that seemed oblivious of my presence.

"What is my destiny?" I asked.

"Ahh, so you didn't leave, Spirit!"

222

I finally saw him: an old man with a long white beard, dark sunglasses holding a walking stick. He was dressed in a handsomely tailored suit with a bowtie that complimented his flashy style. He'd been sitting on a bench bolted to the wall with his back cricked, resting dependently on the wall.

I quickly ran to him, and my movement had been so sudden and fast, I'd sent a gust of air into the physical realm. I examined the man, poking my face into his own; he didn't react. I stepped away from him and noticed he didn't have an aura. I thrust my lips to his ear, and whispered, "Explain how you know I'm here."

The man jumped in his seat and placed his right hand against his chest. "You scared me, Spirit. You almost gave me a heart attack. Though I have no sight, I can hear quite well."

I moved away. "You spoke of destiny. What do you, old man, know of my destiny?"

"You're to become god. The wheels are in motion."

"You are mad, old man," I said. "What is it you're seeking?"

"Only to tell you about your destiny."

"It is as I said, you're truly a madman. Who are you?"

"Just a man like you used to be."

"No man knows of my existence. Therefore you're no ordinary man."

"No, ordinary I'm not. I was given a gift of being able to hear and contact souls. This gift was given to me by you, Spirit, a long time ago."

"I gave you no such a thing."

"Oh, but you did! You see, when I was just a young boy at the innocent age of seventeen, I lived in a moderate house huddled in a small community around a lake. The community was a private one, each house placed on immense pieces of property. Only one of the houses had a fenced in yard so I, the blind boy living around Pleasantview Lake couldn't wander into the water. For three summers I dreamt of being able to dip my feet in the water while I sat on the pier without the aide of anyone else. I could do this and wanted to prove to my parents I was capable of doing things for myself. Well, one day I attempted to do just that. My mother didn't know I wandered beyond the boundaries of the fence, and probably never suspected her boy would be so imprudent to break such a firm rule of hers, that is until she discovered my body floating face down in the water. She frantically screamed and alerted the neighbors that had come for me and pulled me from the water.

"I was dead, Spirit. I was outside my body and you were bringing me towards the light with a group of others. But I couldn't keep up with the group; something was pulling me back into my body. And ever since that day, I began to hear things most unbelievable."

"So you claim this death experience allows you to hear souls. Why did you speak of destiny, how could you know of such things?"

"I really don't know. Everything I see comes to me during sleep. I've heard things, seen things in my sleep no man should ever know."

"Like what?"

"Like the birth of a creature that is the essence of evil. I saw him and I saw you. You defeated him and helped a beings life you later helped reached Godly status."

I was stunned by his knowledge, by his sudden coming into my life. I needed time to think things through. Silently, I moved away from him planning to return at my convenience. I went to the Land of Chova and immediately went inside the House to check Paige's condition. She wasn't around. I ascended the spiral staircase that brought me to the balcony. I walked to the opposite end of the balcony and entered an adjoining hallway that allowed access to two second level rooms. The ceilings to the two rooms were cathedral, reaching ten stories high. Both rooms were unoccupied, and I quickly retreated to the first level and then the outside. Quickly I moved to the path behind the House and journeyed towards the lake. On the way, I heard the voice that called me to the church, summoning me with urgency. I ignored the voice for the time being, deciding my search for Paige to be more important. I pushed my way through the overgrown plant life that began to obstruct the path's passageway, not allowing it to slow me until I emerged in the small clearing before the lake.

Enamored by the picturesque beauty of the mountain and lake, I couldn't help but pause in my haste to look it over.

"Eden," I said, believing my sudden observation could've been true. I moved onwards, moving to the cave behind the waterfall. Using the light that broke through the cascading wall of water to see, I moved deeper into the cave where a faint wind blew about. The wind's soft howl sounded like the weeping of bitter secrets to never be spoke by mans' lips. Looking to the engravings etched into the cave wall, I reflected the day I first saw them. Then, they didn't make sense and only seemed to frustrate my search for answers. Little did I know, those engravings held all the answers. But that was my past, just like the calamitous events that had taken place beyond the door I'd found myself standing before. Hesitant and nervous I paused for some unknown reason.

I felt silly for feeling that way. I pulled the handle and the door creaked eerily as it opened. I peered inside, the blood stained walls and floor bringing painful memories of Amanda's horrific death into my mind. I could see her lying helplessly within the cusp of my arms, writhing in agony. I closed my eyes and let the door swing shut. The latch snapped into place, sealing the painful memories within. The intruding voice called to me again, still desperate in tone. I ignored it and turned to walk away. Something distinct, a faint popping sound like crackling came from the room I stood before. I listened. Undeniably, there was activity within. In one quick motion I pulled the door open and entered the room.

Logs inside the abandoned fireplace had been lit and they burned with fierceness. I inquisitively scanned the room and discovered a piece of paper on the table weighted with a rock. I pushed the rock to the floor, took the paper and read it. It said:

Spirit,

Now that things are going the way you wanted them to, the way you manipulated them to, your life must be perfect. I hold the blood of the untimely deaths of the humans on your hands. You will have to answer for them being it was you who'd sided with that Devil, Navarro. I want to remind you that you can still change, and I hope for your sake you begin to see things for the way they are. For now I must return to my work to try and preserve humanity from the madness unfolding around them.

I threw the letter into the fire and watched it burn. When the fire completely devoured the paper, I pulled the energy from the flames and extinguished the fire. I stood there, searing with anger from the letters contents. I swore if it were Julius that was responsible for taking those human lives, I would make him pay. How dare he hold me responsible for his actions!

I exited the cave and began my journey back to the House. When I came off the path and rounded the rear of the House to the front, Paige screamed, "What have you done to me, demon?"

I looked upwards and saw her dangling over the balconies railing. She jumped and I could only watch her plummet to the ground and land with a dull thud. I ran to her side and looked to comfort her.

"Get away from me, demon fodder! Don't you ever look to touch me!" she growled, the pain partially immobilizing her.

I slowly backed away, deliberated my choices for a few seconds and decided to leave Chova for the physical realm.

Chapter 37

I ultimately decided to leave Chova because Paige's behavior was frantic and unpredictable. Her persisting cruel accusations that I was a demon hurt me deeply. I'd sacrificed everything I could for the betterment of man and I had dreams of grandeur that Paige and I would become the happily forever after you read about in the books. No such luck.

I decided to follow the voice in my head that was calling me to another church. Knowing exactly where it was, I went around to the back of the building I was called to and entered it through the rear wall. Finding myself standing on an altar and looking out on the people that had come to the worship hour, I could only stare in disbelief at the slumped bodies that littered the pews and aisles. Limbs and faces were twisted and grotesque. Death had come for them with warning. The expressions on the people's faces told that horrific story. First terror filled them. Then the fear that it was possible they were going to be a victim. Then their desperate attempt to get away. And then, finally, unbelief it was their turn. How could Julius do something so cruel?

A priest was dead, face down and sprawled at my feet. A message had been painted around the contour of his body starting at his head. It read:

EVERY SOUL COUNTS IN THIS MOST UNHOLY OF WARS

The sounds of emergency vehicles approaching alerted me to the fact that humans would be arriving soon. I fizzled in and concentrated energy onto the floor around the priest's body, burning away the message. I returned to the spirit realm and watched the message continue to burn away and die out without ever having touched the body. I exited the church, lost in direction and tenacity. How could I help put this to an end if Julius was always one step ahead of me? I froze. I spotted Julius before me on the physical realm unaware I was so close.

Unable to take a delicate approach, I fizzled and charged Julius. I grabbed hold of his cloak and forcefully pulled him to the ground, jumped on top of him and began shouting, "Why have you come here, Julius? What have you done?"

He fizzled from beneath me and I dropped to the ground. Julius was suddenly behind me, striking me with thunderous blows that disoriented me and blurred my vision. He was good, masterfully using both realms to give himself an advantage.

"I was going to ask you the same thing, Travis!" he grunted and struck me. "You dare attack me! I assure you I'll fight back, I'm no human."

I dropped through the ground and came back directly underneath his feet. I took a firm hold of his ankles and yanked him downwards as hard as I could. We plummeted and exchanged blows until we hit the ground. The force of the collision took the fight from our fists and the wind from our lungs. We both gasped for a breath of the steamy air that was trapped in the underground cavern that once served as Navarro's lair.

I struggled to stand and regain my breath when a strong wind knocked me down and sent me tumbling backwards. Julius jumped on top of me and grabbed my neck. He hung my head over the bank of the boiling river and began to push my head closer to the water. I could feel the heat of the water blistering the back of my head. I grabbed his hands with my own and fought frantically to break his grip. He was much stronger than I was, and continued to lower my head, grunting like a wild animal as he did so.

"Why?" he questioned through bared teeth, eyes bulging madly. "Why have you ripped the souls from those bodies!"

I looked into his eyes and saw no sense of reason within. Through the glassy bloodshot texture I could only see anger and uncertainty. Realizing I could never overpower him enough to break his grip, I closed my eyes and called out with my mind, commanding a Surefire fish to jump from the boiling river. My plan worked. The fish leapt and hit Julius in the side of his face, freeing my throat of the tight hold and sending Julius scrambling away. I choked and sucked in air, my throat killing me, feeling as though it were crushed. Julius moaned a death wail and I went to him. His hands covered his face and he buckled from the pain, kneeling and trembling. I reached to pull his hands from his face to see the damage the fish caused, when he flailed, and said, "Don't you touch me!"

His skin was melted, stringing from his face to his hands. He jumped to his feet, turned his back to me, and looked over his shoulder. He said, "I'll make you pay for this, Travis!"

He darted to the surface and I let him go. I'd done enough to him and suddenly came to the understanding that he wasn't responsible for the theft of all those human souls. I could see it in his eyes, hear it in the tone he convicted me with. The fruit had to be mistaken.

"Spirit?" that damn voice called again. I pushed it from my mind, insistent on taking a few moments to myself. Everything was so chaotic, so beyond my control it seemed things could only get worse before they got better. I went to Navarro's throne and sat. I reached above my head to caress the face of Navarro that was carved into the stone chair. I studied the empty chains that dangled from the brick walls and began to laugh hysterically. Nothing so simple as chains could ever hold me again.

I began to wonder what it would be like to rule a domain—to have all serve my every command and fear my wrath. I stood from the throne and pointed to the two giant cement bowls located behind the throne. A puff of black soot emitted from the bowls as Hells' flame began to burn again. I sat back down, crossed my legs, rested my chin in my hand and studied the empty cavern. I had an idea.

I stood from the throne and darted to the surface. I immediately located a lost soul that was no older than twenty years of age when he died. I watched him struggle to gain the attention of the people that unknowingly passed him by. He was on the verge of tears. Knowing how vulnerable he was, I knew he would be perfect.

I charged him and wrapped him tightly in a bear hug. He flailed but his strength was no match to my own. I wrestled him through the ground and dragged him all the way into Hell. I forcefully slammed him to the ground to keep him from fleeing, and pulled him to the chains that were mounted to the ground before the throne. I placed the restraints around his neck and wrists. I backed away and watched him tremble as I took my place in the throne.

"What is it you're afraid of?" I asked. He didn't answer and I grew impatient for his respect of my authority. I jumped from the throne and rushed him. He clamped his eyes shut and turned his head away. I grabbed his chin and forced his head forward. "Open your eyes," I commanded and he obliged. "Do you fear me?"

"Yes," he said, obviously shaken.

"Why?" I mumbled and thrust my face into his. "Do I look like the devil to you?"

"No," he said, shaking so the chains that bound him began to rattle.

I retreated to the throne, and said, "Well I am not the devil. I want you to come with me to a place that's much better than this. Would you like that?"

"I would like that."

"Very well," I said and went to him. I knelt to unbind him and smiled in satisfaction while doing so. I knew I could do as I pleased, and there wasn't a soul on earth that could stop me. I discarded the chains to the side, stood, and said, "Take my hand then. I won't hurt you."

He placed his hand in mine and together we ascended to the light. I entered it with him and traveled through to the other side. Divination, the Seraph Angel was there to greet us. "Spirit!" he shouted seeming overjoyed to see me. "Come inside. Our Lord will be pleased to see you've finally decided to make Heaven your home."

"No, Divination, that is not why I've come. Something on the surface that is happening needs my attention."

"What is it, Spirit, do you need assistance dealing with it?"

"No, Divination, I don't, but thank you. I need to have a word with you alone, if that is at all possible."

"Of course," he said, and called for Osiris. Seconds after his summoning, Osiris the Cherub Angel entered the light source with us.

"Spirit," Osiris shouted sprightly. His tiny wings flapped speedily, carrying his body to where I stood. I knelt before him to give him the proper greeting.

"Hello, old friend," I said. "It feels like a lifetime has passed by since I last saw you." I hugged him and he hugged me back. He turned to the badly shaken soul I'd brought with me and he led him away.

Divination waited until they were gone before he said, "What is it, Spirit, is everything alright?"

"I'm not really sure," I said, reflecting. "I've done something terrible."

He laughed. "You, Spirit? What could you've done that's so terrible?"

I hung my head, and said, "Do you promise to keep what I tell you a secret? I'm ashamed of myself and don't need others ridiculing me for it."

Divination moved close and reassured me with his arm around my shoulders. "I give you my word, Spirit. I won't tell a soul about what you have to say to me."

Knowing his word was gold, I said, "I've tried to mingle with man. I built myself an artificial body and walked through their streets and tasted their foods. But the bad part is how much I liked it. I want to do it again."

He began to laugh and he patted my shoulder as he broke away from me. I didn't see the humor in it and thought to tell him so when he said, "Is that all? You scared me there for a moment. I've thought of doing that many times myself. I got the idea when I would enter the physical realm in search of a new Spirit. I see nothing wrong with it as long as you keep your distance."

"Really?" I asked, and allowed my face to be overtaken by a smile.

"Really," he said. "Just don't interfere."

I instantly felt much better about myself. I hugged Divination, showed him my satisfied smile and returned to Chova with a clear conscious.

Chapter 38

The old blind man had been waiting for me on the train platform again. He was sitting on the same bench and still using the wall to hold himself up. As soon as I walked by, he pointed in my direction with his cane, and said, "I've been waiting for you to return, Spirit. I have something important to tell you."

"About?"

"Well, it concerns the voice you've been hearing."

I approached him cautiously, finding myself fearful of this mortal man that knew things he shouldn't have known. "What voices?" I asked using a deep, interrogating tone. I tried to see his eyes that were hiding behind dark sunglasses and couldn't.

"You know exactly what I am talking about," he said, turning to me. "Last night as I slept, I was approached by a young man. He identified himself as Peter and he told me he knows you personally, that he's been trying to contact you. He needs you, but you've been ignoring his plea for help. He came to me out of desperation, asking me to send you to him."

I reached out and pulled his sunglasses away. Both eye sockets were empty. He snatched his glasses from my hand and pushed them up the bridge of his nose, covering the holes. "You didn't see anything, old man. You haven't eyes to see with."

He shook his head back and forth. "Of course I cannot see, Spirit.

I already established that. How I met this Peter was through a dream just like I dreamt about you becoming a God. But let's try and not make sense of that. In time, I promise, it will all make perfect sense to you."

"Why do you insist on being so enigmatic, old man? Why not just get to the point of things?"

"My name is Raymond, Spirit, and I tell you everything exactly as I feel I should."

I quietly observed Raymond and began to feel sorry for him. He looked so helpless and frail in his blindness and old age. Why had I felt fear of him earlier? My fear was unwarranted, ridiculous in fact. I could've taken anything I wanted from him, but he had nothing to offer. I, on the other hand had something to offer him. I wanted to make him strong, return his sight and change him into a Spirit. I was confident he would make a good one. His insight was great.

"I can change you, Raymond," I said. "I can give you sight and give you eternal life. All you've got to do is tell me you want it and I'll give it to you."

"No, Spirit. I am happy with myself and the life I lead. Though I am lonely at times, my life is full. I accept my death, but not prematurely. I am not a quitter."

"I admire your strength," I said, not seeing his handicap anymore. Where he lacked in some things, he made up for it in other places. "That's why I didn't just kill you. If you change your mind just tell me, I'll grant you my offer. Now, tell me where I can find this boy named Peter."

When Raymond told me where to go, I dashed through the spirit realm and went directly to Peter's house. I entered through a locked back door and found myself in a cramped hallway that split off in two directions. To the left of me was a door locked from the opposite side I stood, and straight ahead was a door that allowed access to a basement apartment.

I stepped through the door in front of me and descended a flight of weakening steps. At the bottom, I stood in a kitchen that was immaculately clean excluding a pot of beans that were left to crust on the stovetop. To the right from where I stood was a living room/bedroom combo. I drifted into the room and saw a young man sitting on a loveseat couch that was crammed between a bed and wall. He was watching television while munching on chips and sipping soda.

I stood silent, watching the young man for a while. I decided to test him. I moved through him, sat beside him on the couch and all the while I tried to figure why he too was missing his aura like Raymond was. "Peter," I whispered into his ear and he jumped off the couch. His soda fell from the arm of the couch and splashed on the carpet and entertainment center. The bag of chips flew off his lap and the entire contents of the bag spilled out on the floor. He revolved frantically, searching the room with widened eyes.

"Who's there?" he called out, mashing the chips underfoot.

I quickly fizzled into the physical realm and pushed Peter on the couch and reentered the spirit realm.

"Spirit?" he sought, looking all around himself, unable to see where I'd gone.

"Why have you summoned me?" I asked as I zoomed all around him.

"Spirit? Travis? I can't see you. Show yourself."

I fizzled partially in, holding a near transparent state as I hovered over him.

"Travis," he said with relief. "It has been so long since I've seen you, my friend. I've been lost without you." He stood from the couch and nervously smiled, and said, "It is Eidolon."

"Eidolon?" I said, and stepped completely inside the physical realm. It had been so long since I spoke his name, thought of the soul that abruptly left me. "How in the world did you get inside that body?"

"The owner of this body was toying with a tool that connects his realm to ours. When the opening was created, I stepped through. I wanted to see what it would be like to be human again. But, when I had enough and wanted out, I realized I couldn't get out."

"You know the rules," I scolded. "And you knowingly broke them."

"But it gets worse, Spirit. When I entered this body, its owner remained inside. There are two of us in here and we've been battling for control. When I crossed over, I carried a connection to the spirit realm and when I would sleep, I could see things that were happening in the world. I saw human souls being stolen. It hurts the people, Spirit; I've felt their pain, battled their fear. That's why I've been calling you and another like you. Julius, I believe. But I don't know if he's heard my call."

"Eidolon," I said, things suddenly beginning to clear. "Do you realize you would call me just before these attacks would occur? You need to tell me when this is going to happen next so I can put a stop to it."

"I need to sleep to see, Spirit. It's the only way."

"Very well, Eidolon, sleep then. I'll wait here until you wake."

I fizzled into the spirit realm and remained within the room. It wasn't long before Eidolon found rest and perceived the theft of more human souls. In his sleep he cried out, kicked, and grabbed the sheets as if battling the wrongdoer. I fizzled in and shook him until he woke.

"It was terrible," he said. He was sweating and panting heavily, his concern real. "I saw a church filled with people of all ages. A shrouded man ran from person to person, forcefully pulling their souls from body. He was much faster than their eyes could see. No one could escape him, Spirit!"

After Eidolon named the location, I entered the spirit realm with my adrenaline pumping and heart racing. I journeyed hastily to the Manhattan Catholic Church, knowing my early arrival could save hundreds of lives, and ultimately, their souls.

I arrived at the church and the early morning worshippers were filing through the open doors. Everyone had been dressed nicely. The women wore dresses and the men wore suits with ties. It had been the most pleasant Sunday I could remember since the early days of summer. An unseasonably warm breeze blew gently, fooling all into believing this was going to be a pleasant day. I could only hope to help them.

I figured it best if I were on the physical realm acting as if I were a human that was there to observe the services. I searched for a secluded area behind the church where I would be able to gather some energy so I could animate myself once again. Once the body I imagined had been complete, I had to give myself the proper attire to assure I blended in perfectly. I chose black deck shoes, dark gray slacks, and a white button down shirt with a tan sports jacket. I casually walked to the entranceway of the church and headed inside like I were a regular. A young man and woman no older than twenty years stood inside the doorway and greeted the people that arrived for the service. Their auras were as bright as their welcome.

Upon entering the church, I quickly decided on a seat I thought was best for me to occupy. There were three separate rows, each row consisting of approximately thirty pews. The service was packed and my options for seating were limited. I'd chosen a seat at the rear of the church next to the center isle. The best possible place I could be, I figured, if swift action was needed.

A soothing organ began humming a light tune that was followed by a chorus of voices that consisted of both men and women. I looked up and behind me and noted there was a balcony filled with the members of the churches' choir. As soon as the song came to a melodic halt, a priest dressed in a white alb and chasuble with a white and gold stole dangling loosely around his neck came to the pulpit and warmly welcomed everyone attending the mass. He immediately broke into his planned speeches concerning Christ, taking passages directly from the Bible and quoting them. The room was hushed all except the few people clearing their throats or the restless child that wouldn't sit still. The priests speech continued on as I scanned the physical realm for the slightest abnormality. My eyesight being so sensitive I could see any disturbances in the physical realms very fabric. When Spirit's or other entities cross over from the spirit realm, their transition sends a noticeable ripple through the air, visible only to the trained eye.

I patiently waited and continued to observe, hoping Eidolon's vision was to be. Knowing for sure if the soul stealer was to strike, I would be the one to stop him and end his reign of terror.

The priest stepped away from the pulpit and sat. The organist began playing a soothing tone and the choir joined in. Some members of the church sang along, and others mouthed the words or remained completely quiet. No one judged. Suddenly the organ stopped playing, and then the singing from the choir. The attending members waited patiently for the priest's direction. He stood and looked to the balcony. He began walking down the center aisle and everyone followed him with their eyes. They looked where he was looking.

The soul-stealer jumped from the balcony and into the aisle, charged the priest and grabbed hold of his soul. "I'm sorry Father," he said, and tore the soul from the body.

The priest's body fell to the floor, lifeless and empty of its separated soul. The people around me began to panic, and everyone started shouting, scrambling for the exit. The smaller and elderly were being trampled in the consuming chaos.

I jumped from my seat and charged down the aisle after the soul-stealer. Finally realizing who it was I was after, I shouted so loud my throat burned and the back of my head buzzed. "Sear!" I said, my anger intense.

He looked to me with crying eyes and disbelief. "No," he moaned, "not you, not yet!"

He ran from me and began snatching more souls from their bodies. Without notice to my keen senses, a hand poked through the fabric of the physical realm from the spirit side, grabbed hold of Sear and pulled him through. I threw the energy I held to make my body and stepped into the spirit realm. Julius was holding Sear on the ground by his shoulders and he was violently shaking him, shouting, "What have you done!"

The few souls Sear was able to pull from their bodies stood around and watched us in horror; I couldn't imagine their confusion. One second they were sitting in church enjoying the service, and the next second they were inside the barren spirit realm standing in the shoes of a foreign body. They didn't need to see any of this. I went to them and comforted them as best I could while I escorted them to the light. I offered no explanation while doing so; the shock of the soul-stealers identity still hadn't left me.

As I approached Julius, he pulled Sear to his feet and shook him. "Tell him," Julius said to Sear. "Tell the Spirit what you told me while he was gone!"

"All of this is your fault, Spirit," he condemned, peering at me with eyes of a man possessed. His anger polished by sweat and tightly scrunched brows. He would've struck me if he could get away with it. But, he wouldn't and he knew that.

His accusation, the way he looked at me, his entire demeanor infuriated me. "My fault!" I retorted. I looked to Julius and his face displayed the red gooey wound I'd inflicted with the Surefire fish. Julius didn't seem to notice it anymore. He looked to Sear and shook him again. Sear's arms flailed like a helpless child's would in his father's disciplining hold.

"Your obsession with the old ways has made you delusional! You've been interfering with the natural cycle of life and death, Sear. You know the rules a celestial must follow. It is written if a crime is committed against humanity by a serving celestial, punishment for his neglect is eternity in the Lake of Fire. I would take you there right now and ease you into the burning lava myself, but only God can decide what your punishment will be!"

"God?" Sear erupted; the sweat ran down his face and dripped from his chin. "Our God is the one you both helped Navarro destroy! Can't you see what you and the others have done? But, it isn't too late. Turn away from the Devil now and beg for forgiveness. Judgment day is upon us, and when it's bestowed on you, you don't want to be held responsible for the terrible things you've done!"

Julius laughed and began mocking Sear. "Your supposed 'God' has been destroyed. You've been killing in the wrong name. Therefore, I think it is you who better start praying."

"If you believe our God has been destroyed by Navarro then you're both a bigger fool than I originally thought. He's very much alive and He's watching us play this foolish game with the Devil to see where we stand!"

"You can be such the fool," I said with contempt. Now I'd thought to strike him, maybe the blow would knock some sense into his head. "He was an evil God and He sent forth His godly wrath to punish His own creations. His annihilation and replacing was necessary."

"You, Travis," Sear spat, "have been corrupted by the Devil and it's eating out your insides. Slowly I've seen you becoming more and more like a monster. One Devil holds and corrupts human souls in a false Heaven, and another runs rampant on the earth, spreading his madness with oblivious obedience."

"I spread madness? It is you who is mad enough to kill humans and steal their souls for . . ."

"You damn Spirits are taking human souls and happily handing them over to the Devil!" Sear shouted and began to cry. "I've been gathering the people to keep them from you two until the day God returns to judge us. You can bring me before the Devil and I'll tell him the same thing I've told you two, I don't care. I know he won't punish me for it. No. He'll embrace me and all the chaotic things I've done because he loves turmoil and terror. My reasoning is beyond his understanding. He is simple minded, can't you see this? I fear no evil and I'll stand before him proud of my God. I'll let him know he can't infiltrate my mind as he's done to the rest of you. My faith will never break!"

Julius rolled his eyes and spoke with harmless animosity. "You are merely a simple killer, Sear."

"I am a believer, Julius. A believer that hasn't for one moment doubted his God."

I snickered. "He is a stubborn fool, Julius. Let's take him to God."

Together Julius and I brought Sear into the light. The Seraph Angel, Nature, awaited our arrival at the end of the light and was cheerful with welcome.

"Demon bitch!" Sear muttered and looked away from her.

"Spirit?" she questioned, her eyes bouncing between Julius and myself.

Businesslike, I said, "We need to see God, Nature. The matter is a pressing one. Will you take us to Him?"

"Follow me," she directed, bringing us inside Heaven. Souls were standing all around, some in the streets, others stretched out on the lawns of the giant mansions, and others propped themselves on the stoops. Everyone seemed relaxed and carefree.

"Travis! Julius!" a voice called from the distance, muffled and unfamiliar. Everyone around stood and looked down the street paved with gold. The souls all began to point and whisper to one another as Navarro walked past them and came before Julius and me. "I was just informed that you two had arrived. I hope I didn't keep you waiting."

Julius gave a throaty chuckle, and said, "The devil, huh, Sear?"

Navarro looked to Julius, and then to Sear. Wheels were turning. "Is something wrong?" he asked.

Julius went down to one knee and bowed his head. "It seems we have a situation that is in need of your personal attention, my lord."

Navarro seemed uncomfortable with Julius's formalities. He worked on pulling him to his feet, and said, "Please, Spirit, stand up. All those in this domain are considered equals."

Navarro called Divination forward, and as a group we entered a mansion at the begging of the hill. It was an unoccupied home still undergoing renovations. Gathering inside the spacious living room, I told Navarro in explicit detail about Sear's actions and why we'd brought him to Heaven. Navarro seemed disappointed by Sears' activities, hurt almost. Slowly he knelt before Sear and settled when he was eye to eye with him. He pursed his lips and pleaded with his eyes before he said, "Is this true, Sear, is this what you've done?"

Sear narrowed his gaze and deepened his voice, not attempting to hide his resentment. "I won't allow you to intimidate me, you devil! I know your day is coming and when it does your fallacious empire is going to crumble."

"Do these people look like they are suffering?" Navarro asked, his tone soft. "Isn't that what the Devil does—torture people. Corrupt them? You've done a terrible thing, Sear. I cannot allow you to leave here."

"Do to me as you must, beast! I don't fear you and you can't break my faith."

"I'm not looking to break your faith, Sear, I'm looking to nurture it. In time you will see the error of your ways and in your judgment of me." He turned to Divination and said, "Please, bring me Osiris."

241

"I don't fear his corrupted soul either," Sear interjected madly.

Divination parted and returned with Osiris just before the silence within the mansion became uncomforting. Osiris stood before Sear and studied him inertly. "What have you done?" he finally asked. Genuine compassion filled his eyes and surrounded him like a pleasant aroma. He reached for Sear's hand.

"Don't you touch me!" Sear barked and spittle flew from his mouth. He stepped away from Osiris, and said, "You've betrayed God like all the others have and that makes you no better than any one of them."

Osiris shook his head in dispute. "It is good here, Sear, you'll see."

"It saddens me to see how you've been tainted by lies that roll from the Devil's mouth. It seems it is so easy for him to corrupt, but near impossible for me to show everyone the truth." Sear turned to Navarro, and said, "I warn you, if you've used trickery on their minds to have them accept your lies, then I'll plead with the lord to have you burn!"

Osiris faced Navarro. "We will tend to him, my lord."

"Very well," Navarro agreed, the disappointment still noticeable within his voice. He looked to Julius and me. "I want to thank you both for rectifying Sear's unacceptable behavior. His anger and confusion seems deeply rooted. I'm sure he will learn to trust in my dream and me."

Navarro reached and touched Julius's face. "Given time," he concluded, and a dull spark popped and dazzled me, but frightened Julius. He backed away and palmed his face, his melted flesh healed just like that.

Navarro escorted us out of the mansion and brought us before Heaven's exit. Saying our farewells, Julius and I descended towards the surface, talking in depth about the future of the Spirit's.

Chapter 39

Julius and I hovered between Heaven and Earth. We lovingly admired the world below us that had begun a brand new day.

"Just look at the beautiful world on which we live," he said. "Isn't it amazing the way everything fits together so perfectly?"

I presumed that was a rhetorical question. I liked the profundity of the statement and considered it. Yes, it was a beautiful world, nearly perfect. I felt a sudden closeness to Julius. I admired his strength and wit. He was deep and passionate. These components seemed to be lost to almost every soul I'd encountered throughout the years. He would make a great ally, but an even better friend. "I'm sorry for doubting your pureness, Julius. I'm especially sorry for hurting you."

He smiled softly, and said, "I don't hold any bitterness for what happened between us. Now that we know we're on the same side, we need to work together. Come with me, Travis, I have something I want to share with you."

He dove downwards and I followed. I was led to a fast moving river that was exceptionally wide. We entered the physical realm and traveled on the rocky surface beside the rivers edge. The further upriver we trekked, the larger the rocks underfoot became. Soon we were jumping from boulder to boulder.

Julius paused, his legs spread as he straddled two boulders with a slight gap between them. "We're here," he said.

I stopped and looked up river, down river, and all around. I looked back to Julius. "Where exactly is here, Julius? I don't see anything."

He smiled. "That's because you're looking for something extraordinary. See where that stream branches off from the mighty river?"

I looked a few yards upriver and saw it. "Yes," I said.

"Follow its route with your eyes and see where it goes."

"It disappears underneath the boulders we're standing on," I told.

"It does, Spirit. Now look between the crack of the boulders I'm standing on."

I crouched and peered between the boulders. I saw the stream of water pooled beneath the rocks, the center swirled as if it were draining. I stood, slapped my hands clean and brushed my knees. "I don't see the significance."

"That's a sinkhole, Spirit, an indication that caves have been formed below. I have more to share with you. Come."

He stepped back into the spirit realm and I followed, interested in what he was showing me. He dropped through the boulders and I continued to mimic his every move. Beneath the rocks, a small hole no larger than a baseball drained the pool of water. The deeper into the earth we descended, the larger the drain hole became. Water steadily streamed down the limestone wall. We continued our descent.

Soon we arrived inside an underground cave that was eerily beautiful. Cave deposits called stalactites hung like icicles from the ceiling. Other formations called stalagmites extended upwards from the caves floor. Some of the stalactites and stalagmites joined together forming a pillar. Though the cave was completely dark, I could see the formations varied in color from translucent white to a dusky red and brown.

"I discovered this cave over 5,000 years ago right after I began to play my part as a Spirit," Julius said. "Back then this cave wasn't quite so large and the limestone formations weren't so big. There are many more labyrinths than this one, Travis. They are at all different depths below us. But I find I mainly use this one and the one just below it."

I pointed to the heavy stream of water that ran down the wall, and asked, "The water. Where does it go?"

"It continues to run down the wall and drains into an underground stream that flows like the river above us. It's about 500 feet below us. You know, there are fish in the stream that are blind."

"Just like Raymond," I muttered.

"Who?"

"Never mind."

Julius walked into the labyrinth and with his back to me, he placed his hands on something I couldn't see, and said, "This is the most elegant one down here, Travis."

I walked to him and stopped when I was beside him. I examined the rock formation he was so proud of. It was a rare twisted flowerlike stalactite known as a helictite. "It is the prettiest one, Julius. I agree with you."

He turned his head and looked at me. I felt his eyes burning the side of my face. I purposely kept my gaze from him and continued to examine the odd formation.

"Spirit?" he said with gentle kindness.

I couldn't rightfully withhold my gaze from him. I respectively turned to meet his eyes, and said, "Yes, Julius?"

"Let us resurrect the other Spirits."

I shook my head in disapproval, remembering the warning I received when I bit the fruit I'd taken from the Tree of Knowledge.

"They deserve to be freed, Travis," Julius continued with his plea, his compassion remaining.

"No, Julius, we can't do that," I said, finding it hard to deny his request. "It's not a good idea."

"Why?"

"They're unruly and unpredictable. They present a danger to the balance that has finally been brought to the spirit realm."

Julius pet the rock formation and thought in silence. He said, "Don't you remember what it was like when you were in limbo?"

"Yes," I said, my memory of it still fresh. "It was like being buried alive with full awareness of the world around me."

"It was a helpless feeling for me."

"Me too," I said, remembering. "I so desperately wanted someone to wake me."

Julius bowed his head, and said, "Believe me, I know the feeling." He looked me in the eyes, and said, "Do you feel you have the right to condemn the other Spirits to imprisonment because you feel they're going to disrupt this balance you speak of? Once their usefulness was gone you had them put to rest so they'd be out of the way. I see no justification in your reasoning, Spirit."

I wrestled with the unsettling feeling about my decision to leave them in a restful state. Was it wrong? There was a strong possibility. Julius's point was strong, and besides, it was the fruit that told me Julius was the one responsible for separating the human souls from their bodies and it was wrong then. Was it possible it could've been wrong a second time? This was silly thinking, why should I've even bothered worrying about should and could? If I were to leave the Spirits at rest there would be no way for them to foul things up; I couldn't allow it. I said, "Having the Spirits resurrected could cause some serious problems, Julius. They are an undisciplined bunch and they wield too much power for having such bad qualities. I'm strongly opposed to this."

"We've all been mistreated," Julius said, sounding sympathetic. "Our human lives were stolen from us and we were thrust into a role we wanted no part of. No matter what we do, we can't change what we've been turned into. We are like this forever, and forever is a long time to be locked away because someone doesn't like what you are or what you could be. Free them, Spirit. They deserve that much for all the suffering they've had to endure."

Again, a well thought out point designed to make me think. He was prepared. I considered his words and couldn't deny the validity of his argument; all his points were legitimate, no holes. I wasn't happy about having to free the Spirits, but it was only right no matter how wrong the fruit said it was. I told Julius where he could find the Spirits' bones and immediately following, I regretted having done so.

"Once I resurrect them, Travis, I'll return here with you so we can all reunite. Build a society together."

I shook my head in disfavor and sighed heavily. "I don't want to be a part of your coven," I said. "I saw tragedy following their return when I tasted the fruit from the Tree of Knowledge. If you resurrect them, you're going to have to accept responsibility for their actions."

"You've bitten the fruit, Travis? But it is forbidden!"

"It was necessary and it's already done."

"You're going to turn your back on those who're just like you because a fruit told you so? You said it yourself that God was corrupted. Maybe His fruit is too! What type of reasoning is this?"

Condescending. Belittling. I felt the fuel of anger coursing through my veins as his condemnatory words reverberated off the labyrinth walls. I thought of silencing his unnecessary outburst with force unseen to him before, but I reminded myself he was an ally and I managed to maintain my self-control. I lashed back only with words by saying, "I've told you they are going to be trouble; don't underestimate the insight the fruit has! I've been kind enough to tell you where their bones have been buried. Let's leave it at that." I ascended, truly wanting no part of the madness he was about to unleash on the world.

"I'm sure they'll all be disappointed to hear you've decided to separate yourself from them!" Julius shouted.

That statement I would also ignore.

Chapter 40

Stepping through the void inside the train tunnel, I entered Chova, landing inside the forest in the small clearing. I journeyed the familiar path through the forest and made my way to the House of Chova while I contemplated the consequences of Julius waking the Spirits I'd put to rest. The outcome of this event was obvious to me: the fruit had given me a direct warning not to allow the Spirits to be resurrected and I blatantly ignored it. Tragedy would strike, I was completely confident of this, but was unsure of what exactly would happen and when. How could one prepare themselves for something unknown?

"You!" Paige shrieked from the darkness of the hallway as I emerged from the cover of the forest. She marched out of the House with her fists clenched, her chin down and her eyes narrowed. Her physical appearance improved, changing from an old frail woman with droopy stained skin to a woman with all the beauties associated with youth. She stepped before me, pulled her hand back and swiped it across my cheek, rattling my head violently. "What have you done to me, demon!"

I rubbed the side of my face; the stinging proved her strength had been enhanced as well. That was good, it meant the Spirit seed worked. "I saved you from a slow agonizing death. I've restored your youth and have given you a great gift of strength and magic."

She slapped me a second time, the blow numbing the side of my face. "That's just part of your manipulation," she screeched. "I don't know if any of this is even real. But I do know I don't fear you!" She shoved me.

Her unexpected attack stumbled me. I fixed my garments and returned to her. I shoved her back harder than she did me and she toppled over. "After you calm yourself," I growled, "we can talk. Until then be sure to stay away from me." I turned away from her and paused to say, "I also want you to quit calling me demon!"

I left her on the ground and walked into the House, up the spiral stairs and onto the balcony. I rested my forearms on the railing and Paige stood below me, looking upwards, shouting threats and carrying on how I was a demon. I walked to the adjoining hallway and walked into the room on the left. I opened a door in the back of the room and climbed a second long spiraling staircase that was inside one of the towers.

At the top of the staircase, I popped open a hatch on the ceiling and climbed through. I stood and looked over Chova's entire landscape from the towers crown. It looked as if I were as high up as the mountaintop. The trees below me appeared like twigs I could crush if I were to step from the tower.

Concentrating on the distant rumbling sound of the waterfall, the serene atmosphere pulled me in and began to calm me. Things weren't so bad.

"Where the hell are you, demon bastard!" Paige shouted from somewhere within the House. Her voice was shrilling and constant as she stomped around aimlessly searching for me. I would never escape her fury unless I left the area for a while.

I left the tower and returned to the main floor of the House where she sat with her back against the wall.

"What have you done to me, demon?" she asked without looking up from her lap.

"I told you already: I saved you from rotting away in that damn bed. Your family wrote you off as being dead for years. You were all alone in the world and you were labeled a diseased nutcase. You should be thanking me for what I've done for you, not condemning me. I've allowed you to become something better than you could've ever been. You're strong, you have heightened senses and you'll never know what it is like to suffer physically again."

Her eyes slowly moved to me, and she said, "You've tormented me for years, damn you! You sent your damn demons to try and break my faith. Day after day I resisted you and your corrupt suggestions, you devil bastard!"

"Stop it, Paige! I love you and when you talk like this it scares me to death. I can only wonder if your transformation is strictly physical. Tell me, has your mind improved at all? I just want things to be the way they used to be before I left for the war!"

"You want me to love you, a demon? My love was for a compassionate man that was a devoted honorable husband that has long ago passed into the Heaven's. You are nothing but a poor imitation that hides behind a mask. I can see through your wicked lies. I'm leaving here, demon, I'm going to find my way into Heaven and you're to stay out of my way!"

She stood and walked out of the House without uttering another word or brushing me with a glance. I knew she was really leaving and there was nothing I could do short of battling her to convince her to stay with me: the demon from her dreams. I wouldn't do that. My son was right—his mother was deranged.

I waited inside the House to give her sufficient time to leave. Her parting didn't bother me half as much as her accusations that I was a demon. Why couldn't she see me for who I really was? It really didn't matter I suppose. I had an eternity to convince her otherwise.

When enough time elapsed, I exited the House and entered the thick forest to the left of the House. There, camouflaged within a cluster of bushes was the pitch-black cave that was the only exit out of Chova. I entered the cave and was dropped inside the subway system. I quickly ascended and journeyed swiftly to the den Eidolon was nestled in.

Nighttime had fallen on the physical realm and most humans lay on their soft beds to take a journey into the mysterious world of dreams. The room in which Eidolon occupied was dark and quiet. I hovered over his resting body and looked down on him, serene and unaware, completely vulnerable to me. I would care for him, though, because he was all I had.

I stepped into the physical realm and sat on the bed beside him. I lightly shook him and requested he wake.

"Huh," he mumbled with bad breath and unfocused eyes.

"The soul-stealer is gone and I've returned for you. Are you ready to leave that body now?"

He quickly sat up. "Yes, Spirit, more than you could ever know!"

"Very well," I said. "Lay back down and lay completely flat and still. When I begin to pull you from the body, give me a hand by trying to step out."

Eidolon laid himself flat and closed his eyes. His trust was wholesome and for that he would be rewarded handsomely. I immediately fizzled into the spirit realm and went to work. I stuck my arm inside the body and grabbed onto something that struggled against my hold. I released it knowing I had the wrong soul and continued to search for Eidolon. My hand was grabbed and pulled as Eidolon struggled to free himself from the body he was trapped in. I leaned back and gave a mighty tug. Eidolon slid out of the body and slumped to the ground limp and exhausted.

"How are you fairing," I inquired, leaned down and locked my arms beneath his armpits. I pulled him off the floor and allowed him to hold me until he could stand on his own.

"I'm weak," he said, huffing and puffing.

I eased him down to allow him a few moments rest. I backed away and watched him the way a father would his own son. I knew he'd make a great Spirit, and I would be able to use the powers he would gain from the transformation; he would be willing to work with me because I was his teacher. "You've done something terribly wrong," I scolded. "Have you learned anything?"

"I have learned more than I could ever begin to tell you. What will happen to the boy?"

I showed a gentle smile and looked to the senseless boy lying in the bed. I looked back to Eidolon then sat on the floor across from him, and said, "The boy will be just fine. His will to live is strong and his life aura is shining bright. He'll suffer some memory loss; all recollection of his possession will be permanently forgotten."

A strong ally to stand against the Spirits is what I needed. With a new plan entering my mind, I said, "Do you wish to be strong, like me?"

Eidolon rolled his eyes, and said, "I could only dream of such a thing, Spirit. Why tease me with such a question?"

Inwardly I smiled because I knew my plan would work perfectly.

We stood and together we left the house. "How is Amanda?" he asked.

"She is gone forever," I said plainly. "Navarro is God now and I am in total control of the spirit realm."

He stopped abruptly. He began to laugh so I turned and faced him. His laugh stopped abruptly, and he waved his hand at me. "Yeah, okay, Spirit, but that's not funny."

I drifted towards Chova and mustered a serious tone. "Follow me," I said, and along the way I told him of the events that unfolded from the day of his disappearance until the very moment of his return.

Arriving inside Chova, we exited the forest and entered the House. To my disbelief, Amanda was on the floor, squirming in agony, her self-inflicted wound exposed and bleeding lightly. All questions aside, I dashed to where she lay and dropped to my knees. "Who did this to you?" I asked, my focus knowingly turning to the newly resurrected Spirits. With thoughts of revenge, my eyes brushed over her wound and noticed the missing flesh and bone had begun to reform and repair itself. I knew when Osiris plunged the seed into her chest, it had begun to transform her. This also meant before she made it through the light, she'd been pulled back into her bones when Alex buried her body. Thank God I had her back.

Amanda gurgled as she tried to say something.

"Try and be still," I said and lightly kissed her forehead. "I will care for you this time, I promise."

Amanda continued to thrash and I knew I would have to put her to rest to give her temporary relief of the pain. I began a frantic search of the House for the whereabouts of her bones. "What is going on?" Eidolon asked, following me from room to room. I soon gave up my search, realizing her bones weren't left behind.

"Spirit, answer me! Who did this to her?"

I stopped, turned to him, clenched my fists and gritted my teeth. "Look at her, Eidolon! Ask me nothing more because that's all I know!"

He covered both his ears with his hands and pleaded, "I can't take her cries anymore, Spirit! Do something for her!"

I stomped my foot and grabbed my own hair. "Can't you keep quiet! I can't think straight with her cries and your complaining!" I plunged my fist into my own chest and removed a seed. I clenched it tightly in my hand and plunged it into Eidolon's chest. His eyes opened wide and he looked down at the hand buried deep within his chest. I released the seed inside him and withdrew my hand. His knees buckled and he fell to the floor. I watched him for a moment and saw the affects of the seed beginning to wreak havoc on his bodily functions. He convulsed and foamed from the mouth, his eyes remaining open and aware, staring someplace beyond me. I turned to Amanda, pulled another seed from my chest and plunged it into hers. I released the seed, withdrew my hand, and took a step away. She immediately began to calm as the seed started to benumb her.

I looked back to Eidolon and imagined him overwhelming me with praise for the gift I'd given him. But I couldn't enjoy the idyllic thoughts of my family's adoration for my thoughtfulness for long. The faint sounds of branches snapping within the forest caught my attention and pulled me from my reverie. I darted from the House prepared to attack if necessary. The satchel containing Amanda's bones were left on the steps just outside the House's entrance. Seeing no one around, I sat on the steps and opened the tied cloth bag. I removed all of its contents and examined each piece with special care, twirling them in my hand so I could see details. The remnants of her suicide were evident from the shattered skull bone and the broken off bits and pieces that lay like dust on the bottom of the bag. Maybe, I believed, this was a tragedy that could have a good ending.

I placed her bones back inside the sack and tied off its end. I stood and entered the House again. I walked over to Amanda and placed the satchel on the floor next to her and took her hand into my own. I said, "You're going to go to sleep for a while. I'll come for you again, soon. I promise, things will be much better when you wake."

I kissed her gently and saw tears welling in her eyes.

"Don't you fear, Amanda. You're strong now, but will be stronger when you wake."

I grabbed the satchel and left Chova to bury her bones where she couldn't ever be found.

I've contemplated telling you this, but your loyalty has earned my trust. I buried her bones traditionally six feet down inside the plot that was originally intended for Paige and me.

Chapter 41

After giving Amanda's bones a traditional burial, I headed straight to Julius's labyrinth with the intention of confronting him and all the Spirits. My anger was powerful but caged perfectly; they would never suspect the fury I would unleash to punish the guilty. Amanda's suffering had to be avenged.

When I arrived at the giant boulders beside the stream, I descended through the cracks in the rocks. I floated down through the slim passageway that was formed by the trickling water, and soon I came into the giant labyrinth fancied with limestone formations. Julius was at the caves far end watching me approach without concern to my coming. Perfect.

"I told you," I said, thrusting my plan into motion, "that resurrecting those Spirits meant trouble. Which one was it?" My voice was loud, believably irate, amplified by the hollow interior.

Julius stood upright, and said, "What are you talking about, Spirit?" I sensed certain sharpness in his tone.

"Amanda has been resurrected and left inside the House of Chova," I said being sure to keep the hostile tone to my voice. My plan was going to be easy to carry out knowing what they'd done to her. All I had to do was stay focused, not lose my head until I found out who did that to her. "She suffered terribly, her wounds were raw and exposed. She laid alone on that cold hard floor for hours without reason as to why this was happening to her. But, thankfully, while I was comforting her, someone came and left quickly, leaving her bones on the doorstep to the House. At least I could put her to rest and end her suffering."

"I really don't know what you're talking about, Travis. As far as I know all the Spirits have been here. Have you come here to divert attention from yourself? It is you who needs to be questioned!"

"There is nothing to question me about, Julius."

He chuckled and brushed his nose. "I'm not trying to take anything away from what you're saying about Amanda, Spirit, but we've been watching you. We all saw what you did to the woman that was once your wife."

"Is my wife," I said indefinitely.

"Was, Travis. You've taken a human life. You've murdered a human and turned them into a Spirit. That is against the rules."

"Whose rules, Julius? They are not my rules and I don't agree with them, therefore, I won't follow them. I took her life out of mercy, I changed her out of love!"

"No, Spirit, you didn't change her for any of the reasons you claim, at least not entirely. You changed her to keep her from leaving our plane of existence. You did this for your own selfish reasons." Julius thrust his finger into my face. Veins bulged from his neck as his voice grew deafeningly loud. "But the point here is that you've taken a human life prematurely. You've interfered in the natural balance of life and death, and that, my friend, is breaking the rules."

All the Spirits I had Nature put to rest began coming through the caves' floor and they gathered around Julius. With everyone staring at me with chastising faces of hardened stone, I deceitfully submitted to their castigation by bowing my head. Shamefully, I said, "You may be right, Julius. I did break the rules and I'm sorry for that. I've since reconsidered my decision to not be a part of the Spirit coven. I'm lonely without you and I need your help."

Julius tried looking into my eyes, but I purposely hung my head and kept my chin tight against my chest. "Spirit," he whispered. "Look at me so we can talk about this." I remained still, acting ashamed, hurt and in need of comfort. He lightly placed his pointer finger underneath my chin and guided my head up.

I closed my eyes. "There is nothing to talk about, Julius," I said. "I feel the fool for the way I've been acting lately. I've also been ashamed, too proud to come here and tell you I need you."

"Nonsense, Spirit," Julius said. "You know you are always welcome here. We are all grateful for you having awoken us. You've given us all a chance to pursue our own dreams."

The Spirit named Kane stepped forward and hugged me. Through my touch I quickly read his mind and saw he had no knowledge of Amanda's resurrection before my say so.

"Thank you, Kane," I said and brushed tears from my eyes.

"Divination spoke highly of you, Spirit, and now I know why. Thank you for allowing Julius to wake us," he said, and stepped away.

All the Spirits came forward and embraced me in the same manner, welcoming me to their coven. First Zacharius, then John, and lastly Constantine came to me. I saw their minds were all free of any knowledge of Amanda's resurrection. Germaine remained behind Julius and he stared blankly past me. I approached him and acted hesitant as I did so. Before him, I said, "Can we put the past behind us, Germaine? Can we start to build the Spirit coven into a family?"

Germaine licked his lips, snickered, and then looked to me. "You used us, Travis," he said. "Once you got what you needed us for you threw us away. I'm not finding it easy to forgive you for that."

"I knew most of you were feeling that way and I should've addressed the issue before now. I did that because I thought I was protecting mankind. I had terrible visions of a power struggle surrounding us Spirits when I took a bite from a piece of fruit I'd taken from the Tree of Knowledge. Ask Julius, I told him."

Germaine reeked with ire; he couldn't hide from me what I already knew. Confirmation was all I needed.

"It's true, Germaine," Julius said. "He did raise this concern with me."

I offered my hand to Germaine and he looked to Julius for direction. Julius nodded his approval and Adne placed his hand into my own. 2,300 years of experiences flooded my mind, all seen in under a second. All the information dizzied me, and I knew before I could act on what I saw, I needed to take a moment to gather myself. I hid my face in the cusp of my arm, and said, "Please, give me a moment, this is all so overwhelming."

I quickly ascended to the surface and entered the physical realm and sat on a boulder. I closed my eyes and drew in several deep breaths. Two visions inside Germaine's mind were predominant in my own: I saw an elder Spirit roaming the earth with an unknown purpose, his existence known by but a few. The other vision was Germaine resurrecting Amanda, acting alone and cursing me for the loss of his limbs and his undesired fate. Anger coursed through my veins, bringing me to my feet. I'd told Julius not to resurrect the Spirits, that I had foreseen trouble from them. He wouldn't listen to me. He had to argue his point, and convince me to change my mind. Now look what had happened. It was time to show the Spirits my warnings should be taken seriously.

I scanned the surrounding landscape and watched the rushing river angrily push its way through the formed passageway. I was the river, the Spirits were a foreign object falling onto its raging surface. I would carry them along, jiggle them about and pull them under and hold them there. My essence would fill their lungs and make them fear my power. The deep blue sky that was accentuated by the bright evergreen trees gave me a creative idea I would use to punish Germaine.

I went to the trees and broke off two even limbs. I stripped off all the small branches and entered the spirit realm with the limbs. Descending through the boulders, I returned to the labyrinth where all the Spirits still gathered. All watched me with curiosity.

"Not a word," I said. With tremendous force I embedded one of the limbs into the ground so it stood vertically. The Spirits began to whisper and I ignored them, continuing to work steadily. I tore some fabric from my cloak and tore several long strips from it. About a foot and a half from ground level, I tied the second limb across the vertical limb so it was parallel with the ground. I turned my attention to the Spirits, smacked my hands together, and said, "Who here can tell me what I've just made?"

Everyone studied the formation and considered its' design. "It's and upside-down cross," John answered.

"Exactly! Now, who can tell me what it represents?"

The Spirits looked to one another, unsure of what I was getting at. I said, "Come now, I'm sure someone here knows this."

"Evilness? Satanism?" said Germaine.

I chuckled heartily. "Ah, I find it funny you would be the one to know that. You're exactly right, Germaine." I acted quickly, draining the energy from every Spirit around but Germaine. "Ignore the strange sensation," I said, and one by one, the Spirit's dropped to the floor, awake but helpless.

I lunged forward and grabbed Germaine by his throat and slowly but steadily applied pressure. The ligaments in his neck popped, and Germaine struggled against my hold, but the energy I stole from the other Spirits gave me great strength—strength he could never overcome. "That girl had nothing to do with your anger towards me! She suffered terribly, and for that, I shall make you suffer!"

I pulled a lump of energy from Germaine's body and I watched a pathetic look of confusion cover his face. I released him from my hold and he limply fell to the ground. He passed out. I dragged Germaine's limp body to the cross and I lifted him up feet first. I tore another piece of fabric from my cloak and tied his ankles to the top portion of the vertical limb. I released him and he dangled upside-down. Breaking a small branch off the limb, I made several pegs. I picked up a large rock suitable enough to use as a hammer, and I lined a peg to the center of Germaine's feet, returned some energy into him and struck the peg with the rock.

"Argh!" he screamed, and flopped helplessly.

I struck the peg several more times and stopped once it was through both feet and clearly into the beam. I extended his right arm and tied it to the horizontal beam. I hammered a peg through the palm of his hand and into the limb. I untied his legs and arm and stepped back so all could see and fear me for what I'd done.

I slowly returned everyone's energy, and as I did, I said, "Julius.

Kane. John. Zacharius. Constantine. Let what you've seen here be a lesson to you all."

The sound of wood splintering echoed throughout the labyrinth. The Spirits all cried out in horror and seconds later, the wooden cross exploded into a million pieces. Body parts and wooden shards shot in every direction. Without delay, while shock controlled the surviving Spirits, I quickly retreated to Chova.

Part 4: Revelations

Introduction

Spirit

Hello again, old friend. I can call you friend, can't I? . . . I'm sorry, I don't mean to question your loyalty, it's just that things aren't like they used to be, and I guess neither am I, especially after my confrontation with the other Spirits.

One year, my time, has elapsed since I last contacted you. As I sit here all alone wallowing in self pity, day after day, I try and think of a way I can put the pieces of my shattered existence back together. But it seems that is something I may never be able to do, and it probably serves me right for all the things I've done. I've always wondered if my own self-torment is punishment enough for my actions.

The twist of fate my existence has taken is rather ironic. Me, Travis Winter, the Spirit of Independence, the savior of the human soul is now all alone and treated like a devil or maybe something even more evil than that. Whatever that may be.

Chapter 42

It was several months after the destruction of the Spirit named Germaine that I'd finally gathered enough courage to venture outside the Land of Chova. To my surprise, my existence continued on without divergence. I brought lost souls to the light and I frequently visited the intensive care unit in the hospital Paige stayed in to find these souls. I waited for those who would submit to their illness and step over to my side. From there I would guide them. I can remember sitting beside a bed where an elderly man slowly dying from old age laid. He'd slipped into a coma, and life support was keeping him alive. While I waited for him to die, I would think about Julius' coven. What was its function? Had they been following me since my attack, studying me, watching me from a safe distance until the perfect opportunity presented itself for them to unleash a full-scale attack?

My perception said yes. Could I blame myself for feeling that way? Look what I'd done to them. I'm sure it wouldn't just be forgotten without some sort of retaliation.

An elderly woman no longer in human form walked in the room, and said, "Mr.? He is suffering terribly, I can feel it," she said. "Kenny is my husband. I've been waiting for him to come to me for so long, and it doesn't appear he'll be coming today unless you can help me. His instinct to survive is too strong, his body just won't quit."

She began to sob. The woman was right. Her husband was ready for death and had been for days. I'd witnessed with my own eyes his soul trying to step free of the body that wasn't allowed to quit. He needed to be free of the pain he was in and be reunited with his loved one. I reached my arm into the weakened body and grabbed hold of his fragile soul, looked to the woman, and said, "I do this because I have mercy on your husband." And I tugged forcefully on the soul, ejecting it from the body.

The soul looked to his wife, and then to me. I could see the confusion in his eyes as he looked down to his belly and to the thread that kept him connected to the physical realm. I pushed Kenny back and the thread snapped, releasing him from the pains of the world. He tumbled on the floor landing safely on his backside, looking dizzily around.

I picked him up and slung him over my shoulder. I asked the woman to take my hand, and once she did, I ascended with them to the light. During our journey, the woman unremittingly thanked me for sparing her and her husband any further pain. I mustered up a soft caring tone, and said, "I have favor to ask you in return. Don't ever speak about me or what I've done for you. Tell Kenny what I've asked of you too."

The woman agreed, graciously shook my hand and escorted her still dazed husband into the light. I returned to the surface in complete elation for the gratifying task I'd completed.

Each and every day following this event I went to the hospital to take those who were suffering from their dying vessels. Some of the people would've lived for several more hours if I hadn't intervened, maybe even a few more days. That wasn't the issue to me. What was the issue was freeing them from the bodies that pained them; their suffering was unnecessary. If I felt the person was worthy, I would plunge the Spirit seed inside their chest to give them the taste of power they would never really come to understand. While they were transforming, I would carry them to a secluded place within the spirit realm and leave them. Souls that were weak in the heart and mind would be rejected the gift of the Spirit seed and would be sent through the light.

Reasons why I did this eluded me at the time, but when Julius and the others inside the coven found many of the souls I'd transformed into a Spirit, concern and fear forced Julius to take action against me. He gathered all the Spirits both old and new, and he had them search me out.

My day of judgment came when they caught up to me while I was inside Chova, standing on the balcony, pondering my next move. I looked down on an orderly mass that emerged from the forest and surrounded the House. I chuckled to myself; the assembly reminded me of a group of fear filled people coming to the castle to burn the beast that lived within.

"Spirit!" Julius shouted to me; he looked miniscule from where I stood. "We've come to take you to Navarro. Everyone here has shown concern over the things you've been doing."

He was confident. Cocky. I would return the attitude. "What is it I've done, Julius?"

"Look around me, Travis! It appears you've been busy interfering in the natural balance of life and death."

I scanned the large group of newly created Spirit's and I didn't recognize one of them. They were of all different ages and gender.

"Have you taught them well enough to battle me, Julius?" I asked. "That is what you've come here to do, isn't it?"

"If that is what we must do, Spirit. But I assure you we would rather you come willingly."

I leaned over the railing, and said, "Fear is for the weak, Julius. I fear not one of you! You know me well enough to say that, don't you, Eidolon?"

"Fear can keep someone smart," Eidolon said. "I feared you, Spirit. The day you pulled me from the body is the day I noticed there was something different about you, something eerie. That's why I left you and sought out the other Spirit from my vision."

"And you think it wise to pass judgment on me? I wonder how smart you'd be if the other Spirits weren't here!"

"Can't you see that is what our point is? You can't see what you've become. This type of behavior cannot be tolerated any longer. With or without a fight we are not leaving here unless you are with us. Navarro is expecting us to bring you."

"Very well, Eidolon, for you I'll go. Besides, I'm interested in knowing what Navarro has to say."

I left the balcony and descended the spiral staircase, exited the House and walked into the center of the group Julius assembled. "Let us go then so we can get this over with," I said.

My children escorted me out of Chova, and together, we ascended to the light.

Chapter 43

Before I arrived inside Heaven, advanced preparations had been made for my coming. All of Heaven's residents had been cleared out of the area, moved atop the hill. Navarro remained alone, kneeling on the altar and praying.

"Lord?" Julius said being careful to use a tone that wouldn't startle him.

Navarro said, "Amen," and stood. "Welcome home, Spirit," he said with delight.

"Chova is my home. This is your home," I muddled. His cheerful welcome didn't fool me.

"You helped it become what it is today, Spirit. Therefore, it is your home too."

Navarro turned to Julius, and said, "Take the others with you and return to your deeds. Spirit and I need to be left alone."

The Spirits quietly organized and departed. Once they were gone, Navarro said, "I'm concerned about you, Spirit. I would only hope if something were troubling you, you'd come and tell me."

"What could be troubling me?"

"I'm not really sure. But I have been made aware of your actions by the other Spirits, and because of the concern they've expressed, I've come to a decision that will deter you from ever harming another human. To do this, I know I must keep you here, inside Heaven."

I was outraged. How dare he think he could punish me like I were a child! I wouldn't stand for it! "The Spirits can pass judgment on me, that doesn't matter, but you, Navarro? You above anyone should know what it is like to be accused wrongly for something you're doing that you know is right."

"There is no right in what you've been doing, Spirit. Your premature involvement is interfering with people's lives."

"I end their suffering."

"You're murdering them as Sear did!"

"How dare you!"

"I should be saying that to you. You're depriving the people of what we've fought so hard for. Why?"

"There are people down there suffering terribly. I have mercy on them and will continue to so as long as there are nerve endings in their bodies."

"No, Spirit, you cannot do that. You're no longer free to roam the earth."

"And who are you to dictate to me what I can and cannot do, Navarro?"

I paused and waited for a response. His jaw dangled open and he said nothing. I began to walk backwards, moving towards Heaven's exit, and while doing so, I said, "That's exactly what I figured, nothing to say. But I have plenty to say about what you would be without me: a sniveling god without resilience. I gave you your life back and put the toughness inside. I made you a God! You show me your gratitude by condemning me?"

Navarro grinned. I saw right through it. He was nervous, unsure what his next move should be. He said, "You're being irrational, Spirit. Just look at the way you behave now."

"Freedom has been granted to the other Spirits and they're nothing but menaces. You wish to steal mine away? Do you think I'll kneel to you and accept your punishment and obey it? I'm leaving here because I refuse to argue about this any longer. Don't try and stop me, Navarro, and don't dare look to send your Spirits to Chova again. I'll take such a move as an act of war!"

I turned my back and briskly marched towards the exit when I'd suddenly become weak, sickly weak like the old man in the hospital bed had been. I warbled but caught my balance. I turned and faced Navarro, baring my teeth, as I roared with a tone so fierce it stung my lungs and split the air. "What do you think you're doing to me!"

Navarro shuddered, his fear unhidden behind that stupid grin. From somewhere deep inside my raging mind, an unseen force of destruction leapt. The very ground on which we stood trembled with a mighty earthquake powerful enough to sink continents into the seven seas. The ground split and shifted, wailing while it did so. Mansions crumbled and molten earth bubbled from the massive cracks that exposed the earth's guts. The River of Life carried giant tidal waves, and Heaven's sky began to fall.

When my destructive rage ended, I pored over the wasteland, disbelieving I could tap into such power, create such devastation. All of Heavens' souls and celestials were scattered on the ground in twisted disarray. I saw many of the souls had fallen into the bottomless giant cracks that curved throughout the vast land. No one was moving, but cries of distress were abroad.

I ran from Heaven panic-stricken and confused. What had I done? I sought sanctuary inside Hell knowing I would be safe there until I could sort things out. Ever since that day I'd remained there nervously awaiting word on Heaven's condition.

I thought it would do me some good to write you this, but it doesn't. Time feels as though it is dragging, and in contemplating the meaning of time, I've come to realize something: time is both enemy and friend. The longer I spend alone here is the longer I have to reflect on my actions; the anguish can be unbearable. But, the more time I have to reflect on my actions is the longer I have to sort through the mess I've created.

If only I could turn back time . . .

Part 5: Judgment Day

Chapter 44

Spirit

Two weeks after I wrote my last entry to you, I began to grow restless and decided to return to Chova. I figured if anyone were to search for me, Chova would be one of the first places they'd go.

Upon entering the Land, I went to the House and hurried to the top of the tower. There I spent many hours continuing to ponder the state Heaven was in. Why hadn't they sent anyone out to search for me, to hunt me down like I was a witch in need of being burnt at the stake? Had I killed everyone there?

As I searched for a solution, I perceived something beyond the mountain was calling out to me, requesting my immediate attention. I couldn't resist the urge to obey the call so I left the House and journeyed the path that led me to the mountain. But this time I was able to continue on the path that went beyond the falls and wrapped around the opposite side of the mountain. I had an eerie feeling tickle my spine as I rounded the path to the other side. I stood on the mountainside gawking over a valley that had one edifice in its center apparently constructed from gold. The edifice was a typical church. Two spires reached upwards off the rooftop holding crosses proudly against the blue backdrop. A small bell tower was between the two spires, and the bell began to clang, its beat sounding like a voice ordering me to the church.

I walked down the side of the mountain, sticking to the path that turned to gold beneath my feet. I approached with the utmost caution, scanning to the left side of myself, the right and behind. It was a ghost town.

I entered the unlocked front doors and halted my progression to examine the interior of the building. One oak table was positioned in the center of the room. A high cathedral ceiling peaked above the table, and a bright source of light projected on the tabletop from a skylight. Illuminated on the tables' top was a small rolled scroll with a velvet string tied in a simple knot.

I picked up the scroll and removed the string as if being instructed to do so although I heard no voice. I exposed yellow parchment that had fancy calligraphy writings written in the English language. The contents of the scrolls read as follows:

Travis,

Destiny. Was it your karma to become as you are today? I will answer that question for you, but concern yourself not as to who I am because we will be meeting soon.

Yes, it has been your destiny but not totally. You see, I present certain situations to you and give you freewill to choose your own path while I watch you and pray the proper choices are made.

In writing this, I do not yet know what path you've chosen after you became a Spirit. But that path, Travis, is very important to me, and in time you will learn the reasons why.

As for the path you've chosen. You could've assumed only one of two possible paths I've offered to you. I ask you, Travis, where are you now? Fighting to preserve your soul and the soul of humans against the unrelenting corruption of the devil? Or are you seeking refuge because the devil tempted you and you've destructively begun to assume control with greed and force?

If the first is your path, then I extend my overwhelming state of bliss. But, if the second is your path than I am morbid for your failure.

I read the scroll over twice and it became apparent that Julius and Navarro had ingeniously planted it inside the church for me to find. I'm sure they hoped it would've left me besotted by its mystery, which would've left me in an addled vulnerable state, but I knew better. I tossed the scroll over my shoulder and exited the church. I began my journey back to the House and I scanned my surroundings with an alertness so in tune it would've been impossible for anyone to sneak up on me.

Chapter 45

Upon entering the House of Chova, I was greeted by an ordinary man that was sitting on the steps of the spiraling staircase. He had short brown hair that was neatly parted to the side, peach colored skin, and he dressed himself handsomely in a suit.

"You took longer than I anticipated, Travis. Please make yourself comfortable, we have much to talk about," said the man with a voice that couldn't be questioned.

Feeling at ease, I sat on the floor and rested my back against the wall.

"I knew this day was to come," the man continued. "But the outcome was something I never wanted to know until the actual moment, and that moment has come. I take it you've read the scroll I'd placed inside the church?"

"Yes," I said, and he shook his head knowingly.

"So tell me, Travis, in what way are you living out your life today?"

"Day by day."

"I see. Please, Travis, I need you to stand for me." I did, and the man nodded towards the entranceway, and said, "I've summoned everyone else here."

Navarro, Julius, Paige, Nature, Divination, Sear, Alex, Osiris along with the rest of the Dezrects, and the rest of the Spirits filed into the House. Everyone was silent and orderly as they settled into a circle around the man. The ordinary man waved his hand in the air, and said, "First, let me take away the cloak of deception that has been placed on you all."

The air crackled and popped, and everyone appeared as they did before Navarro transformed them. The man walked before Navarro, and said, "How may times have we gone through this? I pray you come to view things differently. The way you act saddens me, but no matter what elaborate scheme you concoct to try and convince those around you to view me as something evil, you're still my child. And Nature?" he turned to her, and said, "I thought you would've learned by now. I gave you a mind of your own. You don't need Navarro thinking for you, he only gets you into trouble."

"But Lord," Navarro said. "I did it! I've recreated Heaven and I was its leader. Isn't that so, Nature?"

"It is, my love. We did it all right. We fooled each and every one of them. Just look at the expressions on their faces, it's priceless, isn't it?"

"It is," Divination said to my surprise.

I looked to the other Spirits and Julius had stepped forward and stared disbelievingly at Divination. "Why?" he questioned aggrieved.

"Because I was left alone without cause or purpose," Divination said. "Navarro came to me with an opportunity to gain what I'd lost and I accepted it. It was an offer I couldn't refuse."

"What is it you've lost, Divination, that you'd scheme against us?" I asked, unexplainably calm.

"More than you'll ever know, Travis! My purpose was to protect God's supreme being called the Spirit, and none of you are this Spirit I speak of. The Spirit had long ago abandoned me, leaving me alone without purpose and hope. That is when Navarro came to me with a way I could once again have my Spirit back; a desperate man will do desperate things. This plan Navarro concocted was so creative, so intricately complex I was sure no one would be able to see through to its lies. You see, we've created our own Spirits, and those Spirits are all of you standing here with us. The seed used to transform you is a corrupted seed sown by the Devil himself. How, for even a moment, could you think the creation of a celestial by God's hands could be done by such a simple minded mean as a seed?"

"Oh, Travis," Navarro praised. He began to dance joyfully. "Here comes the good part. Remember me?"

Navarro shook his body until it became a blur to my eyes. When he stopped, he was standing before me as an old man with a long white beard. Dark sunglasses covered his eyes, and he held onto a walking stick.

"Raymond . . ." I muttered.

" . . . Yes, Travis, Raymond! You're to become a God, remember that? It's complete now. You're the God I said you would be. Everyone, meet the God of the fools!"

"I told you he was evil!" Sear howled and grabbed everyone's attention. We all watched him walk before the man that was standing in the center of the room. "They have all been played by the Devil, my Lord, and I warned them about him. Day after day they fell deeper into his trap, and soon they began sending him lost human souls in a false Heaven they helped him create. Out of mercy I began separating human souls from their bodies. I did it with the intention of preserving them and their faith in you, my Lord God. I chose those within your churches because I knew their faith in you was already instilled, and if Navarro was able to cross over completely, then those people would've been his first target for corruption. I was alone and afraid, Lord, and the only thing I had was my faith in you and your coming."

The man smiled and placed his hand on Sear's head. "Your faith has been tested against insurmountable odds, Sear, and your actions were always for me and the benefit of others. And for that, you've earned your way into Heaven."

Sear dropped to his knees and began kissing the man's feet. "Thank you, Lord," he praised, and kept repeating.

"Navarro?" the plain man asked, unfazed by Sear's reverence. "Why don't you use your real name? Does Lucifer seem unfitting to you?"

Navarro shook off his false shell and remained quiet.

"That's just great," I huffed. I turned to Navarro, and said, "What about the story you told me? The one about God rejecting His creations and placing the evil seed inside them?"

"It was a lie," he said.

"And what about the destruction of God and the wasted lives that were casualties of the war? I saw the destruction with my own eyes."

"Followers of mine that were expendable, Travis. Souls willing to sacrifice their lives so I could suck you all into my game. Just like the images I showed you while you were in Limbo; great lie from a great deceiver. The big hero thought he was coming back to save the world. A dream of grandeur, Travis, has made you cocky, careless, and my puppet. You have been played the fool... you've all been played the fool! Nature, Divination and I have created chaos and confusion, a scheme, I must admit, to top all others before."

I was still for a moment, whirling from the confusion. "Why?" I questioned the man in the center of the room I'd come to realize was God. "Why allow this to happen? Why allow Navarro to taint us with his seed of corruption?"

"Its' corruption has no effect on any of you. The corruption comes from within, by choice. I allow freewill to everyone, and if your faith was strong like Sear's and Paige's is, you would've seen through his lies. But you didn't because that is what you chose."

"Faith! That is what this is all about? I've suffered and I've been tormented for over fifty years!"

"You haven't been the first to suffer in my name, Travis. You should've turned to me, called out to me for direction. I would've shown you."

"But how was I to know he wasn't God like he claimed to be? His deception is beyond my comprehension."

"Lucifer, show the Spirits your wrists."

The Devil stepped forward and opened his hands, palms facing up. I examined his wrists and saw nothing from the ordinary. I turned to God and questioned Him with my eyes.

"Now," He said. "Look at mine." He displayed His wrists to me and everyone else in the room. I saw obvious circular scarring in the center of His wrists. "With all of his powers of deceit, the Devil can never mock the scars I bear that releases man of their sins. I am there for you all, Travis. All you have to do is have faith in me."

God led Paige and Sear into the center of the room with Him, and He took their hands into His own. "It saddens me to leave with only two today. But, I promise to return soon."

And just like that He was gone and so were all the others, displaced elsewhere without a trace. There I found myself standing alone inside the House of Chova, dazed and confused by the palpably false incident.

To be continued in Spirit of Independence: Repentance coming soon from Barclay Books, LLC

A Spectral Visions Imprint
Now Available

Riverwatch

By
Joseph M. Nassise

From a new voice in horror comes a novel rich in characterization and stunning in its imagery. In his debut novel, author Joseph M. Nassise weaves strange and shocking events into the ordinary lives of his characters so smoothly that the reader accepts them without pause, setting the stage for a climactic ending with the rushing power of a summer storm.

When his construction team finds the tunnel hidden beneath the cellar floor in the old Blake family mansion in Harrington Falls, Jake Caruso is excited by the possibility of what he might find hidden there. Exploring its depths, he discovers an even greater mystery: a sealed stone chamber at the end of that tunnel.

When the seal on that long forgotten chamber is broken, a reign of terror and death comes unbidden to the residents of the small mountain community. Something is stalking its citizens; something that comes in the dark of night on silent wings and strikes without warning, leaving a trail of blood in its wake. Something that should never have been released from the prison the Guardian had fashioned for it years before.

Now Jake, with the help of his friends Sam Travers and Katelynn Riley, will be forced to confront this ancient evil in an effort to stop the creature's rampage. The Nightshade, however, has other plans.

Ask for it at your local bookseller!

ISBN 1931402191

www.barclaybooks.com

A Spectral Visions Imprint
Now Available

Night Terrors

By
Drew Williams

He came to them in summer, while everyone slept . . .

For Detective Steve Wyckoff, the summer brought four suicides and a grisly murder to his hometown. Deaths that would haunt his dreams and lead him to the brink of madness.

For David Cavanaugh, the summer brought back long forgotten dreams of childhood. Dreams that became nightmares for which there would be no escape.

For Nathan Espy, the summer brought freedom from a life of abuse. Freedom purchased at the cost of his own soul.

From an abyss of darkness, he came to their dreams and whispered his name . . .

"Dust"

Ask for it at your local bookseller!

ISBN 193140248

www.barclaybooks.com

A Spectral Visions Imprint
Now Available

The Apostate

By
Paul Lonardo

An ancient evil is spreading through Caldera, a burgeoning desert metropolis that has been heralded as the gateway of the new millennium. As the malevolent shadow spreads across the land, three seemingly ordinary people, Julian, Saney, and Chris, discover that they are the only ones who can defeat the true source of the region's evil, which may or may not be the Devil himself. When a man claiming to work for a mysterious global organization informs the trio that Satan has, in fact, chosen Caldera as the site of the final battle between good and evil, only one questions remains…

Is it too late for humanity?

Ask for it at your local bookseller!

ISBN 193140132

www.barclaybooks.com

A Spectral Visions Imprint
Now Available

Phantom Feast

By
Diana Barron

A haunted antique circus wagon.

A murderous dwarf.

A disappearing town under siege.

The citizens of sleepy little Hester, New York are plunged into unimaginable terror when their town is transformed into snowy old-growth forests, lush, steamy jungles, and grassy, golden savannas by a powerful, supernatural force determined to live...again

Danger and death stalk two handsome young cops, a retired couple and their dog, the town 'bad girl', her younger sister's boyfriend, and three members of the local motorcycle gang. They find themselves battling the elements, restless spirits, and each other on a perilous journey into the unknown, where nothing is familiar, and people are not what they at first appear to be.

Who, or what, are the real monsters?

Ask for it at your local bookseller!

ISBN 193140213

www.barclaybooks.com

A Spectral Visions Imprint

Now Available

Psyclone

by

Roger Sharp

Driven by the need to recreate the twin brother who had been abducted more than twenty years ago and using himself as a model, renowned geneticist David Brooks develops the ability to clone an adult human being. His partner, Dr. Williams, is closing in on a break-through that will let them implant a false set of memories, thoughts, and emotions into the newly formed clone's mind to give it a sense of the past. Before Williams succeeds, however, an ancient demon possesses the clone's empty shell and takes the doctors hostage. Is what the demon reveals about the fate of his brother true? Can they escape and stop the demon clone's rampage before too much damage is done?

Ask for it at your local bookseller!

ISBN 193140019

www.barclaybooks.com